Dear Mystery Reader:

Forensic pathologist Andy Broussard is back in D.J. Donaldson's latest DEAD LETTER offering, SLEEPING WITH THE CRAWFISH. Donaldson, a professor of anatomy and neurobiology, is no stranger to the grotesqueries of police forensics. His expertise shines on every page.

This time around, Donaldson pairs up Broussard with his former colleague Kit Franklyn to find out the true identity of a mysterious cadaver. With only fingerprints to go on, Andy discovers that the deceased is actually a convict who is supposed to be behind bars in the Louisiana state prison. When Kit arrives at the prison to fingerprint and photograph the convict, she's met with some shocking news. According to the prison official, the convict in question died during the night and was cremated. As the story unravels, it's clear that Broussard and Kit are falling deeper and deeper into a plot to cover up murder on the bayou.

If you're a Patricia Cornwell fan, I strongly advise you to check out D.J. Donaldson's forensic mystery series. He combines eerily authentic forensic details with a vivid Louisiana flavor that makes for an engrossing read. But beware: Donaldson's books can be very habit forming!

Yours in crime,

Joe Veltre
St. Martin's Press DEAD LETTER Paperback Mysteries

SLEEPING
WITH THE
CRAWFISH

D. J. DONALDSON

St. Martin's Paperbacks

Library of Congress Catalog Card Number: 97-20036

ISBN: 0-312-96681-4

Printed in the United States of America

St. Martin's Press hardcover edition/November 1997
St. Martin's Paperbacks edition/December 1998

10 9 8 7 6 5 4 3 2 1

Acknowledgments

They say to write what you know. My problem is that I don't know much, certainly not enough to fill a book. This means I'm constantly relying on the kindness of strangers and friends for information. For this book, I'm indebted to Dr. Mel Park for filling in my almost-nonexistent knowledge about guns and for taking me to the firing range that appears in this story. Thanks also to Bob LeNoue for a thorough discussion of the cremation process, to Nancy Loggins for instruction on embalming procedures, and to Dr. Harry Mincer for information on dental matters. I particularly enjoyed talking dart-poison frogs with Charles Beck, curator of reptiles and amphibians at the Memphis Zoo. And yes, his office was *very* warm. It was fun, too, learning a bit about signing for the deaf from Dr. Jennifer Lukomski. My apologies to anyone who told me things I've used in this book but who wasn't mentioned here. As much as I want every fact to be correct, sometimes things go awry. If that's happened anywhere in this story, the blame is all mine.

1

"All right, Warden Guillory . . . thanks. It's a puzzle, no question. But if he's there, he can't be here, too. I'll be in touch."

Chief Medical Examiner Andy Broussard hung up and stared into space, his hand remaining on the phone. Then he picked up the file that had come over from Central Records and looked again at the mug shot of Ronald Cicero.

The man in the picture and the guy on the table downstairs in the morgue were obviously the same person. The photo had been taken nineteen years ago when Cicero had been booked for killing a clerk in a liquor-store robbery. Now, at sixty-eight, he didn't look much different . . . and his prints matched. He'd been sent to the state prison at Angola for life, and the warden had just said he was still there.

Broussard closed the file and tossed it onto his desk. He reached into the fishbowl of lemon drops next to the wooden sign that read THOSE WHO DON'T BELIEVE THE DEAD CAN COME BACK TO LIFE SHOULD BE HERE AT QUITTING TIME and popped a candy into each cheek. He then rocked back in his chair and folded his stubby fingers over his ample belly, his mind going back to the odd lesions he'd found in the depths of Cicero's brain—clean holes of degeneration without signs of inflammation. That was perplexing enough . . . one puzzle to a customer. Now the warden at Angola says *he's* got Cicero.

Broussard reflected on the situation for about ninety seconds, the lemon balls in his cheek clicking around his mouth like marbles in a sack. Hitting on a way to solve two of his problems at the same time, he rocked forward in his chair and reached for the phone book.

"Oh, it's *gone*," the woman moaned, stomping her heel on the floor. She turned to Kit and pointed at the wall. "Yesterday, in that spot there was a scene of Jackson Square right after a rain, with the light reflecting off the wet bricks . . . kind of eerie."

"I remember it," Kit Franklyn said.

"Is it in the back somewhere?" the woman asked hopefully.

"I'm afraid it's sold."

"Why'd you do that?"

"People give us money, we give them pictures—it's kind of a business thing."

"You don't have to be snotty about it."

She was right, of course. The customer should always be right, even if they ask stupid questions. It was just hard for Kit to adapt to her current status. Five weeks earlier, she'd been the medical examiner's suicide investigator and psychological profiler for the police. Now . . . a clerk.

No one had forced this on her. It had been her choice. To Broussard and everyone else who knew her, a totally puzzling one. Of course, they hadn't been degraded and humiliated by a pair of psychotic kidnappers. It was all still fresh in her mind—the Ph.D. . . . the big psychologist . . . totally dominated by two bottom-feeders. Who wouldn't suffer a loss of confidence after that?

She'd felt like a fraud—like if she had a CAT scan, they'd find that the ventricles in her brain were hugely enlarged and she was getting by on a thin shell of gray matter. It could happen—had already, in fact—to another woman in this country. You could look it up. Such a person shouldn't be investigating anything. They should be a clerk. And right now, she wasn't even doing that well.

"I'm sorry," she said to the irritated customer. "Would you like to order a print of that photo? I'm sure the owner has the negative and would be happy to make one for you."

"Tell him he can take his negative and shove it."

As the woman stormed out, the phone rang.

"Boyd's Gallery."

"Kit, is that you?" Andy Broussard said.

"Sometimes I wonder myself."

"It's good to hear your voice."

"You, too."

"Say, I've got a problem over here I was hopin' you'd be willin' to help me with."

"I'm not good at solving problems."

"This one is pretty straightforward. I just don't have anyone I can put on it."

"I don't know . . ."

"Please. As a personal favor."

He was hitting below the belt now. After all they'd been through together and how much she respected and, yes, loved the old curmudgeon, granting him a small favor didn't seem like too much to ask. Still . . . "I've got responsibilities here at the gallery."

"I understand, but maybe you could get free for a while and drop by the office."

She hesitated, wishing she was the person Broussard thought she was. She pictured her office, sitting there empty, the chapters of her unfinished manuscript on suicide languishing in her desk.

A book. She'd actually had the nerve to believe she could write a book. Utterly self-delusional.

"Kit, you still there?"

"I'm here."

"What do you say? Will you help me?"

"Umm . . . I don't know if I can. . . . Maybe . . . I don't know. I'll call you."

She hung up without giving him the opportunity to coax her again. Remaining by the phone, she watched the foot traffic pass by the window on Toulouse. Andy needed help.

Outside, a kid on his father's shoulders looked at her through the glass and waved happily. She waved back, envying the child, his life stretching before him, no choices yet made, a fresh, unstained existence, everything to come, his potential still a mystery.

Nolen Boyd, the owner of the gallery, came through the door, eating a Lucky Dog from the pushcart on the corner, a Coke in the other hand. He was a big, overweight guy with a soft, slack face and a deep, resonant voice Kit suspected could do a killer rendition of "Old Man River." He subsisted, it seemed, on Lucky Dogs blanketed with chili that frequently dripped onto his paunch, where the stain usually disappeared into the psychedelic floral pattern on the Hawaiian shirts he favored.

"Did I see a woman come out of here empty-handed?" he asked.

Kit pointed at the empty spot on the wall. "She wanted that rainy Cabildo scene."

"You tell her I'd make her one?"

"I did, but we sort of got off on the wrong foot."

"Whose fault?"

"Mine. She asked a goofy question and I didn't handle it well."

"Done that myself from time to time. Trouble with having a business open to the general public is, that's who comes in. Forget it. She obviously didn't deserve one of my pictures."

He took another bite of his hot dog.

Andy needed help.

"Nolen, would you mind if I left for an hour or so? There's something I have to do."

He waved his hand theatrically. "Away, then."

"Thanks."

She picked up the phone and called Broussard.

"Hi, it's me, Kit. I'll come over and listen, but I can't promise anything. I should be there in twenty minutes."

She hung up and left by the back door. Like most buildings in the French Quarter, there was a courtyard behind the gallery. Two hundred years ago, the place had housed a single family, the owners living in the wrought iron–decorated two stories facing Toulouse, the servants occupying the two floors of plain brick that formed the left and back boundaries of the courtyard. The rear wing had recently been declared structurally unsafe and there was a chain-link fence across that part of the courtyard to keep people a safe distance away. Kit's apartment and one other were on the second floor of the refurbished left wing. Because there was so much street noise at night, Nolen had put his darkroom above the gallery and lived in the apartment below Kit.

Avoiding the drops of blood from Nolen's miniature dachshund, which had been menstruating all over the place for the last three days, Kit mounted the gray cypress stairs that led to the second floor. "Lucky . . . here, boy."

Her own little brown dog wiggled out of a tall patch of straw grass and bounded toward her, tongue lolling. At the steps, he skidded to a stop and sat down, his hind feet facing forward like a child, waiting for her to tell him what she wanted.

"I'm going out for a while and I want you to be a good boy." Brown eyes glistening, Lucky cocked his head, trying *so* hard to understand.

"Can you do that? Can you be a good boy?"

Jesus, he was cute. She stepped off the stairs, knelt, and ruffled the fur on Lucky's head with both hands. When she started to go, he grabbed her shoelace.

"No, Lucky . . . no."

He released the lace, sat again, and watched her go up the stairs.

As Kit passed the apartment before hers, the door flew open and the occupant came out holding a tray filled with disturbing objects.

"Kit, dear. I've just developed a new line and I wanted your opinion. It's been so long since I've seen one, I wasn't sure I got it right."

It was Eunice Dalehite, a rail-thin woman with straight gray hair and eyes that functioned independently of each other, like those of a chameleon.

"What do you think?" she asked, one eye looking at Kit, the other glancing over Kit's shoulder. She thrust the tray at Kit's face, forcing her to take a step backward. Eunice made erotic candy for the Naughty but Nice shop two blocks down Bourbon Street. On the tray were six chocolate erections, complete with shaved chocolate pubic hair.

Kit was speechless.

"Is it accurate?" Eunice said.

"I . . . I'm no expert, but they look good—ah . . . accurate to me."

Eunice beamed. "It's my own special blend of chocolate. Try one." She thrust the tray forward.

Even if she'd wanted to sample one, Kit hadn't the slightest idea how one would do it and retain a shred of dignity.

"It's tempting . . . but I'm allergic to chocolate," Kit said.

"Oh dear. How terrible for you."

"It's a burden, but I manage."

"Maybe I'll make you some nice open-zipper cookies instead."

"You're too kind."

Kit's apartment was Lilliputian: a living room, one bedroom, a bathroom, and a tiny kitchen with a counter between it and the living room. Last week, a crack had developed in the center of the living room ceiling, ominously creeping a couple of inches a day, so it now formed a large nasty smile. Uncomforted by Nolen's assurance that it was just the old building settling and meant nothing, Kit looked up to check its progress, noting with alarm that it was several inches longer than it had been a few hours ago.

Tired of worrying about the crack, Kit's mind drifted back to the wonderful old house she'd once owned in the uptown section—its beautiful Victorian beadwork and solid oak columns in the entry foyer, the glistening quarter-sawn oak floors . . . the human remains she'd found buried in the backyard.

Reminded of why she'd had to sell, her thoughts shifted to the gorgeous Italianate villa she'd lived in next. But that image, too, was sullied . . . by the faces of the two kidnappers. Trouble, it seems, always knew her address.

But this was now her home and she'd have to make the best of it. Making a detour around the *x* she'd taped on the carpet to remind her of the danger overhead, she went into the bathroom, where she put on a fresh coat of lip gloss, then brushed her long auburn hair and reset the faux tortoise-shell combs that kept it out of her eyes.

She paused and studied her reflection, looking for outward evidence of the changes she'd experienced internally. But her eyes were still brown, there were still sixteen freckles scattered across the bridge of her nose, and her neck was still one of her nicest features. On the surface, she was still Kit. Inside . . . who knows?

There simply wasn't enough room in the French Quarter. This applied particularly to cars, which, if you lived there, were a financial liability of ruinous proportions because of the cost of garage space. This caused many of the Quarter's residents to give them up. Without convenient transportation, and finding they could satisfy all their needs in the Quarter, a large number of the carless became exiles who rarely, if ever, ventured out of its boundaries. Not so depressed that she was willing to join their number, Kit had taken the job at the gallery mostly because Nolen had thrown in a parking space in a garage three blocks away on Dauphine Street, her next destination.

It was a beautiful late-spring day in which the slit of sky between the balconied buildings lining Toulouse was blue and cloudless and the temperature was cool enough to keep the Quarter from smelling like an errant compost heap, as it did in summer. The sidewalks were crowded with tourists, street magicians, singers, and mimes, giving the place an aimless energy that made Kit feel as though she lived on the grounds of an insane asylum. At the corner of Bourbon and Toulouse, a mechanical mime in a tuxedo and white gloves offered her a carnation, his every rachety move accompanied by a convincing whirring noise. Leaving the flower for one of the tourists, she stepped over a spilled ice cream cone and kept moving.

At Dauphine, a dirty old man with a sooty gray beard came around the corner, pushing a grocery cart. Tied to the cart and leading the way was an equally sooty Sheltie, who began straining at his leash when he saw her. Curtis and Jimmy.

Upon reaching her, Jimmy put his front paws on her shoes and bowed in a doggy greeting. Protocol observed, he then began jumping against her legs, deliriously happy to see her.

"I've told him to play hard to get," Curtis said. "But he just won't listen."

Kit knelt and pulled on Jimmy's ruff. "That's because we're old friends."

"Are you well, then?" Curtis inquired, leaning on the handle of the cart.

Kit had definitely been better, but she wasn't about to complain to poor Curtis. "I am well," she said, giving Jimmy one last rub. "And you?"

"Not an hour ago, a fine young man from Mobile gave me five dollars, so Jimmy and I have had a grand meal and are feelin' like we could whip a small polar bear."

"We can't have out-of-towners doing more for our friends than we do," she said, digging in her purse. She took out a ten she could ill afford to part with and gave it to Curtis, whose eyes had told her there had been no man from Mobile.

"You're a saint," Curtis said. "And surely the prettiest of the lot. Give Lucky our regards." Curtis pushed his cart forward, tightening the leash and pulling Jimmy reluctantly away from her.

Watching them leave, Kit was heartened that Jimmy didn't seem to know his master was homeless, which meant Lucky probably wasn't aware of her own altered circumstances.

Broussard's filing system consisted of books and letters and Xeroxed articles stacked around his office in piles that made the place an obstacle course. Kit found him with half of one of those piles in his arms.

"Kit."

He dropped his load onto the only available spot on his green vinyl sofa and steamed toward her, arms spread wide, as if intending to embrace her. But the closer he got, the more his arms sagged, until when he reached her, he touched only her hand, grasping it firmly in his chubby fingers.

"I . . . everyone's missed you," he said.

"Me, too."

It had been Kit's strongest desire since she'd joined his staff to hear Broussard praise her work. A childish need, she knew, but it was there nevertheless. And he had never done it. She'd once believed the fault was his. Now, confidence shattered, she was sure she'd simply never deserved his approval.

It had been six weeks since she'd last seen him, and outwardly, he hadn't changed, either—still hugely overweight, his hair and beard no grayer, his small eyes just as clear and bright, glasses still equipped with a lanyard that let them dangle within reach when he worked at the microscope, a real bow tie at his throat, not a clip-on.

"I see you still have your sweet tooth," she said, referring to the lemon ball pushing his cheek out.

Broussard eagerly dug in his pants pocket and produced two cellophane-wrapped lemon balls, which he put in her hand. He folded her fingers over them and covered her hand with both of his.

When she'd first come aboard, he'd frequently offered her naked lemon balls from his pocket, which she consistently refused. Realizing she was concerned about the other things he touched during a typical day, he'd begun carrying wrapped ones just for her. Her reference to his sweet tooth had been a test to see if he'd continued the practice. The fact that he had touched her.

They exchanged a few more pleasantries and then Kit said, "What is it you wanted me to do?"

Broussard led her to his desk, where he picked up a stack of Polaroid morgue photos. Shifting through them, he selected one and handed it to her. "Yesterday afternoon, that man stabbed a woman coming out of the Walgreens on Gentilly Boulevard. He was shot and killed in the act by an off-duty policeman." He waved her into the wooden chair in front of the desk and went to his own chair behind it.

"How's the woman?"

"In serious condition, but they think she'll be okay."

"Any idea why he did it?"

"Doesn't appear to be any rational explanation. She didn't know him, and he made no move for her purse. I suspect it had somethin' to do with the degenerative lesions I found in both temporal lobes of his brain."

"What kind of lesions?"

"Nothin' like I ever saw before."

"Where do I come in?"

"He wasn't carryin' any ID. When we ran his prints, it came back that he was servin' a life term in Angola."

"So he was paroled?"

"Not accordin' to the Angola warden. When I talked to him half an hour ago, he said this man was still there."

Broussard was encouraged that upon hearing this, Kit sat straighter in her chair, indicating she was definitely interested.

"What is it you want of me?"

"I'd like you to take a camera and a print kit to Angola and get me some reliable data."

"Couldn't the prison send you that stuff?"

"The key word in what I just said was *reliable*. With no direct link to that information, I wouldn't know what weight to give it. No, I need you to go over there."

Kit sat back in her chair, mulling over the situation, Broussard watching her intently, hoping she'd agree and, through this commitment, be drawn back into her old life.

"How far is Angola?"

"You could be there in three hours," Broussard said brightly.

"I dunno. . . ."

Broussard hurriedly wrote a number on a scratch pad, tore it off, and handed it to her. "That's the warden's number. It's too late to go today. So I'd suggest you set up an appointment for tomorrow."

Kit stared at the number for what seemed to Broussard like a very long time.

The old pathologist's heart characteristically thumped along at a glacial fifty beats a minute. But as he waited for

Kit's decision, it seemed to have slipped a flywheel, for he could feel it racing in his chest.

Kit began to shake her head almost imperceptibly. A look that Broussard interpreted as indicating a negative decision crossed her face.

She looked up. "So where's this camera and print kit?"

2

Angola lies 125 miles northwest of New Orleans, near the Louisiana-Mississippi border. Calling from home, Kit arranged to meet the warden in his office on prison grounds the next day at 4:00 P.M. The following afternoon, she left New Orleans at one o'clock, heading toward Baton Rouge, wishing she hadn't agreed to go.

The city had been without rain for nearly three weeks, so the resurrection ferns growing on the boughs of the biggest oaks looked dead. This was, of course, an illusion. One good deluge and they'd be back again, green and happy. And from the look of the white clouds with promising dark centers filling the sky, that moment might soon be at hand.

By the time she'd left urban clutter behind and started across the marshy edges of Lake Pontchartrain on the long portion of I-10 resting on piers sunk in mud, the clouds had massed in front of the sun, forming a huge dirty cauliflower with luminous edges. Apparently disturbed by the impending storm and unsure of what to do, dozens of egrets crisscrossed high overhead, their white feathers glowing with cold fire in the diffused light.

Then, heat lightning began, pulsing and rippling behind the cloud's folded contours, one jolt after another, with barely a pause between them, the streaks showing a cloudy substructure not previously visible. On and on it went, the actual lightning trails masked by cloud cover, creating the fanciful illusion that the occupants of an extraterrestrial transport might be back there engaging in high-voltage mischief.

It was an impressive and diverting performance that lasted for nearly forty miles. Eventually, the cloud dispersed and it became just another day in which the resurrection ferns would sleep awhile longer.

At 3:10 P.M., on the other side of Baton Rouge, following the directions on a small green sign that pointed to Angola, she turned onto the Tunica Trace Scenic Highway. Twenty miles later, she came to another, larger green sign advising her that anyone entering a Department of Correction facility was subject to a physical search that might include an examination of body cavities. Oddly, this made her reluctant to continue, and she remained for several minutes at the sign, appraising the prison entrance fifty yards ahead.

On her side of the requisite chain-link fence topped with razor wire, this consisted of a couple of small single-story yellow brick buildings with burgundy trim, a tower of the same color, and a guardhouse that straddled the road. As she sat there, she thought of the scene in *The Silence of the Lambs* where Jodie Foster walks past all the occupied cells to get her first look at Hannibal Lecter. The recollection made her wish she'd brought a raincoat and an umbrella.

But this wasn't getting her job done. She nudged the gas and rolled up to the guardhouse, which disgorged a blue-uniformed trooper type wearing a gray Smokey the Bear hat and sunglasses. His request that she state her business was so cold, she wouldn't have been surprised to see his breath.

"I'm Kit Franklyn, from the medical examiner's office in New Orleans. I have an appointment with Warden Guillory."

"Wait here."

The trooper went into the guardhouse and picked up the phone.

While he made his call, an eighteen-wheeler came down the road from inside the prison and stopped at the guardhouse. The other trooper on duty made the driver open the cab door. Satisfied no convict was hiding on the floor, the trooper went around to the rear of the truck, opened the back door, and looked inside. Kit wanted to see if he'd use mirrors to look under the truck, but her attention was diverted by the return of her trooper.

"Ma'am, the warden said for you to wait out here. He's on his way. You can park over yonder." He gestured to a graveled lot in front of the public toilets.

Kit had expected to be shown in by a guard, so she was surprised at this. Apparently, the warden had overestimated her importance and was giving it the personal touch. She nodded, backed her car up, and put it where the trooper had indicated.

Because the day had grown warm and the trooper's manner made her uncomfortable, she elected to wait in her car with the air conditioner running. Five minutes later, the yellow metal arm blocking the prison's exit lane lifted at the approach of a black Cadillac with tinted windows. It stopped at the guardhouse and the driver exchanged words with the trooper she'd spoken with. Seeing the trooper point at her car, she cut the engine and got out.

The Cadillac came to meet her, crunching to a stop a few feet away.

In it were two men. The driver had a broad Cro-Magnon face and dark hair that edged over his forehead in a series of robust commas. The passenger in the backseat was difficult to see.

The rear window rolled down and his face appeared in the

opening, allowing the late-afternoon sun access to a thick head of copper-colored hair that reflected the rays like a new penny. His fleshy face spread in a dentured smile.

"Dr. Franklyn?"

Kit moved over to the car, expecting to be invited in and then driven back to the warden's office. But the door remained closed. Instead, a hand came through the open window. "I'm Warden Guillory. Good to see you."

Kit shook the hand as best she could with it so high in the air; then it was drawn back into the car.

"I'm afraid we've encountered a difficulty," Guillory said, bringing his face back to the window.

"What kind of difficulty?"

"Last night, the man you came to see had a heart attack and died."

"I can still get a picture and his prints."

"Ah, well, that's the problem. . . . I left clear orders that nothing be done to the body until you arrived. But there was a mix-up and . . . I'm afraid it's been . . . cremated."

"How could you do that so fast? Don't the relatives have to be notified or something?"

"He had no living relatives. Hadn't had a stick of mail in years. I'm afraid no one cared whether he lived or died."

"Pretty sad, even for a felon."

"In such cases, we're free to move quickly to dispose of the body, and we usually take full advantage of that."

"What do I do now?" Kit said, thinking aloud.

"There's nothing you *can* do but go back to New Orleans and tell Dr. Broussard how sorry I am this happened. If it helps any, I brought this for you." He turned and picked up a manila envelope, which he handed her through the window. "It contains the photographs of him we took when he arrived, and his fingerprints."

Kit opened the envelope and examined its contents. The photo was of a man in his late forties.

"How long had he spent here?"

"I believe it was . . . nineteen years."

"You don't have a more recent picture?"

"Sorry, no."

"Can you tell me how he'd changed?"

"His hair had a lot of gray in it and his face showed his age and his years here."

"Can you be more specific?"

"I don't know what else to say. He was an average-looking old con."

"Was he thin or heavy?"

"Thin, I *can* tell you that."

To return home with only the manila envelope would mean her trip had accomplished nothing but to provide Broussard with data he could have obtained by mail. He'd sent her to do more. But what else was possible? "Where are the ashes from the cremation?"

"At the funeral home where it was done."

"Where's that?"

"I hardly think you can learn anything from those."

"Probably not, but I'd like to see them at least."

"Of course that's up to you. The funeral home is about fifteen miles from here in a small town called Courville. Guillory proceeded to give her directions and she was soon on her way, the warden's car behind her until, at the road to Courville, they separated.

Died . . . of a heart attack . . . and then cremated. . . . Oh sure, this assignment is a snap. She should have just politely told Broussard, no thanks, and gone back to the photo gallery when he'd brought it up.

She was still whipping herself about this when she saw the tasteful green sign for Courville. A HISTORIC COMMUNITY. That's all it said—no satellite signs advertising the Rotary Club or the Lions Club or the Optimists, no statement about the population.

About a mile beyond the sign, the houses began—large white structures, mostly wooden, with columned porches and green shutters. They were widely spaced from one another on well-tended grounds dotted with ancient live oaks whose branches curled outward in sweeping arcs, reminding Kit of the trunks on compliant pachyderms.

It was rumored that Spanish moss was becoming endangered and was slowly disappearing from Louisiana trees. Whatever was causing that situation was obviously not operating in Courville, for its oaks were generously shrouded with it, giving the place a timeless beauty.

Two miles down the road, she came to the Courville Funeral Home. Under its name on the sign out front, it advised passersby, TAKE YOUR FINAL TRIP WITH TRIP. The sign made no sense until she saw in smaller letters that the proprietor was Trip Guillory. Guillory was a common Louisiana name, but she was prepared to bet heavily that this one and the warden were related.

She pulled into the oyster-shell drive and followed it to the funeral home, which was housed in a striking two-story brick house with Gothic arches topping the front door and all the windows. There were three gables on the front, each trimmed in white Victorian gingerbread. The Gothic arch theme was repeated on more white gingerbread trimming the columned porch, the roof of which was enclosed by a white picket fence.

She parked in a lot on the right of the house, hoping the absence of other vehicles didn't mean the place was closed. She checked her watch: 4:35. But who knows what hours they keep out here? she thought.

Despite her eagerness to get on with her business, the wonderful silence that greeted her when she left her car made her pause. For the next minute, the only sound she heard was a sharp creak as her car's engine cooled. Then a single frog began calling out in a small reedy voice. From a nearby tree, an unseen bird added its chatter, earnestly enjoying its own sweet counsel. A distant crow vocalized its displeasure at something, the sound bittersweet, like being stabbed in the heart with a long-stemmed rose. Struck by the thought that Courville would be a far better place to live than the French Quarter, she headed across the lot toward the house.

There was a big mat on the porch and a small sign that asked visitors to wipe their feet, which she did. She tried the front door and found it unlocked.

The foyer floor was covered with an Oriental rug of muted colors and the walls were lined with dark oak paneling the same color as the oak beams on the coffered ceiling.

Coffered . . . Kit let the word roll around in her brain, finding its resemblance to *coffin* so appropriate.

There were four doors off the foyer, one on each side and two straight ahead, with no signs identifying anything. "Hello . . . is anyone here?"

She listened for an answer but heard none.

She crossed the room and tried a door. It opened into a small chapel with several rows of pews.

"Hello . . ."

She went to another door and found another chapel that was also still and empty.

The door on the left side of the foyer was locked, which left her only one more choice.

That door led to a room with a cement floor and lots of metal cabinets. Over by a metal bench hugging the wall to her left were two stainless-steel gurneys and something called a Porti-Boy, with tubes coming out of it.

She saw a set of double metal doors standing wide open in the far-right corner. The room beyond emitted a whirring sound like the one made by the mechanical mime who'd offered her the flower. She closed the door hard, hoping the sound would announce her presence. The head and shoulders of a red-haired man with pale skin appeared from behind one of the open doors.

"You must be Dr. Franklyn," he said.

Kit crossed the room and entered a thin cloud of drifting ash. When she reached him, he offered his hand. "I'm Trip Guillory. George said to expect you."

He was standing turned to the side, and as Kit shook his hand, her eyes went past him to the large green metal oven behind him and the ash and bone inside it.

Noticing that her attention was on the oven, Guillory said, "That doesn't bother you, does it? Since you're from the medical examiner's office, I assumed . . ."

"No, it's fine," Kit lied, looking him in the eye. "George is . . ."

"My brother . . . the warden at Angola."

Beyond hair color and complexion, there wasn't much resemblance between the two men. Whereas George wore his hair long, Trip's was short. Trip was also about fifteen years younger and thin, with a long face and apparently real teeth.

"George said you're interested in the cremains of the fellow who came in this morning."

Cremains . . . another appropriate word, Kit thought. "Are we talking about Ronald Cicero?"

"Right, Cicero. Say, I'm running a little late. Do you mind if I keep working while we talk?"

"Not at all."

Guillory turned to the wall and reached for something that looked like one of those rakes croupiers use to move chips around a roulette table—only this one had a handle about eight feet long.

"We made a big mistake when we designed this area," Guillory said, carefully running the handle past her. "If we'd realized how long this cleaning tool is, we'd have laid it out so the retort could be emptied without having these doors open."

He slid the business end of the cleaning tool into the retort and began pulling the ash and bone into a narrow trough that ran down the center of the retort's floor. Many of the bones were still intact, but the skull had separated so that its individual elements lay in a disarticulated pile. As the cleaning tool gathered the cremains, the bones broke into smaller fragments.

"Not much left, is there?" Kit said.

"Usually not more than a couple of pounds." As Guillory worked, the amount of ash in the air increased, settling on Kit's clothing. The thought that particles derived from a human liver or tongue or toe were settling on her like dandruff was bad enough, but the likelihood she was also inhaling them was just about more than she could take. But she had a job to do, so she held her ground and tried not to breathe so deeply.

"Is that him in there?" she asked.

"Cicero? No, I did him this morning." Guillory pulled the cleaning tool down the center of the trough, scraping the cremains forward, where they disappeared down a hole.

"What exactly did you hope to accomplish here?" he said, reaching into the ashes and plucking out a metal strap with three screws attached. He tossed it into a nearby trash can.

"What was that?" Kit asked.

"A mending plate. Orthopedic surgeons use them to stabilize fractures. You'd be surprised how much metal comes out of here in a month. Take a look."

Kit stepped over and peered into the trash can, which contained, in addition to an impressive number of mending plates, a couple of much larger metal replicas of the upper end of a thighbone.

"Those big things in there are artificial hip joints," Guillory said. "Watch your head."

He pulled the cleaning tool out of the retort, returned it to the wall, and took down an equally long-handled brush, which he used to sweep out the remaining bone and ash.

"The only kinds of surgical artifacts we have to watch out for are pacemakers—they can explode and damage the lining of the retort—and silicone breast implants—when they melt, they make a helluva mess."

Kit hadn't answered Guillory's question about what she'd hoped to accomplish by coming, because she hadn't yet figured that out herself. But now, having learned there can be various kinds of surgical artifacts in cremains, as well as some fairly large pieces of bone, it seemed possible that even if Guillory *had* culled the bigger pieces of metal, Broussard might learn something useful by examining what came out of the retort.

With the retort tidied up inside, Guillory went around to its left side and slid out a large metal drawer that obviously contained the cremains he'd just collected. What happened next made Kit's heart sink.

Guillory began rummaging through the cremains with a magnet that quickly became bristly with bits of wire and other metal.

"We usually cremate bodies in a cardboard box," he said. "This picks up all the staples that held the box together."

As well as any metal artifacts that might be used to identify the body, Kit thought glumly. Then things got worse.

Guillory carried the drawer over to something that looked like a small ice chest and began pouring the cremains through an opening in the top with a plastic scoop. When they were all inside, he shut the door in the chest and flicked a switch that turned on some machinery.

While pistons and gears meshed and groaned, he put the retort drawer back where it had come from, then returned to the chest, which he let grind away for about half a minute, the noise so loud that conversation was impossible. When he turned it off, silence had never sounded so good.

He removed a drawer at the bottom of the chest and showed Kit that the machinery had ground and pulverized the bone in the cremains until it all resembled fireplace ash.

He sat the drawer on top of the chest and looked at her. "Did you ever say what you wanted from me?"

The process Kit had just witnessed had probably made the cremains of Ronald Cicero totally useless for identification purposes. But she had been with Broussard long enough to know the old pathologist should never be underestimated, which is why she said, "I'd like to take Cicero's cremains back to New Orleans with me."

Up to that point, Guillory's manner had been open and congenial. Hearing her request, his face hardened. "I don't know about that. I couldn't give them to you without George's permission."

"Can you call him now?"

"I guess. . . . It'll take a few minutes, though."

"I can wait."

There was a phone on the wall near the Porti-Boy, but instead of using it, Guillory left the room. Figuring the wall phone was probably just some kind of intercom, Kit thought nothing more about it.

While waiting, she went over to the retort and idly looked inside. Seeing nothing of interest, she turned her attention to a recording device in a box on the front.

Some kind of data regarding the retort's operation were being recorded on a circular piece of paper divided into many concentric circles that she quickly realized represented 50° increments in the retort's temperature. Lines perpendicular to the concentric circles divided the paper into hours of the day.

At 12:30 P.M., the temperature had risen steeply to 1,700° F. The smooth line indicating this then turned horizontally, became a tight little zigzag for about thirty minutes, then straightened, continuing along the 1,700° line for another ninety minutes. At this point, it dropped to baseline.

Following the time of day around the circle, she saw a similar but not identical heating pattern that had begun at 8:30 that morning—the run for Ronald Cicero.

A few minutes later, the door to the foyer opened and Guillory returned. "George says it's okay. All you have to do is sign this form."

They met in the center of the room and Kit took the clipboard Guillory offered. She read the form and signed it with the pen clipped to the board.

"Keep it," Guillory said, referring to the pen. "We write them off as advertising."

Even though he'd seen her sign it, Guillory checked her signature as though she might have tried to pull a fast one by signing someone else's name. Satisfied that everything was in order, he opened a nearby cabinet and removed a circular metal container about a foot long and four inches in diameter and handed it to her.

"Have a nice trip back. I'll see you out."

When they parted, Guillory remained on the funeral home's front porch only until Kit stepped off it. Then he went back inside.

Before getting into her car, Kit brushed the ash off her clothing and checked the metal cylinder to be sure it couldn't come open during the ride home. Seeing that the screw top was sealed with a bead of solder, she confidently put it on the backseat.

It was now a little after five, which would get her into New Orleans around eight. Cicero, it appeared, would be spending the night in her apartment.

After consulting the rearview mirror and brushing some ash from her hair, she buckled up and turned the key in the ignition. The car remained as quiet as one of the chapels she'd seen. She tried again, with the same results. The third try was no charm. Distinctly less thrilled with silence than she had been earlier, she got out and walked back to the funeral home.

Guillory was in the cremation area, putting the top on a decorative urn.

"My car won't start. Is there a mechanic nearby?"

"What bad luck. Yeah, there's one a few miles from here."

"Will they still be open?"

"I'm sure someone will be there." He got an idea. "Right across the street from the garage, there's a really good restaurant. I could drop you off at the garage. You can give them your car key, then have a nice meal while they're fixing things."

"Now that you mention it, I *am* kind of hungry. Sorry to put you out like this."

"Forget it. I'm finished here, and it's right on my way. I'll lock up and we'll go out the back."

"I need to get the cremains and some other things from my car."

"You get them and I'll come around and pick you up."

At her car, Kit retrieved the manila envelope and the metal cylinder, locked her doors, and waited for Guillory, who soon appeared from behind the funeral home in a long black hearse.

He stopped beside her and rolled his window down. "Hope you don't mind riding in the wagon."

"I never find fault when someone's doing me a favor."

She crossed in front of the hearse, got in, and they were on their way.

Accustomed to economy transportation, the plush, quiet ostentation of the hearse made it seem like a traveling church.

"How about some music?" Guillory said.

"I'm just along for the ride. Whatever you want."

Guillory flicked on the tape player and the hearse was filled with circus music. "It's a calliope tape I got when I was in Amsterdam last year for the IFDA meeting." Realizing she might not know what that was, he added, "International Funeral Director's Association. The calliopes just sit on the street cranking away. Great, isn't it?"

She didn't tell him, but even allowing for the New Orleans tradition of jazz funerals, the tape made her uneasy—as if they were committing some kind of blasphemy. The next tune, though, was so infectiously toe-tapping, it would have made even the Pope's eyes sparkle. So, despite her car troubles and the Cicero situation, she was in good spirits when they arrived at Albert's Auto Repair.

She was thankful for its existence, but there was no denying the garage was a candidate for EPA superfund cleanup money, for every inch of the dirt drive and the half acre surrounding the place was saturated with grease and oil. There were at least twenty derelict cars and a scattering of rusty farm machinery littered across the front of the operation, which was housed in an unpainted cement-block building with a corrugated metal roof. The dirt drive continued into the garage, where Kit saw a shower of sparks coming from the undercarriage of an old truck.

"I guess you could say the town has a love-hate relationship with Albert," Guillory said. "He and his people are the best mechanics for fifty miles, but you can see what the place looks like. But then, what is life but compromise?"

Kit turned her keys over to Albert's son, Henry, a lanky young man with grease in his hair, under his nails, and probably in his veins, who promised to put a clean cloth over her car seat before he sat in it. Though she doubted there was a clean cloth anywhere in the place, there was little she could do but trust him.

Guillory wrote his home phone number on his card and told her to call him if she needed anything. He then got back in the hearse and continued on his way, the calliope tape making him sound like a Ringling Brothers advance man.

Henry followed him out of the driveway in a tow truck and set out for the funeral home.

The restaurant Guillory had touted was called Beano's. Presumably that was Beano's face on the giant neon crawfish adorning the big sign out front. With the manila envelope tucked under her arm and the metal cylinder in her hand, Kit crossed the road.

The restaurant, too, was cement block, but it sported a fresh coat of white paint. Its windows were clean and the newly paved and lined parking lot was litter-free. The presence of a dozen vehicles in the lot, mostly pickups, supported Guillory's opinion of its food.

Inside, it was as cheerful as red-checked plastic tablecloths and a plastic dahlia on each table can make a place. Kit took a booth at the window so she could keep an eye out for the tow truck's return.

"Hi there. I'm Belle. You got car trouble, right?"

The waitress was a fat girl with curly dark hair. Despite the weight she carried in her face, she was pretty. Knock off forty pounds and she'd be gorgeous.

"I saw you talkin' to Henry," she explained. "You break down at the funeral home?"

"You saw me arrive in the hearse?"

"Big front window like this, it's hard *not* to see what's goin' on. What's in that metal thing? You an artist?"

Rather than tell her what she was really carrying, Kit thought it best simply to say, "Sort of."

"You visitin' somebody at the prison?"

"Yes, I was."

"Thought so. Never seen you before, so figured it was the prison. Who is it? Husband . . . boyfriend?"

"It's kind of a long story."

"Tell me about it. Me . . . it's my husband. He's comin' up for parole day after tomorrow." She glanced back at the kitchen pass-through, then leaned closer and dropped her voice. "He gets it, I'm outta here. So, what ya gonna have? We got red beans and rice so good, it'll make you cry."

"How could I pass that up? And iced tea."

"You got it."

Her food was brought out in just a few minutes and it was indeed very good. Before she'd finished eating, the tow truck returned with her car. Figuring Henry would need some time to figure out what was wrong, she didn't hurry her meal.

Through the window, she saw Henry lower the car to the ground and move the tow truck out of the way. He came back and fiddled around in the engine for a couple of minutes, then pulled his head out and went into the garage. He returned wheeling some kind of machine with a long cord trailing behind it and spent another few minutes under the hood. Finally, leaving the hood up, he hurried toward the restaurant.

When he came through the door, Kit waved at him, bringing him to her booth.

"Miss, your battery's shot. I ain't got one in stock, but I can fetch one from Retreat. And puttin' it in is easy."

"How long will it take?"

"Hour maybe."

"How much will it cost?"

"Depends on the battery."

"The cheapest one you can find."

"I can get you runnin' again for between fifty and sixty dollars."

"Okay, do it."

Kit spent the next hour and a half drinking coffee and watching it grow progressively darker and darker through the restaurant's front window, until night had Courville firmly in its grasp. About the time she'd begun to think something had happened to Henry, the tow truck turned into the garage's drive. Another ten minutes and he had the new battery installed.

She was so happy to hear the engine start on the first try, the fifty-eight bucks it cost her seemed survivable. The prospect that she'd now arrive home much later than planned was far less objectionable than spending the night in Courville, so as the road stretched away before her headlights, she felt centered and comfortable.

A few minutes later, while listening to Michael Bolton singing "When a Man Loves a Woman," a pair of headlights suddenly appeared in her rearview mirror. And the idiot had his brights on.

She flicked the mirror to its night setting and tried to keep her eyes on the road. But the lights grew brighter. Checking to see why, she saw that the car was now tailgating her. Then she heard a crash and her car gave a sickening sideways lurch.

She hit the brakes, but her momentum carried the car off the road. It greased across the shoulder and jolted over cobbled terrain. The steering wheel was ripped from her hand and her head was thrown from side to side, rattling her teeth and casting the combs from her hair. Suddenly, the ground dropped away and the car was airborne. A moment later, it returned to earth with a shattering impact. At practically the same instant, it rolled, causing her head to strike the side window, so as the car landed upside down in the waiting bayou and slowly began to sink into its dark waters, she sat limply strapped in her seat, unconscious.

3

The driver's floor mat lay on the back of Kit's legs. Her thighs were pressed against the steering wheel. Both arms dangled, the car's scant headroom folding them at the elbows. From around the doors, water seeped into the car and pooled on the inside of the roof. As the level rose, it lifted her hair and covered her hands. Still unconscious, she knew nothing about any of this.

Gradually, the water deepened, creeping over Kit's wrists, the spilled contents of the glove compartment quietly spinning in tiny eddies. Her watch went under and stalled. The drooping floor mat on the passenger side let go and splashed into the water, creating ripples that pushed a floating Paper Mate pen in her direction, where it became moored in the auburn sargassum of her hair. A minute later, the rising water caressed the crown of her head. Outside, in the weeds along the bank, a hundred pairs of amphibian eyes watched the car sink lower in the water, their owners as oblivious to Kit's plight as she was.

Fifty yards up the road, Ozaire Chevalons was listening to

"Ma Petite Fille" on a Blackie Forestier tape, an open beer bottle nestled between his legs. A few yards before his headlights picked up the skid marks that would have led him to Kit's car in the bayou, he threw his head back and sang a few bars himself. By the time he looked back at the road, he'd missed her.

When the water reached Kit's eyebrows, she woke.

For an instant, she was disoriented, her head throbbing from the blow she'd received and the blood pooling in her brain from being upside down.

Then she knew.

There in the dark, the water rising, she was seized by dread as black as the watery grave claiming her an inch at a time.

But as frightful as her situation was, she wasn't dead yet.

Her mind went wild. What to do? . . . Think. . . . Damn it. . . . The seat belt . . . Have to get loose.

She reached up and fumbled for the release button, her hands clumsy and slow. Where was it? . . . There.

No longer held in her seat, she dropped six inches. Surprised at the fall, she took a breath, sucking water into her nose and mouth as her face was submerged up to her chin. Gagging and coughing, she lifted her head out of the water.

Dimly, she realized her lower body was draped over the steering wheel. Kicking and pushing, she fought free and toppled sideways, her legs buckling the open glove compartment door before her feet struck the passenger door, wrenching her ankles and knees. With the car rocking sickeningly, she pulled in her legs and dropped into the water.

Again disoriented, she groped into the darkness. Her fingers found the steering wheel. The other side . . . easier to get out the passenger side.

She pushed herself up and became tangled in the seat belt. A scream of frustration bulled into her throat as she clawed at the strap, trapping her. Then, she was free of it.

She moved to the passenger door on her knees, the water

now up to her waist. Hands fluttering like a wounded bird, her fingers scrambled over the door, looking for the lock pin.

A fingernail caught on something and bent back.

Where was the pin. . . . Damn pin . . .

The scream in her throat slid forward, pushed at her lips.

She found the pin and yanked it. Then she lifted her hands, sliding them in wide circles that put the door handle in her grasp.

Now things were about to get worse, but it had to be done. She took three deep breaths to saturate her blood with oxygen, hoping to stretch the length of time she could go without breathing. She pulled the handle and leaned on the door.

The weight of water pressing from the other side made the door open slowly, so the bayou rushed in madly before there was any hope of her squeezing through the opening. It came with such force, it filled the car instantly, knocking her off her knees. She was now totally submerged, the way out lost.

Dread . . . Trapped . . .

The car's wheels slipped below the water's surface. With its intrusive shape out of sight, a young frog croaked its approval. A female six yards away answered.

As the car sank to the bottom of the bayou, which was well over twelve feet deep, Kit was sharply aware that she needed to move more quickly than she ever had, yet the water held her back, subverting every action into slow motion.

Soft . . . The seat . . . The other way . . .

Steering wheel . . . Oh God.

Dread . . .

Turning what seemed like 180 degrees, she pushed forward. Her hands hit something that gave way. . . . The door . . .

With the pressure equalized, the door opened more easily than before, but still too slowly. A balloon in her chest compressed her heart. Another filled her skull.

She pushed harder, crowding the opening. The inflated orb

in her chest dissected up through her neck and filled her mouth.

Open . . . She pushed through.

She was going to make it.

Her foot—something had hold of her.

She kicked madly to free herself but couldn't. Turning, she followed her leg to the trouble. Whatever reserve she'd created by the three breaths was long gone and her body screamed for air. Behind her eyes, beacons from a hundred arc lights crossed each other, cone shapes cutting the darkness, filling the night with ozone in an incandescent extravaganza announcing her death.

She exhaled, releasing some of the pressure that seemed about to blow her eardrums. Her fingers found her ankle and the seat belt strap that had twisted improbably around her shoe. Tearing at the shoe's lace, she loosened it and slipped free. A clot of slimy vegetation floated into her face. Fighting madness, she clawed it away.

Which way to the surface? Her sense of direction was gone. Which way?

Cupping her hands to her mouth, she forced the tiny residuum of air from her lungs, hoping to learn which way the bubbles went, but they were too few or too small to feel.

No time left . . .

Blindly, she began to swim, her head throbbing. Dig . . . dig. There was only water . . . How much farther? . . .

Dig . . . dig.

How much farther?

Then her head punched through into the night air. Her gasp silenced every frog for a hundred yards up and down the bayou. And it was a terrible sound, so full of need and terror that even two armadillos in the bushes thirty yards away stopped mating to listen.

The air was so sweet, she couldn't get enough of it. She sucked it in and let it out . . . so sharp and fine.

She dog-paddled and concentrated on breathing until her arms began to tire. Then she struck out for the bank, keeping her face well above the duckweed floating on the bayou's surface. In just a few seconds, her knees hit bottom. When she stood, she felt her shoeless foot sink in muck.

Up on the pavement, from the direction of the restaurant, she saw headlights. Still thigh-deep in water, she began waving her arms. Afraid she was too far off road to be seen, she scrambled for the bank, her feet slipping on the slime coating the floor of the bayou.

The car was nearly upon her. Using some weeds for a handhold, she hauled herself out of the water, aware now that she had a major-league headache. She scrambled up the bank, ignoring the sharp stubble poking her shoeless foot and the piston slamming against the inside of her head. Gaining the shoulder, she threw her arms up and began wiping the air.

The oncoming lights blinded her to the driver's intent. Just when she was sure the car would speed by, twisting blue lights cut the night.

Thank God . . . a police car.

Arms at her side, her body racked with a shivering spasm, she watched the car slide past and ease onto the shoulder, where it sat idling for a moment before the driver got out and walked toward her, the beam from a powerful flashlight showing the way.

"Someone forced my car off the road," she said through chattering teeth. Hugging herself, she added lamely, "It sank."

The flashlight beam swung along the course her car had taken into the water, then returned and explored her from head to foot.

"Are you hurt," a male voice said. "Should I call an ambulance?"

She lifted a hand to shield her eyes. "Please . . . the light . . . it's blinding me."

"Sorry." The beam shifted to the ground.

"I don't think I'm hurt . . . just cold."

"Come on back to the car."

In the light from the flashers on the police car's roof, Kit could see the cop was thin and had a mustache and large ears. Staying on the shoulder side, he led her to the car's back door and opened it.

"There's a blanket you can use on the seat. Watch your head."

Kit climbed in, sat down, and wrapped herself in the blanket.

The cop shut the door and went around to the other side. He got a notebook from the front seat and climbed in beside her.

"I'm Heath Hubly, ma'am, the sheriff around here. Who are you?"

"My name is Kit Franklyn. I live in New Orleans."

"Where in New Awlins?"

She gave him her address.

"Now, what exactly happened?"

"Do you have an aspirin? My head is killing me."

"Sorry, I don't. You want some coffee?"

"I'd love some."

He got up and reached over the seat for a thermos. Returning to the seat, he unscrewed the lid, thought about pouring some into it, then offered her the whole thing.

The coffee, strong and heavily laced with chicory, lit a welcome fire in Kit's stomach. She took another swig and handed the thermos back. "Thanks."

"Can you talk now?"

As proof she could, she related how the car with its brights on had hit her from behind, spinning her out of control.

"Did he do it on purpose?"

"I don't know."

"Can you describe the car?"

"I never got a real look at it. Its lights were so bright, that's all I could see."

Hubly then asked her a series of questions that gradually took her all the way back to the reason for her visit to the area and what her job with Broussard entailed.

"I don't see you gettin' back to New Awlins tonight," he said when she was through. "You have any friends in the area?"

She thought about Trip Guillory, then said, "None."

"My wife and I have a big house with a couple extra bedrooms just up the road. You can stay with us tonight while we get this worked out."

"That's very kind."

"Least we can do after the poor welcome you've been given."

He left the backseat and got behind the wheel.

"My car," Kit said. "My handbag is in it and that metal cylinder I mentioned."

"We won't be able to get your car out until mornin', when we can see what we're doin'. Meanwhile, I'll get my deputy over here to make sure nobody disturbs anything."

He reached for his radio. "Car one to car two. Car two, come in." Only static came back. He repeated the call.

More static, then a voice. "Car two here. Sorry, Heath, I was takin' a leak. Whatcha got?"

Hubly thumbed the mike. "A lady's car went into Snake Bayou. . . ."

Hearing what it was called, Kit shuddered.

"Car's under with her handbag and some other things of value. I want you to come over here and ensure nobody makes off with anything that might float up durin' the night."

"You mean spend my entire shift over there?"

"Maybe you'd rather I find somebody else to do your whole job."

"Roger. . . . Snake Bayou. Be there in five minutes."

Still holding the mike, Hubly looked over his shoulder. "I'd like to wait until he shows."

Kit nodded and pulled the blanket tighter.

"I'm sure we've got aspirin at the house." Hubly lifted the mike to his lips. "Car one to Dispatch. Dispatch, come in."

A female voice answered. "Dispatch here."

"Donna, call my wife and tell her to get the back bedroom ready for a young woman who's had a traffic accident and will be spendin' the night with us."

"Roger, will do."

Hubly's deputy showed up a few minutes later. Hubly went back to the deputy's car and they spoke briefly. Upon Hubly's return, he apologized for the delay and they were on their way.

He lived a short distance past the funeral home on the opposite side of the road, in one of the simpler white two-story houses Kit had admired coming in. They were met at the door by a dark-haired woman who wore her short hair in the same style as the Angola warden's driver. She had a small nose with practically no bridge, so the frames of her oversized horn-rimmed glasses sat directly on her face. Kit thought the glasses a bad choice as they emphasized her thin lips.

She held her arms out to Kit as though they were old friends. "You poor thing. What on earth happened?"

Kit had not been thinking about her own appearance. From Mrs. Hubly's shocked expression, she realized she must look frightful.

Mrs. Hubly hugged her. Unsure of how to respond, Kit merely allowed it, keeping her own arms under the blanket.

"Somebody forced her car into Snake Bayou," Hubly said. "She needs some aspirin."

"Of course." Mrs. Hubly took Kit's blanketed arm. "Come on back to the kitchen."

"Beverly, you take good care of her," Hubly said. "I've got some things to do. Be back in an hour."

Hubly's admonition to his wife had a sharp edge on it, and Kit saw a faint shadow of resentment cross her face. The shadow departed with Hubly.

Beverly led Kit through a high-ceilinged entry hall papered with yellow-stained murals depicting old plantation scenes, then into a country kitchen with a redbrick floor and pots and pans hanging over an island cooktop. She sat her at a dark wooden breakfast table in front of a large window that looked onto what in the outside gloom seemed to be swampy wilderness.

Moving efficiently, Beverly soon placed an open bottle of aspirin and a glass of water in front of Kit and watched approvingly as she downed two of the white tablets.

"It's always amazed me that as long as aspirin has been around, they still don't know how it works," Beverly observed. "That's quite a bump on your head."

Following Beverly's eyes, Kit's hand went to the left side of her forehead, where it found a distinct bulge.

"Would you like some tea?" Beverly asked. "Or maybe you'd rather get cleaned up."

"Could I have both—cleaned up first?"

"Of course. Your room is upstairs. Can you make it?"

"I'm actually not hurt. But I guess I look pretty awful."

"Let's just say you wouldn't want your picture taken."

Despite all she'd been through, Kit managed a tepid smile. Hesitantly, Beverly's lips, too, crept up at the corners.

They went back to the entry hall and up a simple staircase missing a few spindles, and Beverly showed Kit to a room overlooking the main road through a fan-shaped window. The walls of the room were covered with a small floral-print fabric with a blue ground, a trick commonly used to hide walls too damaged to paper. The tall ceiling was covered with the same fabric, hanging in festoons that radiated outward from a decorative plaster ceiling medallion for the light fixture.

With her recent escape from a watery death still fresh in her mind, Kit felt as if she was in a coffin with a lot of headroom. Even with her sunken car subtracted from the equation, she wouldn't have liked the decor. Considering all the Hublys were doing for her, she was ashamed of herself for repaying their kindness with a critical thought.

"Sorry the room doesn't have a connecting bath," Beverly said. "In fact, there's only one bathroom on the whole floor. It's directly across the hall. You wait here and I'll get you something to wear."

While Beverly was gone, Kit took the opportunity to look at herself in the dresser mirror.

It was worse than she'd imagined. Her hair hung in limp ropes and it was decorated with little green rosettes of duckweed and strings of pond scum. Except for a slash of mud cutting across one cheek and the pallid lump on her forehead, her face was red and raw. She let the blanket drop and saw that her blouse and slacks, too, were decked with mud, pond scum, and duckweed. Her slacks had also picked up several hundred dried thistle seeds. Mud caked her remaining blue canvas shoe and oozed between her toes.

Mud . . .

She looked at the beige carpet and saw a trail of little mud smears.

Beverly returned with an armful of clothes, which she took to the big iron bed. "Here're a pair of pajamas, a robe, and slippers. We're about the same size, so I think they'll fit."

"I'm so sorry," Kit said. "I've tracked mud all through your house."

"It's nothing my husband doesn't do every day of the week.

I'll put a pot on for the tea. Leave your clothes outside the bathroom door and I'll throw them in the washer."

When Beverly was gone, Kit took off her muddy shoe and carried the dry clothes across to the bathroom, trying to walk only on the clean part of her mud-caked feet. From all the clutter on the bathroom sink and in the niches of the tub and shower surround, it was obvious this was the bathroom the Hublys used. Beverly had been given practically no warning of Kit's arrival, so in order to shower, Kit had to overcome not only her reluctance at once again being immersed in water but her aversion to other folks' pubic hair, which decorated the tub like characters in a foreign alphabet.

All that was forgotten as the hot, cleansing water banished even the most stubborn of her bayou souvenirs to the drain. Instead of getting out when she was clean, she explored the settings on the shower head until she found one whose pulsing jets hitting the nape of her neck sent ripples of pleasure down her back. Civilized water, she concluded, was far better than its wild cousin in Snake Bayou.

She dried on a clean towel she found in a small linen closet tucked into one corner of the bathroom, then combed her hair with her fingers. She slipped into the cotton pajamas Beverly had provided, added the terry-cloth robe, and put on the slippers.

Less than an hour ago, there'd been a good chance she would die in Snake Bayou. When she'd been fighting that seat belt wrapped around her shoe, survival had been all that mattered. She'd have given anything, stripped herself of every possession, if that's what it took to live. When she'd surfaced and taken that first lungful of air, the joy had been indescribable. Now, some thirty minutes later, she was suddenly engulfed in a cloud of self-pity. Not only was her apartment in New Orleans a dump; she'd used up her savings, nearly maxed out her credit cards, and now had no car.

Worse, she was standing there dressed in someone else's clothes.

Despite all this concern for her own welfare, she remembered that Nolen had agreed to feed Lucky and keep him inside after dark until she got home. She needed to call and tell him what had happened.

She unlocked the bathroom door and stepped into the hall, noting that Beverly had taken her dirty clothes to be washed, as promised. She went to the head of the stairs and was about to start down when she heard a sharp sound like a single hand clap, followed by Heath Hubly's angry whisper.

"I told you to put her in the *back* bedroom, not the front."

"Donna didn't say anything about the back bedroom," Beverly said, on the verge of sobbing.

"Keep your voice down."

"Besides, the back bedroom has that big water stain on the ceiling and the bed's not comfortable."

"All right, what's done is done. It wouldn't look right to move her into a worse room. We'll just have to deal with it."

4

Not wanting the Hublys to know she'd overheard their conversation, Kit retreated from the stairs and went to her room, where she tried to imagine why Hubly didn't want her there. It didn't look like a room being kept just as it had been when a child died. It seemed like an ordinary guest room. Maybe it was next to the Hublys' room and he was afraid she'd hear them making love. But was that any reason to slap Beverly, for that's what the sharp sound almost certainly had been.

There was a tapping at the door.

"Come in."

It was Beverly with a small tray bearing a teapot and a cup and saucer. "I thought you might prefer having this up here," she explained. Her left cheek had a distinctly ruddy hue.

"That was very thoughtful."

Beverly put the tray on the dresser.

Feeling partially responsible for what Hubly had done to

Beverly, Kit wanted to reach out to her. Puzzled over how to do this without revealing what she'd heard, she said, "Beverly is my mother's name."

"Really. . . . Do you and she get along well?"

"Not at the moment, I'm afraid."

This quick reversal into Kit's troubles and Beverly's apparent reluctance to pry terminated that line of conversation. At a loss for another thread, Kit said, "I need to make a phone call . . . to New Orleans. I'll reverse the charges."

"We've got a portable phone downstairs. I'll bring it up."

While waiting for the phone, Kit went to the tea tray, which also held a small plate of cookies. She poured herself some tea and took it to the window, still wondering why Hubly was so upset that Beverly had given her this room.

Outside, streetlamps she hadn't noticed until now were on, set so far apart, the dark patches between them made the illuminated areas look like a series of translucent tents. A car whose muffler was so loud that she could hear it through the glass rattled by, making her think Hubly's time would be better spent out ticketing loud cars than at home hitting his wife.

Down to her right, beyond a line of trees that blocked her view of the funeral home, she could see its illuminated sign. TAKE YOUR FINAL TRIP WITH TRIP. When she'd first read that, she had no idea how close she was about to come to *her* final trip.

Beverly tapped on the door and came in with the phone.

"I'm afraid I'm being a terrible burden," Kit said.

"Not to me," Beverly said, putting the phone by the tea tray. "After you've made your call, you've got a number of options. You can come downstairs and watch TV, I can bring up an extra set that will get only three channels, or I could find you some books."

"Let me make my call and see how I feel. By the way, the tea is excellent. Darjeeling, isn't it?"

Beverly nodded, obviously pleased at the compliment. "It's imported." Then, realizing what a silly comment that was, she added, "Like we grow a lot of tea in this country. I'll let you make that call."

When Beverly was gone, Kit picked up the phone and carried it to the bed.

Nolen picked up on the second ring. When asked if he'd accept the call, he said he would.

"Nolen, I'm afraid I won't make it back until tomorrow."

"Nothin' wrong, I hope."

"Not much. My car just sank in a bayou, with me in it."

"You don't sound dead."

"How would you know?"

"You got me there. Are you dead? 'Cause if you are, I'm takin' your dog."

"How is he?"

"You've only been gone a few hours. What could have happened to him?"

"He could have gotten out of the courtyard and run off."

"He didn't run off. He's right here. Want to talk to him? Never mind, he's gone after Mitzi. You sure he's been disarmed? I may have to charge you a stud fee."

"I think you've got it backward."

"Wouldn't be the first time. Guess you won't be openin' the gallery for me tomorrow."

"I don't know when I'll get back."

"Don't worry about Lucky. He'll be safe. I might even feed him. Seriously, is there anything I can do?"

"I'm not sure. I'll see how things develop in the morning, and if I need anything, I'll let you know."

She sat with the phone, thinking she ought to call Broussard and maybe her boyfriend, Teddy LaBiche, who ran an alligator farm in Bayou Coteau, 125 miles from New Orleans. Upon further reflection, she decided those calls would accomplish nothing except disturb the recipients. Teddy would probably want to come right over and get her, but she needed to stay, at least until they found her handbag.

God, what all was in there that would have to be replaced? Driver's license, Visa card, hospital ID . . .

There was a knock at the door, different from the way Beverly had announced herself. She pulled her robe closed more tightly. "Come in."

It was Heath Hubly, with another man behind him.

"Miss Frankly, this is Dr. Chenet. I thought, just to be safe, he should take a look at you."

Kit believed there were two kinds of doctors—young ones who didn't know what they were doing and old ones who had been in the dark a lot longer. Chenet was the latter.

"Heath told me about your narrow escape," Chenet said, coming toward her.

He was short and heavy, with a face that reminded her of Danny De Vito as the Penguin. He seemed mesmerized by the lump on her head, his small eyes fixed on it as though it were a holy relic.

Hubly walked over and pulled the drapes. When Kit glanced his way, he said, "If they're left open at night, we get a lot of condensation on the inside that runs down the glass and pops the paint."

"Please look this way, miss," Chenet chided.

Kit turned back to the doctor, who bent down and studied her lump. He placed his fingers gently on the surrounding skin. "Does that hurt?"

"No." She didn't tell him about the aspirin.

"Have you been experiencing any dizziness?"

"No."

He took a penlight from his pocket. "Please look straight ahead."

Rather than argue with him, Kit did as he asked. While Chenet examined her eyes, Hubly remained at the window, fiddling with the drapes.

Chenet put his penlight back in his pocket and picked up her arm by the wrist. The whole time the doctor was taking her pulse, Hubly stayed by the drapes.

"I don't think there's any problem here," Chenet said finally, releasing her. "But . . ." He moved his cracked leather bag from the floor to the bed, opened it, and began clattering through it, eventually producing a bottle of pills from its interior. He picked up Kit's hand and tapped two tablets from the bottle into her palm. "I want you to take those. What you need now is rest. They'll help you sleep, and there's also a little something in them to reduce that swelling."

Kit shook her head. "I don't need—"

"Miss, you're in no position to know *what* you need. But I am. Trust me. I know what I'm doing. I graduated from medical school and everything."

He turned and walked to the dresser, where he poured some more tea into Kit's cup and took it over to her. "Here you go. Be a good girl."

"I think you should listen to him," Hubly said from his post by the drapes.

Kit lifted her hand to her mouth, threw her head back, and reached for the teacup. She took a sip, swallowed, and handed it back.

"Very good," Chenet said, his Penguin face beaming. Hubly moved away from the drapes.

Chenet snapped his bag shut and looked at Kit. "And there's no charge."

"You don't have to stay in here," Hubly said. "Beverly's watching TV downstairs. I'm sure she'd like some company. I'm going back out."

"Maybe it's those pills," Kit said. "But I'm suddenly feeling very tired. I think I'd just like to turn in."

"That's probably best," Chenet said.

When they were gone, Kit went to the door, opened it a crack, and listened until she was sure they were downstairs.

Then she darted across the hall and into the bathroom, where she flushed the pills she'd tucked into a fold of her robe when the two men weren't watching.

From the way Hubly had hovered around the drapes and the interest they'd both shown in getting those pills into her, it was obvious Hubly was afraid she'd see something through that window.

Back in her room, Kit looked to see if it was possible to lock the door. She found a thumb bolt below the knob, but the mechanism was too crusted with paint to move. No matter. Since they thought she'd taken the pills, they'd probably assume she'd soon be asleep and wouldn't check on her.

She pulled the armchair by the dresser over to the window. She then tied the drapes together at eye level, using the tassels on the edges. She tossed the pillows from the bed onto the floor beside the chair and flicked off the lights.

Returning to the chair, she sat and propped the drapes open with the pillows, trusting that with the panels tied at eye level, the small opening below wouldn't be noticeable from the street even if Hubly should check. She hadn't the faintest idea what she was looking for, but from Hubly's actions, she believed it should be obvious.

For the next few hours, she watched the road out front diligently, her curiosity staving off boredom. In that time, probably thirty vehicles went by. Other than seeing the car with the loud muffler again, nothing jogged her interest. She was sure, though, something was going to take place she wasn't supposed to see.

With her watch broken and no clock in the room, there was no way to judge time. So she couldn't say whether it was passing slowly or quickly. But she did feel that whatever was supposed to happen was still in the offing. Or was it? Maybe Hubly had overestimated her. Maybe the event had already taken place and she'd been too dense to see it.

Having allowed that wedge into her thinking, it was a lot

harder to keep looking. She stayed alert for a while longer; then her eyelids began to droop. She fought back by lifting one leg and holding it up until it hurt. Then she switched legs. A little water on the face would help, but as soon as she ran across the hall, that's when *it* would happen.

Soon her eyes felt like the zoom lens on a camera unable to find the right focus. Chenet had been right. She needed rest . . . sleep. Nothing was going to happen. It had all been in her imagination.

The bed beckoned . . . soft and warm.

As she bent to pick up one of the pillows, a vehicle unlike any she had seen since beginning her vigil came into a light tent to her left.

A hearse, and behind it, a silver pickup.

The hearse passed in front of the house and then the pickup went by. The hearse was a different model from the one Trip Guillory drove—taller and boxier. The truck was jazzed up with elongated red crescents that crisscrossed on the door panels.

When the hearse reached the driveway of the funeral home, it turned in and the pickup followed. The trees prevented her from seeing any more.

Was that it? Could that be what Hubly hadn't wanted her to see?

It couldn't be. It meant nothing.

Unable to fight off sleep any longer, she got up and turned on the lights. She threw the pillows onto the bed, untied the drapes, and pulled the armchair back where she'd found it. With her foot, she erased the drag marks the chair had made on the carpet, then headed back for the light switch. She was asleep practically before she hit the bed.

5

"We got to do somethin' about those flies," Broussard said over the noise of the compressor for the pneumatic chisel.

Ten feet away, a fireman in full gear was using the chisel to cut a steel drum from the block of concrete inside. Nearby, two other firemen stood next to a gasoline-powered concrete-cutting saw.

The flies were attracted to the decomposing human feet and ankles protruding from the cement. Each time the chisel struck the drum, they rose in a throbbing mass, only to settle again quickly on the exposed flesh. The fireman paused in his work to chase a few flies away from his nose.

"I'll run back to the morgue and get some masks," Charlie Franks, the deputy ME, said.

Suddenly, over the compressor noise came the sound of a chopper. Looking up, Broussard saw the traffic helicopter from Channel 3 hovering over the site.

"Looks like were gonna be on the news again," Broussard said.

Franks shaded his eyes and looked up. "I thought the wall around this place would let us work in peace."

"There's no mind more devious than a reporter's."

"I'd never let *my* sister marry one."

"I've got an appointment with Phillip for lunch," Broussard said. "So I'm gonna head over to Grandma O's."

"And I've got to get those masks. I hope the next case you get makes you wish you'd drawn *this* one."

"Nobody's that unlucky."

As he passed the cop guarding the entrance to the parking lot where they were working, Broussard pointed at the chopper. "You got my permission to lock up that whole crew when they land."

Broussard owned six 1957 T-Birds, all with the original paint. With his large girth, he didn't so much drive them as put them on. Today, he'd worn the white one. As he pulled away from the curb, with the steering wheel wedged against his shirt, a rental truck equipped with a pneumatic boom turned onto the same side street. When it passed, the driver, Nick Lawson, crime reporter for the *Times-Picayune,* gave him a big grin. Having already lost site security to the chopper, Broussard allowed them to proceed with just a resigned shake of the head.

Phil Gatlin, oldest homicide detective on the force, was waiting at Broussard's perpetually reserved table in the rear of Grandma O's when he arrived. Even seated, Gatlin was tall.

"Where you been?" Gatlin said. "My stomach has been saying some rotten things about you."

"Pretty big enemy to have," Broussard replied, sitting down.

"Guess you don't put much faith in what mirrors tell you."

"Keep that up, you're gonna hurt my feelin's."

"'Bout time you got here, city boy."

The rustle of Grandma O's trademark taffeta dress had alerted Broussard to her arrival well before she spoke.

"Dis fella here's been starin' at other folks' food so hard, dey're beginnin' to think he's dangerous." She smiled broadly, showing the gold star inlay in her front tooth, poised to swat away any defense Broussard might offer.

"I'd tell you where I've been, but I don't think you'd want to know."

"Well, Ah hope you washed your hands."

"Excuse me, are you the owner of this restaurant?" a man who'd come up behind Grandma O asked.

"After a few hundred more payments to da bank," she replied.

He flashed a shield. "I'm Special Agent Willis, state Fish and Wildlife. Did you know it's illegal to kill a pelican?"

Grandma O glanced at the mounted pelican on the shelf over the bar, which also displayed a couple of stuffed armadillos and a nutria. "Ah *didn'* kill it," she said. "Ah bought it jus' like you see it from an antique shop on Royal Street."

"Well, it's also illegal to possess a pelican carcass. I'm going to have to confiscate it."

Grandma O pulled herself up to her full height, seemingly also to increase in circumference. "How come you didn' confiscate it *before* Ah bought it?"

Inflated like that, she was a magnificent sight, towering over the Fish and Wildlife agent by at least six inches and vastly outweighing him. Unlike most who were confronted by this wall of defiance, the agent never faltered.

"You are required to appear in court, where it is quite likely you will be assessed a hefty fine." He pulled an envelope from his back pocket and handed it to Grandma O. "You can find all the details of your appearance and the charges in there. I'll be back in thirty minutes. That should give you time to get the pelican down from its shelf. Please have it ready." He turned and made his way between tables, heading toward the door.

For the first time since Broussard had known her, Grandma O was speechless. "That's a bit of bad luck," he said. "I've heard those fines can run in the thousands."

"Is dat fair? Ah didn' kill da bird. Though Ah wouldn' mind gettin' mah han's on dat agent."

"Don't you see," Broussard said, "by buyin' it, you create a market for stuffed pelicans. Havin' sold it, the dealer you bought it from will buy another to replace it. The person he bought it from will do the same and so on, until somebody goes out and kills another pelican to satisfy the demand. As much as it hurts me to see a good friend in this kind of trouble, I'm afraid the law is correct."

Grandma O dropped her chin and looked menacingly at Broussard from the tops of her eyes.

"Yes, I'd have to agree," Gatlin said.

"Ah didn' know about any of dis."

"They can't let you off for that," Gatlin said. "The burden for being properly informed has to lie with the people."

"Open the envelope," Broussard prodded.

Her face wrinkled with disgust, Grandma O tore open the envelope. She removed the single sheet of paper inside and unfolded it to read, "Not everyone who says he's a Fish and Wildlife Agent really is." It was signed "Andy."

Growing even larger than when she'd tried to intimidate the fake agent, Grandma O turned on Broussard. "Well, ain't you a million laughs. You two mus' like to live on da edge, doin' somethin' like dis to someone who could put jus' anything dey wanted in your food." She smiled angelically. "Now, what can Ah get you?"

"Roast beef po' boy, alligator chili, and iced tea," Broussard said quickly.

Gatlin hesitated, apparently considering what she'd said.

"Come on, funny boy, Ah ain't got all day."

"A muffaletta, gumbo, and tea," Gatlin said. "And hold the strychnine."

"Dis ain't Burger King," Grandma O said. "Here, you have it my way."

After she was out of earshot, Broussard said, "I was afraid I was gonna get here too late to see the show."

"She was kidding about putting something in our food, wasn't she?"

"Of course."

"But you know she's going to get even somehow."

"Wouldn't be any fun if she didn't."

Thinking that the joke didn't seem as funny now, Gatlin began playing with a sugar packet. Noticing that Broussard's expression had grown serious, he said, "She's got you worried, too, huh?"

"Who?"

"Grandma O."

"It's not that. I sent Kit up to Angola yesterday to work on resolving the identity of that John Doe I've got. She was to take a picture of the inmate in question, print him, and come back. Shouldn't have taken more than a day. I expected to hear from her this mornin', but I didn't. I called the photo gallery where she's been workin' and learned she's been in a car accident. The gallery owner said she called him last night. Apparently, her car went into a bayou. He said she didn't sound hurt."

"She wasn't."

"How do you know?"

He pointed toward the door. "There she is."

Broussard turned and, sure enough, there was Kit, heading for their table. Both rose to greet her.

"I heard you had some trouble," Broussard said.

"Who told you that?" Kit replied.

"Owner of the gallery."

"He told you right. I don't know where to begin. . . ."

Broussard pulled a chair out for her and they all sat.

"I can start by giving you these," Kit said, handing Broussard a manila envelope and the metal cylinder.

"What are they?"

"I'll get to that."

"Hello, Kit darlin'," Grandma O said, arriving with the food. "Ah ain't seen you in awhile. You doin' okay?"

"No, I'd have to say I'm not."

Grandma O put her tray on the edge of the table and started setting out its contents. "Soun' like you got a story."

"I was just about to tell it."

"Oh, chil' Ah'd love to siddown, but Ah got to keep movin'. Will you tell me some other time?"

"If you like."

"What can Ah get you?"

Kit looked at Broussard's sandwich. "That looks good. I'll have one of those and a Coke."

"Comin' up." Grandma O looked slyly at Broussard. "Course it won't be *exactly* like his." Then she was gone.

"What did she mean by that?" Kit said.

"It's just a game," Broussard said. "She's tryin' to make us think she's gonna poison us for a prank we pulled on her. It's nothin'. So what happened?"

Gatlin lifted the top of his sandwich and poked suspiciously through the contents.

"First thing is, the warden doesn't let me in, but he comes out to meet me. And he says Ronald Cicero died of a heart attack night before last."

Hearing this, Gatlin suspended inspection of his muffaletta and listened harder. Broussard's interest, too, sharpened.

"But that didn't keep you from photographin' and printin' him," Broussard said.

"It wouldn't have, except that due to a miscommunication, the body had been cremated by the time I arrived."

Gatlin's heavy eyebrows jigged together. "That's two."

"Two what?" Kit asked.

"Pieces of bad luck," Gatlin replied. "I'm just keeping track."

"At this point, I didn't know what else to do, so I went over to the funeral home where the cremation took place, thinking I could at least bring back Cicero's remains, for whatever good it would do."

"That's not him in the metal cylinder, is it?" Gatlin said.

"I guess that's what we have to find out."

The old couple at the next table had been trying hard to eavesdrop. Hearing they were having lunch next to the remains of a dead man, they pushed their plates back and began waving for the check.

"How were you treated at the funeral home?" Gatlin asked.

"Pretty well. The owner had to check with his brother before he'd release the cremains."

"Who's his brother?" Gatlin said.

"The warden."

"Tidy little arrangement," Gatlin remarked.

"But they *did* turn the cremains over to me."

Grandma O arrived with Kit's food and put it in front of her. She eyed Gatlin's and Broussard's untouched meals. "You know you two ain't leavin' here 'til you finish dat."

"We're just caught up in Kit's story," Broussard explained. "We'll eat."

"You better."

Grandma O then went over to deal with the two eavesdroppers.

Gatlin raised his sandwich and took a small bite.

"I was ready to come back to New Orleans, but when I left the funeral home, my car wouldn't start.

"That's three."

"The owner took me to a garage and the mechanic there put in a new battery while I had dinner at a restaurant across the street. When I finally got on the road after dark, a car with its brights on came up behind me and hit my bumper. I lost control and flipped over in a bayou.

"I must have hit my head, because I was knocked out for a few seconds. When I came to, the car was sinking. Everything was black. . . . I couldn't tell up from down. . . . I managed to get out of my seat belt and open the door, but the water rushing in knocked me down and I got disoriented. I thought that was it for me . . . that I'd had it. But I was able to get out. I'll tell you, whatever troubles you think you're having, they don't seem very important when you've just escaped death."

"Don't suppose you got a look at the car that shoved you off the road," Gatlin said.

"Its lights were too bright."

"That's four."

"I flagged down a car that turned out to be the sheriff's."

"Any other cars pass you before that?" Gatlin asked.

"No, why?"

"Nothing. Go on."

"Not much more to tell. The sheriff took me to his home and he and his wife put me up for the night." She paused, wondering if she should mention Hubly's odd behavior about the window. Deciding that it hadn't amounted to anything, she skipped it. "In the morning, they pulled my car out. The guy at the garage, the one who fixed it earlier, thinks it's a total loss."

"Were you present when they retrieved your car?" Gatlin asked.

"No." She waited for him to reply, but he said nothing.

"They found my handbag and the cremains, but the photo and the prints the warden gave me were ruined. The sheriff drove over to the prison and got me another set. I know they're not what you wanted, but I felt like I should bring them. I wish I could have replaced the camera you gave me as easily. It's ruined, too, I'm afraid." Not wanting to give Broussard time to think about the camera, she hurried on. "The sheriff took me to a place where I could rent a car, and here I am."

Still worried about losing the camera, she tried to cover it up by putting Broussard on the defensive. "Thanks for sending me on such a simple assignment."

"Who could have known it'd turn out like that?" Broussard said. He picked up his sandwich, took a big bite, and chewed thoughtfully.

Kit had awakened that morning with no appetite and had politely declined Beverly's offer of breakfast. Now famished, she turned her full attention to her food.

They all ate for a few minutes without talking. Finally, Gatlin broke the silence. "Kit, you know everything that happened to you was choreographed, don't you? Your car not starting when you came out of the funeral home was intended to keep you in the area until dark, so you wouldn't be able to get a look at the car that forced you off the road. Whoever was responsible probably pulled one of your battery cables off or loosened it. . . . And let me guess, the guy who sold you the new one had to go somewhere to pick it up, right?"

Kit nodded.

"And the first person you encounter when you need help is the sheriff? Unlikely."

"That all crossed my mind," Kit said. "But why . . . why'd they do it?"

"I don't think they necessarily wanted to kill you," Gatlin said.

"Well, they almost did."

"That would have been a bonus. Running you off the road to kill you is like that crap they do in those James Bond films—put a snake in his hotel room and hope it bites him, when it's just as likely to go under the door, down the hall, and look for mice under the ice machine. No, it's more likely—"

"They wanted her separated from the cremains they gave her," Broussard said.

"I know I'm saying this a lot, but why?" Kit asked. "If they hadn't wanted me to have them, why give them to me in the first place?"

"They didn't want to appear uncooperative," Gatlin suggested.

"So why not just tell me the cylinder was lost in the bayou? They gave it back to me. Why?"

"I don't know," Gatlin said. He looked at Broussard, who could often fill in the blanks when blanks were about all they had. Kit, too, waited for a sage pronouncement.

"I think that . . ." Broussard began.

His two companions waited expectantly, the detective side of Gatlin wanting an answer, the competitor in him hoping Broussard hadn't beaten him to the explanation.

". . . we should go back to the morgue and examine those cremains."

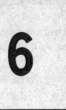

6

Kit had parked her rental car near Charity Hospital, where Broussard had his offices. She'd walked to Grandma O's after learning from Broussard's secretary that he was there. Going back, she rode with him in his T-Bird. Gatlin followed in his aging Pontiac, which he preferred over a departmental car because it was home to fewer cockroaches.

Nothing had happened on Kit's Angola trip to change her mind about her competence to conduct an investigation, unless it was to undermine it further. Some triumphant return—ruined the camera, lost her car, and never even got a look at Cicero. Better she'd stayed at the gallery.

She glanced at Broussard, molded against the T-Bird's interior like foam-fill insulation, wondering how this man had gotten to her so thoroughly that she'd once lived only for his approval. It had been her shameful secret—a grown, self-sufficient woman with an advanced academic degree pining for a pat on the head from her boss. It was absurd even when she'd believed herself to *be* self-sufficient and valuable. Now, realizing the truth, it was simply sad.

She should just go back to being a clerk—but not yet. She hadn't wanted to be involved in this puzzle, but now that she was, she couldn't walk away, especially if there was a possibility the Guillorys and the sheriff were responsible for nearly killing her.

Ten minutes later, they were all in the morgue. Guy Minoux, one of Broussard's morgue assistants, had used a soldering gun to free the top on the metal cylinder and it was now open.

Gatlin looked inside. "Jesus, how are you going to tell anything from that?" He crossed himself for saying "Jesus."

"Maybe we can't," Broussard replied. "First thing to do is X-ray it. Any bits of metal will show up clearly on the films. Often there are clues there—an eyeglass screw, a surgical clip, or a piece of a dental fillin' . . . that's really the best. If you can match an object in the cremains to a fillin' on a set of dental X rays, that's as good as it gets."

"Fillings don't melt during cremation?" Gatlin asked.

."Amalgam does. Porcelain crowns just sag a little. Dental gold and silver aren't affected at all."

"And being nonferrous, they wouldn't be picked up by the magnet funeral homes use on the cremains before packaging them," Kit said.

"Exactly."

"You got any dental films of this guy Cicero?" Gatlin asked.

"Arrived this mornin' from the military records depository in St. Louis." Broussard looked at his assistant. "I need a chest X-ray cassette and a piece of posterboard about the same size."

When Kit had worked for Broussard, the morgue was a place she avoided. She was there today only because she just *had* to know who was in the metal cylinder. During the interlude, while Minoux rounded up the requested items, the faint odor of Clorox crept up her nose and tickled her throat. Looking now at the morgue's stainless-steel benchtops, sinks, and human-sized drain boards, she saw that *washable* was the watchword here, right down to the ancient yellow tile on the walls. And they kept it uncomfortably chilly, at least for those still capable of feeling. But it probably did keep the odors down. She looked at the pitted concrete floor with its coat of shiny green paint and wondered if it was slippery when wet. Broussard had once said that when two surfaces come in contact, something of each is transferred to the other. What would she carry away from the morgue on the soles of her shoes?

Minoux returned with the things he'd gone to find.

Broussard put the cassette on a stainless gurney and laid the posterboard on top of it. He donned a plastic apron and a pair of rubber gloves and picked up the cylinder holding the cremains. Taking the cylinder to the gurney, he poured the contents onto the posterboard and carefully spread them until they were evenly distributed.

Understanding what Broussard wanted next without being told, Minoux rolled a portable X-ray machine over to the gurney and swung the arm holding the X-ray source over the cremains. He adjusted the height of the arm and looked at Broussard, who nodded his approval.

Minoux briefly turned the power on, then off.

"One more to be sure," Broussard said.

He lifted the posterboard so Minoux could turn the cassette over and expose another film. When that was done, Minoux took the cassette away to develop the pictures.

"This is gonna take a few minutes," Broussard said. "Might as well wait down by the snack machines."

The vending machines were just inside the entrance where bodies were delivered. For seating, it contained four dingy orange vinyl sofas. On one cement-block wall was a faded print of a flower-filled mountain valley.

While Gatlin and Broussard perused the offerings of the

vending machines, Kit found the cleanest cushion on the sofas and sat down.

"Didn't you two just eat?" she said.

"Window-shoppin'," Broussard replied.

The elevator doors opened and Charlie Franks got off. "Look at this," he said, "the whole brain trust in one place. What's going on?"

"It's a long story," Broussard replied.

Franks looked at Kit. "Does this mean you're coming back, I hope?"

"We don't know what it means," Kit said. "But I wouldn't think it means that. It's good to see you, though."

Franks turned his attention to Gatlin. "Hey, Phillip. How's it going?"

"My blood pressure's up, I got a case of athlete's foot I can't cure, and there's a varicose vein as big as a sausage sticking out of my ass. Otherwise, great."

"And how's the wife? On second thought, maybe I shouldn't know." He turned to Broussard. "We got that body out of the cement."

"Didn't take long."

"Once we got started, we were able to follow cleavage planes between the cement and the victim's clothing. We found the chain saw used to cut him up in there, too. They're dusting it for prints even as we speak."

The buzzer at the door sounded. "There are the remains now."

He went to the double doors and unlocked them, then looked back. "You all might want to hold your breath."

He opened the doors and two uniformed men wheeled in a gurney with a body bag on it.

"Room two," Broussard said. "We're workin' in one."

Kit held her breath until the gurney had passed through the swinging double doors leading to the autopsy rooms. In doing so, she was transported back to Snake Bayou, back to the moment when the seat belt had her shoe and the bayou was about to pour into her mouth and nose. She gasped for air, drawing curious stares from the two men.

"You all right?" Broussard asked.

"I just held my breath too long."

Gatlin sat on the sofa against the wall opposite Kit. He stretched his legs out and rubbed his face with his big mitt, fuzzing his eyebrows. He checked his watch.

Hands in his pockets, Broussard paced.

"I can't wait much longer," Gatlin said.

"Go on, then. . . . I'll keep you informed," Broussard said.

"A little longer maybe."

Five minutes later, Gatlin slapped his thighs and stood up, giving every indication his patience was exhausted. Before he could speak, Guy Minoux's voice came over the intercom.

"Dr. Broussard, those X rays are ready."

When they reached the autopsy room, Minoux already had the film clipped to a view box. With Kit close on his heels, Broussard went to the view box and perused the film.

Amid a hazy background of crushed bone fragments, half a dozen sharp images stood out. In the upper-left corner was a staple Kit recognized as one like those Trip Guillory had said were from the cardboard box the bodies were cremated in. Kit pointed this out and Broussard grunted in reply.

She saw two more staples, but refrained from saying anything. In the lower-right corner were two round objects that looked metallic.

"Ha." Broussard pointed at an image, slightly right of center. "That's the kind of thing I'm lookin' for."

Kit and Gatlin moved in for a closer look. Broussard was referring to a forked object about three millimeters wide and five long, with one leg shorter than the other.

Broussard again donned his apron and a pair of rubber gloves. He picked up a pair of forceps from a porcelain tray on the counter, slipped a pair of jeweler's magnifying lenses over his head, and returned to the X ray. After a quick refresher on the location of the forked object, he went to the cremains, nudged the magnifying lenses down over his glasses, and began picking through the ashes with the forceps in the general area where the film had located the forked object.

In less than a minute, he found it and put it in his palm. Moving to where the light was better, he examined the object briefly, nudged his magnifiers up, and looked at Kit and Gatlin, obviously pleased. "This is a pin-and-post casting— to hold a crown on a multirooted tooth," he said. "It's an important find for two reasons: The first is its distinctive shape. No two castings from different teeth can be identical. The second is that castings are not done much anymore. Most pins these days are little threaded rods commercially made in a variety of sizes that come with matching drill bits. So this was likely done a long time ago."

"Oh, I get it," Gatlin said. "If that work was done *after* the army X rays upstairs were made, it'd be worthless to us."

"It still may be," Broussard replied. "As it stands now, there's at least a chance it'll be helpful." He turned to Minoux. "We're goin' up to my office. Now the X-ray machine is workin' again, I'd appreciate it if you'd get John Doe number two out of the fridge and get me a full set of dental films. I'll want to see 'em soon as they're ready."

Broussard put the casting in a small snap-top vial. He shucked all his gear, put the vial in his pocket, and pulled the X ray from the view box. "Let's go."

Reaching his office, Broussard went directly to the view box behind his desk and hung the film he'd brought from the morgue. He retrieved the dental files from the military records he'd received and hung them, as well.

Still smarting from Gatlin beating him to the windup of his discourse on the significance of cast pins versus commercial ones, Broussard made sure he blocked Gatlin's view of the films while he gave them a quick once-over. It took only a few seconds to spot a familiar forked object. Not believing his eyes, he took another look at the film from the morgue, then glanced back at the dental film. Deep in thought now, he wandered away from the view box and began to pace.

With him out of the way, Gatlin and Kit studied the films for themselves. Seeing what Broussard had seen, Gatlin said, "I'll be damned." He looked at Broussard. "I'd have bet you a hundred bucks we wouldn't find that casting on these films."

"So the guy who was cremated at Angola really *was* Ronald Cicero," Kit said.

"That would seem to be the case," Broussard replied.

"Which means everything is on the up-and-up over there. And your suspicions that my misadventure was choreographed are wrong."

Broussard stared at the bookcases on the wall, his thumb under his chin, his finger rubbing the bristly hairs on the tip of his nose. Knowing he was now too far away to reach, Kit looked at Gatlin for a reply. But he just turned his palms to the ceiling and shrugged.

This little tableau was brought to an end by a knock at the door.

It was Guy Minoux, looking shell-shocked.

"You didn't bring those X rays," Broussard said, stating the obvious.

"I couldn't."

"Why not?"

"John Doe number two is gone."

7

Sam Parker, the night morgue man, couldn't believe it, either. "You say somebody stole a body from us? What for?"

Parker had skin the color of lightly creamed coffee. His normally friendly, steady eyes were now jittering in their sockets. When he said, "What for?" his voice slid up two octaves. He looked imploringly at each of his interrogators.

"We don't know why," Broussard said. "Right now, we're just tryin' to find out *how* it happened. There's so much activity in the morgue durin' the day, it seems extremely unlikely it was taken then. That's why we asked you to come in. Was there any time last night when the morgue was unattended?"

Parker's forehead became a ridged landscape. "Am I gonna lose my job over this? 'Cause I can't lose my job. I got two kids an' another comin'. I can't lose my job. I can't. . . ."

Broussard put a chubby hand on Parker's shoulder. "Sam, your job is safe. What happened?"

"I was just tryin' to be charitable, like First Corinthians

says. 'Though I speak with the tongues of men and angels and have not charity, I am become as soundin' brass or a tinklin' cymbal.' I wasn't tryin' to promote myself, just do somethin' for somebody who needed help. An' look what happens."

"Who did you help?"

"About eight o'clock, I hear the buzzer at the entrance. I go down there an' find an old lady with her arm in a sling leanin' on the buzzer with her good hand. I open up an' she says her car has a flat tire an' could I change it for her. I ax her couldn't she call the auto club or somebody, but she don't belong to one. Don't have any friends she can call an' can't afford to have a service station come an' do it. So what am I gonna do, tell her no? So I say okay. Wouldn't you?"

Broussard nodded. "Probably so."

"And her car is far enough away that when you reach it, you're out of sight of the morgue entrance," Gatlin offered.

"Yeah, but at the time, I don't think she's tryin' to lure me away. I just think I'm bein' charitable, you know? But I guess she had watcha callit . . . accomplices who broke in while I was gone."

"I'm sure she did," Broussard said.

"You know what the worst kind of crime is?" Parker said. "The kind that takes advantage of charity. I don't care if she *was* an old lady, they oughta throw the book at her and whoever helped her. 'Cause when you take advantage of somebody doin' a charitable thing, you make people afraid to help anybody. And then where are we? You tell me that. Where are we? Not a worse kind of crime. Oughta give 'em the death penalty." He looked at Gatlin. "What can you get for stealin' a body, anyway?"

"Never had a case like that. I'd have to check."

Broussard thanked Parker for coming in and assured him again he wasn't going to lose his job. When he was out the door, Kit was finally able to speak. "I've got it figured out," she said, leaping out of her chair. "When I was at the sheriff's house, I overheard him and his wife arguing about her putting me in the front bedroom. He wanted me in the back. He was so upset about it, he hit her."

"Any man who hits a woman is a danger to the entire fabric of society," Broussard said. "I'd never trust a man who did that."

"Outrage noted," Gatlin said. "Now can we hear the rest of her story?"

"Sorry. Go ahead."

"Later, when he came in with a doctor to see about the bump on my head, I noticed the sheriff seemed overly concerned about the drapes being open, kept fiddling with them. And the doctor tried to get me to take some sleeping pills, which I hid in my robe.

"After they left, I pulled a chair over to the window to learn what it was they didn't want me to see. I don't know what time it was because my watch was ruined in the bayou, but I'd guess it was at least eleven o'clock when I saw a hearse and a pickup go into the drive of the funeral home operated by the warden's brother."

"You're saying the body stolen from the morgue was in that hearse?" Gatlin said.

"Doesn't it all fit? The warden never expected me to want Cicero's cremains, but, like you said, they gave them to me to appear cooperative, except they weren't Cicero's cremains, because he was in the morgue here. Feeling that the cremains they gave me could be used to prove they'd lied about Cicero dying in the prison, Trip Guillory, the owner of the funeral home, disabled my car when he went to call his brother about giving them to me. They had me pushed into the bayou like you said, to separate me from the cremains. Then, during the night, they stole the body from here, ran back to the funeral home with it, cremated it, and switched those cremains for the ones they'd given me."

Gatlin looked at Broussard. "It sounds good."

"I agree, but before I raise a stink about this, I wish I had a little more proof. Right now, from their point of view, everything is correct. They gave you a set of cremains they said were those of Ronald Cicero. And we just proved they *are*. We haven't got much to support our position."

"What about the photos and the prints you made of Cicero?" Kit said.

"There's certainly that. But I'd like somethin' more."

Kit lapsed into thought. After a few minutes of mental reconstruction, she remembered the patterns she'd seen on the cremation retort's heat recorder. "I don't know if this is significant, but when I got to the funeral home, he'd just finished cremating the second body of the day. The first was supposedly Cicero. . . . I noticed the patterns drawn by the retort's heat recorder weren't the same."

"How'd they differ?" Broussard asked.

"I need something to draw with."

Broussard provided a pencil from a cache of pens, pencils, and probes in an American Academy of Forensic Sciences mug on his desk and gave her a sheet of paper from a stack next to his laser writer.

"This is the pattern of the cremation that took place immediately after the one they said was Cicero."

Leaning over the desk, with Gatlin on one side and Broussard on the other, Kit sketched the butte-shape the recorder had drawn just before she'd arrived at the funeral home, being sure to include the inch-long tight zigzag after the line had turned horizontally. She added vertical dividers indicating elapsed time and horizontal ones marking off temperature, explaining what they meant as she worked.

"In contrast, the earlier pattern looked like this." She drew the quickly rising line as before; then her pencil turned to the horizontal leg. She sketched a short stretch of zigzag, then drew a distinct upward bulge that had lasted for about thirty minutes. The rest of the pattern was like the first one.

She looked at Broussard. "What do you think?"

"Very interestin'." He put his thick finger under the zigzag on the first drawing. "This is where the body was actually burnin'—the combustion of the soft tissues caused these temperature fluctuations. This one"—he moved his finger to the other pattern—"obviously burned at a higher temperature."

"Any idea why?" Kit asked.

"Fat. The more fat present, the higher the temperature when the body burns. This was a man carryin' a lot of weight."

"But Cicero was thin," Kit said excitedly. "You can see that in the morgue pictures. . . ." She thought a moment. "And when I asked the warden what Cicero looked like, he was pretty vague, except he did say Cicero was *thin*. That *couldn't* have been him. We've got them."

"Don't know about that. But we have enough to contact the state prison board and ask for an investigation."

"Why haven't we got them?" Kit asked.

"If they realize the heat recorder is inconsistent with Cicero's weight, they'll probably doctor it or substitute a different record for the one you saw."

"Sounds like they're trying to cover up an escape," Gatlin said.

"Why cover up something like that?" Kit said.

"Maybe the warden's on thin ice. One more screwup and he's gone," Broussard suggested.

Gatlin looked at his watch. "Now I *really* have to go. Let me know what happens."

After Gatlin left, Broussard said, "I better get busy and write this up for the prison board." He picked up a file folder. "I've got a case here we're pretty sure was a suicide, but I'd feel a lot better if you'd check it out."

"I lost the camera and the print kit on my last assignment. I think I'll pass."

"Didn't we just prove that wasn't your fault?"

"If I'd been more alert, maybe I'd have seen it coming."

"There was nothin' to see."

"They couldn't have done to you what they did to me."

"Your givin' me way too much credit."

"I don't think so."

"I had your office repainted."

"That was nice."

"You ought to go look at it."

"I've got things to do."

"Go on, take a look. I think you'll be surprised."

"I'm sorry. I've got to go." Wishing she *could* return to work, but knowing that was impossible, Kit walked to the door and paused.

Thinking she might have changed her mind, Broussard's hopes rose. But then she opened the door and was gone.

For several seconds, Broussard stared at where she'd stood. He then went to the door, cracked it, and watched her until she stepped onto the elevator. Shaking his head, he walked down to Kit's office and unlocked it. Inside, on her desk, where he'd put it that morning, was a large bouquet of spring flowers in a cut-glass vase. He crossed to the desk and retrieved the card he'd written: "There's no one who can do your job better. Please come back."

When it had become clear she wasn't going to look at her office, he should have told her what was on the card, but it was so much easier to write than say. Ah well . . .

He dropped the card into the empty wastebasket, picked up the flowers, and took them to the main office for his two secretaries to enjoy.

Kit moved her rental car from the lot near the hospital to Nolen's garage, then set about reconstructing her life, such as it was. First, she walked over to the five-and-dime on Dauphine Street and bought a pair of tortoiseshell combs to replace those she'd lost in Snake Bayou, paying for them with a still-damp bill. Tired of having her hair hanging in her face, she didn't wait until she got home, but put them on outside the store, using the front window as a mirror. In the big picture, it was a small accomplishment, but it was surprising how much better it made her feel.

When she walked into the photo gallery, a well-dressed middle-aged woman was asking Nolen, "What does this mean?" She showed him the back of the picture she'd chosen. "'Nolen Boyd, intaphotography.' What's intaphotography?"

"It's what I do," Nolen said. "I'm into photography." He saw Kit and his smile at his own cleverness widened to a grin.

Usually when he told people what the phrase meant, they groaned or shook their heads at how corny he was, but this woman laughed, like bubbles streaming from a child's soap wand. She paid cash and Nolen bagged her purchase.

"Thanks a lot. . . . Come back."

When she stepped away from the register, Nolen looked at Kit. "Hey, kiddo, how are you?"

"Still a little frazzled."

"How'd you get back? Your car okay?"

"They think it's shot. I came back in a rental. Did Lucky give you any trouble?"

He waved away the thought. "Nah. He's out in the courtyard. I don't mean to be insensitive to what you've gone through, but would you be up to puttin' in a couple of hours here today? There's some darkroom work I just gotta get out."

"I can do that, if you'll give me an hour to take care of some things."

"That's fair."

Kit went out the back door and called Lucky, who burst out of some weeds as if he'd been launched. She knelt and held out her arms. A foot from reaching her, he jumped, the impact when he hit nearly knocking her over. She lifted him away and laid him on his back.

"Did you miss me, you little curmudgeon?"

She grabbed his ruff with both hands and gently worried it while his mouth hung open in ecstasy. A couple of yards away, Nolen's dog, Mitzi, sat and watched the action with obvious interest.

Kit rolled Lucky from side to side and scratched his belly. "What a sweet varmint you are."

Playing with Lucky like this pushed her close call in Snake Bayou further into the past. If it were left to Lucky, this would have gone on much longer. "Okay, that's all for now." She gave him a final shake and stood up. Remaining on his back, Lucky wiggled and squirmed.

Kit was six steps up the stairs before he got to his feet and bounded after her. As happy as she was to see him, she didn't allow him inside, a denial that bothered both of them.

Inside, seeing the x on the carpet, she looked up and saw that the ceiling crack had grown longer, now forming a half circle. She went to the bedroom and took her wallet out of her still-moist handbag. After spreading the wallet's contents over the bed to dry, she went to the dresser and sorted through a shoe box of warranties and other papers until she found the little booklet the store had given her when she'd bought her bag.

She took the booklet to the phone and punched in the number for customer service. When they answered, she asked for instructions on how to care for a bag that had been submerged. The voice on the other end told her total submersion was not a good idea for a handbag. And things didn't get any better, so when she hung up a few minutes later, she'd learned nothing, except that "maybe it'll be okay."

She called her insurance company next and told them what had happened and gave them the name and address of the garage in Courville where she'd left her car. They said they'd send a local claims adjuster over there to take a look. Meanwhile, her policy would cover the cost of the rental.

They promised to call and let her know as soon as the adjuster had made a decision.

Now that all the practical things had been addressed, Kit faced a yawning emptiness. Since it had happened, she'd told her story several times, but not yet to anyone who loved her.

She thought of her parents in Speculator, New York, and longed to let her fingers tap in their number . . . just call them up as though she'd never cut them out of her life. She believed they'd welcome the call, but it was not in her to make it.

Instead, she punched in the only other possibility.

"Hi, this is Kit. Is Teddy around? Sure, I'll hold."

At the moment and for the foreseeable future, Teddy was the only romantic interest in her life. With so much distance between them, they usually saw each other only on weekends, when Teddy would drive from his alligator farm to New Orleans early Saturday morning and leave early Monday. Before her recent slide into self-insufficiency, she'd generally been satisfied with that arrangement, happy not to have him underfoot all the time. Today, it seemed highly unsatisfactory.

"Hey LaBiche, where were you?"

"Out in the feed shed with one of my local women, quite an affectionate girl."

"Does she like men in traction?"

"Men in Traction . . . what is that, a rap group?"

"It's somebody we both know if he doesn't watch his step."

"I believe . . . yes, there she goes now, on her way home. I don't think she'll be back. Kind of unusual for you to call in the middle of the day. I must be some great guy."

"It's your money."

"I don't think so. You were hooked before you ever knew I was loaded."

"So you think."

"Listen, anybody who won't let me provide them with a nice place to live rent-free isn't after money."

"Maybe I'm just being devious."

"If you are, it's working. How about I jump in my pickup and drive over?"

"Can you?"

"I'm the boss, remember?"

"I'd like that."

"We'll go to Gautreau's for some of their great tilapia. I'll see you about six?"

"I'll be waiting. And Teddy . . . don't let 'em get behind you."

Kit hung up and sat by the phone, feeling much less empty inside, even though she hadn't gotten around to telling Teddy what had happened. She'd do that tonight.

With her own needs met, her thoughts turned to Beverly Hubly and how her husband had treated her. On impulse, she punched in the number for information. When the operator asked for the city, she said, "Courville," then "Heath Hubly, I'm not sure what street."

Fortunately, there was only one Hubly in Courville. She broke the connection to the operator and punched in Hubly's number, hoping *he* wouldn't answer.

He didn't.

"Beverly? This is Kit Franklyn. . . ."

"Yes, hello. Did you get home all right?"

"I'm there now. Listen, I want to thank you for all you did."

"There's no need. I'm sure you would have done the same for me."

"And . . . there's something else. I like you, so I'm going to be frank. I heard how upset your husband was because you put me in the wrong bedroom. And I heard him slap you."

She said nothing in reply, and Kit imagined that Beverly's face was now crimson with embarrassment. "I wanted you to know you don't have to take that from anybody. You don't deserve that kind of treatment and it doesn't have to continue.

There are people at your regional Department of Human Services who can help you. I hope you'll talk to them."

"It's not really so bad," Beverly said. "He just gets like that sometimes."

"He shouldn't *ever* get like that. Make the call."

"I'll . . . think about it. Oh . . . there he is. I better go."

The line went dead.

As she hung up, Kit was sure Beverly wasn't going to make that call. But maybe she wouldn't have to. Once the prison board figured out what was going on over there, Hubly himself might be getting some jail time. Then Beverly could easily get free of him. The one thing Kit saw as a possible impediment to that scenario was that this was all happening in the state where corruption and graft had been invented.

Still feeling dirty and slimy from her experience in Snake Bayou, Kit was as pleased at the opportunity to get dressed up as she was at the prospect of seeing Teddy. In going through her wardrobe, she found that merely touching her silk dress with the ruby paisley print reminded her of algae sliding over her skin. Once her favorite, she doubted she could ever wear it again. She chose instead a black short-sleeved linen dress with a white yoke and crisp white rick-rack trim, accessorizing with spectator heels, a five-strand pearl bracelet, and pearl earrings caged in gold. Looking at herself in the mirror, she felt for the first time completely out of the bayou's grip.

Teddy buzzed to be let in just as she finished putting a few essentials in her purse. She pressed the button, releasing the gate lock, and went to meet him.

Stepping onto the porch, she saw Lucky bolt across the courtyard, his tongue lolling at the sight of old Teddy, who barely had time to wave at her before Lucky was on him.

Teddy squatted on his haunches and gave Lucky what he wanted—a hard Dutch rub, so Lucky's eyes rolled back in their sockets in sheer pleasure.

Kit went down the steps. "I think he loves you more than he does me."

Teddy looked up at her. "Oh, did you want your head rubbed, too?"

"I was talking to you, not Lucky."

Teddy gave the little dog a final scratch under the chin and stood up.

Teddy's dress code contained very little latitude, its dictates usually putting him in jeans, a denim shirt, alligator boots, and a rakish straw hat, a look only someone with his lean good looks could pull off. When the occasion required, though, he could adapt. Tonight, he was turned out in pleated Bedford cord slacks of an olive hue that picked up one of the colors in his Algarve checked shirt. A woven cowhide belt and Amalfi loafers ensured he was, at that moment, the most cosmopolitan generator of alligator skins in the state.

Teddy looked Kit over and shook his head. Between visits, he'd often think of her large feline eyes. Sometimes he'd picture her lips, which, despite the little girl spray of freckles across the bridge of her nose, gave her face an elegance that made his whole body ache with pleasure. Sometimes, his memories never reached her face. "Franklyn, you're a handsome woman."

She stepped closer and he kissed her lightly on the lips.

"We'd better go," he said. "Our table is for six-thirty."

Gautreau's sits quietly on Soniat Street in the uptown section of the city, the only whisper of its identity a *G* in the tiles on the front steps. The maître d' greeted Kit and Teddy by name and showed them to a table back by the oak wine and liquor cabinets that had held medicinals for the half century the place served as a pharmacy. Without being told, the waiter brought two glasses of white wine and withdrew to let them study the menu.

Kit had thought it would be hard to recount to Teddy what had happened to her in Courville, because she'd have to relive it in the telling. But here, with soft piano music in the background, surrounded by dark paneling and gilded ceiling fans turning lazily overhead, it all seemed so improbably far away, the tale began pouring out.

"You know that car I used to have?"

"What do you mean, 'used to have'?"

Teddy sat speechless for the next ten minutes, his lower jaw dropping farther and his eyes growing wider with each new twist in her story.

"So I ended up losing my car, Andy's camera, and the print kit. And I never saw any of it coming. Another effective performance . . ."

Teddy shook his head in amazement, then looked into her eyes in silence, something obviously on his mind.

"What?" Kit said.

"I've never said anything about the effects those kidnappers had on you, because I figured you needed time to sort out your feelings. But I hate seeing you continue to beat yourself up over it. I was there. I know what you went through. You can't experience something like that and not be changed by it. But this feeling you have that you alone should have been able to reverse the situation is unrealistic. No matter how competent and self-sufficient we are, sometimes we all need help." He reached across and took her hand. "We're a team. With you, I'm stronger than I am by myself. And I'd like to think I make you stronger. We die alone, but life is to be shared."

"You're saying I should go back to work for Andy?"

"Actually, I *have* been thinking that your taking a leave wasn't a good idea. But . . . I swear, he can get you into more trouble—"

Kit pulled her hand free. "That's not fair. It wasn't *his* fault I got shoved into that bayou."

"I like Andy a lot, you know that. But whose idea was it to send you up there?"

"He couldn't have known what was going to happen."

"My point is . . . it's a dangerous job. Are you thinking of returning to it?"

In Kit's mind, whether she did or didn't return was a decision for *her* to make, not Teddy. But since she *wasn't* going back, there was no reason to make an issue of it. "For now, I'm staying at the photo gallery. And to be fair to Nolen, I should work Saturday and Sunday to make up for the time I took off. Would you mind that we won't be able to spend the weekend together?"

"I'll miss you, that's for sure. But as you said, it sounds like the fair thing to do."

After a wonderful dinner, they returned to her apartment to take Lucky on his usual evening walk with Nolen and Mitzi. Though he could easily afford the best suite in any hotel in the city and surely couldn't find Kit's apartment any more agreeable then she did, when Teddy visited, he never pressured her to stay with him at a nice place, but accepted her world as his. Tonight, as she fell asleep in his arms, she thought about his comment that life is to be shared. She had no quarrel with most corollaries to that view, especially agreeing with the one that had brought him into her bed. But when she reviewed her many failures over the last two months, including the Courville fiasco, his words brought her no comfort.

8

Bubba Oustellette waved at Kit through the window of the booth guarding the entrance to the New Orleans Police Department vehicle-impoundment lot. Believing he'd be right out, she left the rental car running.

The day after she'd explained about her "accident" to the insurance company, they'd called back to say the car was indeed a total loss and their claims adjuster had set its value at $2,500. Thinking this was criminally low, she'd called Bubba to ask his opinion.

Bubba was Grandma O's grandson. He was the one who kept Broussard's fleet of T-Birds running, and he knew just about all there was to know about cars and engines. When she'd told the insurance company Bubba believed they were a thousand too low, they'd suggested she and her adviser meet with the adjuster and negotiate, which meant she'd have to drive all the way back to Courville. As she was in no position to write off a thousand dollars, and since Bubba was willing to use some of his accumulated overtime leave to go, she'd reluctantly agreed.

A man in gray shirt and pants came out of the lot and went into the booth. He and Bubba exchanged a few words and Bubba came out and walked to Kit's car. He opened the passenger door and looked in.

"Hey, Doc Franklyn, how's it goin'? You sure we're not gonna need da gun?"

He was referring to the times Kit had asked him to accompany her on expeditions where there was an element of danger. In such cases, he always brought a pistol with a very long barrel.

"Today, we're just going to talk to a claims adjuster."

"So we *are* gonna need da gun." His bushy black beard parted, revealing enough white teeth to rival Teddy Roosevelt's smile on Mount Rushmore.

"We're negotiating, not committing armed robbery. Come on, get in."

He did as she asked and settled into his seat, his short stature causing his feet to barely brush the carpet. Kit backed up, slipped the car into drive, and they were off.

For most of the time Kit had known Bubba, his clothing had consisted of many copies of the same outfit—blue T-shirt, blue coveralls, and a green baseball cap bearing the Tulane logo of an ocean wave showing its teeth and carrying a football. A few months ago, after reading a *Cosmo* article on personal growth, he had abruptly discarded this combination in favor of a brown T-shirt, brown coveralls, and a purple Saints baseball cap bearing a fleur-de-lis. Today, he was back to the old costume.

"What happened to your new look?"

"It jus' wasn't me. Nice car . . . could use some new shocks, though. You see dat piece in da paper yesterday about somebody stealin' a body from Andy?"

"I saw it. Nick Lawson's byline, of course. I swear I don't know where that man gets his information. You can't keep *anything* from him."

"He sure made it soun' like Andy was runnin' a sloppy operation."

"It wasn't Andy's fault at all. It's not as though stealing bodies from a morgue is something you always have to be on guard against. I'll bet that's the first time it's ever happened anywhere."

"Why you figure somebody did dat?"

She hesitated, wondering if she should tell Bubba what she knew. Lawson apparently was still in the dark over the reason for the theft, and with an investigation now under way, it was best he stay that way. Bubba certainly knew how to keep quiet, but if Lawson found out the rest of the story, even she might wonder if the leak had been Bubba. To spare him that, she dodged the issue.

"Good question."

She hadn't lied, not by the strictest interpretation of the word. But that didn't make her feel any better about the path she'd taken, especially since Bubba was doing her yet another huge favor. Her discomfort over this lasted all the way to Courville, where the tire marks her car had made as it had flown off the road into Snake Bayou generated other thoughts.

On the way over, they'd seen a wreath on some skinned trees near the highway, obviously the site of a fatal accident. If she'd drowned here, would there be a wreath for her? No. She'd just be dead.

Bubba noticed her interest in the water and the marks on the road. "Is dat where you almos' slept with da crawfish?"

"That's the place."

"Ah saw a drowned person once. It ain't somethin' Ah'd recommend . . . drownin', Ah mean." He thought a moment, then added, "Seein' da victim wasn't da most fun Ah ever had, either."

Long before leaving New Orleans, Kit had decided that if she saw Henry, the mechanic who had likely been part of the scheme to delay her departure on her first visit, it would be best to say nothing. She reminded herself of that a few minutes later as she rolled into the garage's driveway for their one o'clock appointment.

Her car was sitting out front by an old cement mixer. Standing beside it was a man with a leather folder the size of a legal pad.

"That looks like him," she said, pulling in so the front bumper nearly touched the cement mixer.

Apparently realizing who they were, he moved toward their car as they got out.

"Dr. Franklyn?"

Kit walked over and offered her hand.

"Ah'm Dewey Lancon, your claims adjuster."

Lancon had black hair and a full black beard that looked as soft as cat fur. His smile was forced and unnatural, like the fit of his suit.

"Before we proceed, Ah should warn you dat Ah have been generous in mah assessment of dis vehicle's value. So Ah'm afraid you have made an unnecessary trip. Ah tried to explain dat to da people in New Awlins, but city folk don't listen. However, Ah *am* willin' to hear you out."

Bubba stepped up beside Kit.

"This is Bubba Oustellette, my mechanic. He'll tell you why we think the car is worth more than your assessment."

While the two men shook hands, Kit took a moment to glance at her poor car, which was covered with a dried scum.

"Lancon," Bubba said, trying the sound of the name on his tongue. "Where are your people?"

"Plaquemines Parish mostly," Lancon said, "aroun' Delacroix."

"Your daddy's name wouldn't be Cezaire, would it?"

"Sure is."

"Mama's name Oline?"

"How'd you know all dat?"

"You remember fishin' for buffalo an' gaspergou with Alcide Oustellette an' his two boys in Coon Lick Swamp?"

"Well kick me an' turn me aroun'. Bubba Oustellette. You remember how your momma used to clean da nasty out of dat buffalo meat in a washin' machine?"

"Lot of folks today don't know how to clean buffalo or cook gaspergou."

"Didn' we used to have some fine Christmas boucherie?"

Bubba looked at Kit. "Dat's a crawfish boil."

"You know what Ah remember most bout your momma?" Lancon said. "Dat awful alligator-fat cough syrup she gave me one day." Lancon's smile was now genuine.

"It stopped you from coughin', though."

"Least in front a her it did."

Feeling about as out of place as she ever had, Kit said, "If you two will excuse me, I'm going across the street and wait. Bubba, when you finish, come on over."

Kit crossed the road and went into Beano's restaurant. Since it was a little after one, the place wasn't crowded. Two men wearing overalls were sitting in the booth she'd chosen the last time she was in, so she went instead to one nearer the back, where if she looked between the *O* and *S* on the name Beano's written in red across the front window, she could see Bubba and the claims adjuster in animated conversation.

"It's you, ain't it?" a voice said. Belle, the waitress. "The artist from the other day."

"You've got a good memory."

"Not really. Ain't been long enough to forget anything."

"Did your husband make parole?"

Belle's face fell. "Those tight asses on the board? No."

Kit had doubts that parole was a useful concept. But the situation called for some expression of sympathy. "It's hard to have your hopes crushed like that."

"Our trouble was, we let our lives get in the hands of other people. I'm just afraid if he stays in there long enough, he may never get out."

"I know what you mean. Prisons are dangerous places."

"This one more than most, and it's not only the other inmates you have to worry about."

This perked Kit's interest. "What do you mean?"

Apparently sensing that Kit was no longer making casual conversation, Belle shied. "Nothin' . . . I didn't mean nothin'. What can I get you?"

"I'm expecting a friend. So for now, coffee."

While waiting for Belle to return, Kit looked out the window and saw Bubba heading for the restaurant. He located her as soon as he came inside.

"Well, what happened?" she asked even before he got seated.

"Thirty-five hundred. Check should arrive in a couple days. You can keep da rental car till da money comes."

"You're a genius."

"Ah'm jus' well connected. An' hungry, too."

"Lunch is on me."

"Might not be much left of dat thirty-five hundred after Ah order."

"I can handle it."

They had a good lunch and were lingering over pecan pie and coffee when, during one of Kit's frequent glances out the window to make sure the rental car wasn't in anybody's way, she saw something that sent a jolt of current down her spine.

"We've gotta go," she said, digging in her bag. She found a twenty and a five and threw them on the table. "Come on."

Bubba took another mouthful of pie and hurried to catch her, but it wasn't easy. Once she was out the door, she broke into a dead run. Bubba was sure she'd hold up at the road to wait for the oncoming dump truck in the near lane to pass, but she didn't, scooting across its path in a perilous maneuver that made him close his eyes in horror.

By the time the truck had passed and Bubba could cross, Kit was already in the rental car. She backed up in a tight turn and waited for him to get in. As soon as his legs were clear of the door, she dropped her foot onto the gas. Spitting dirt, the car surged forward, slamming Bubba's door closed.

"What are we doin'?" Bubba said, wide-eyed.

"No time to explain." The car bounced onto the road and fishtailed before she got it heading in the direction of the funeral home.

In a few minutes, she caught the dump truck, which was dropping little clay bombs onto the asphalt from the mountain of dirt it was carrying. She swung out to pass, hoping to see—yes, there it was, about a hundred yards ahead: the pickup she'd seen tailing the hearse that night at the Hubleys'.

Not wanting to attract the pickup driver's attention, as soon as she was clear of the dump truck, she pulled back into the proper lane and eased up on the gas. She followed the pickup for about a mile and then it turned right, toward the Courville business district. When she reached the turnoff, she followed.

This road was lined by single-story houses and there were numerous side roads that emptied an exasperating number of cars into her path, so her view of the pickup was soon blocked.

The street eventually dumped them onto the Courville town square, whose focal point was a military figure astride a bronze horse. Fearing she'd never lay eyes on the pickup again, she proceeded around the square, checking the cars and trucks parked nose-in to the curb.

Then she saw it . . . same color, with elongated crescents on the door, primer spot on the rear fender . . . no question. She continued around the square and eased into the first available parking place.

Now what?

The same question was on Bubba's face.

Her pursuit of the pickup had been an instinctive act flaring from the smoldering anger she'd felt since realizing her off-road adventure at the bayou had been no accident. Sure, there was an investigation under way, but she wasn't involved in it. This was personal.

She turned to Bubba. "I have reason to believe the pickup I followed over here was involved in the theft of that body from Andy." Now Bubba surely knew she'd held back when they'd discussed the theft earlier. But he gave no indication of it. "I'm going to look through its glove compartment. Will you come with me?"

"Ah had a hunch dis trip wasn't gonna be as simple as it sounded. Le's go."

There was no way to know how long the driver would be away from the pickup. That made Kit want to reach it as quickly as she could. But since no one else in town seemed in a hurry, she and Bubba tried to blend in by strolling to it on the sidewalk.

When they were nearly there, Kit waited for an aging Marlboro man and his Irish setter to pass, then gave Bubba his instructions. "You wait on the sidewalk and keep an eye out for the driver."

"How am Ah gonna know who dat is?"

"Body language—the direction he's looking, car keys in his hand, things like that.

"An' the gun he's pointin' at me?"

"And position yourself so if he's in that hardware, he can't see me through the window."

Bubba took up his post. Wishing it was Broussard's far more ample frame shielding her, Kit stepped off the curb and reached for the pickup's door handle.

Locked.

She returned to the sidewalk. "It's locked. Can you open it?"

"You sure we oughta be involved in dis? Dese rural towns,

police can do anything to you. Ain't no civil liberties union here."

"I'll take full responsibility."

"Ah can see it—ten years from now, Ah turn to my new cellmate an' say, 'She tol' me she'd take full responsibility.' "

"It's okay. We're investigating a crime."

"An' you won't have any trouble provin' dat?"

"Just open the door."

Sighing, Bubba reached into his pocket for his Swiss army knife and stepped off the sidewalk.

Kit checked the door to the hardware, then looked to her right. Coming toward her a block away were two women with a little kid between them, hands linked like cutout paper dolls. Nothing to her left. When she turned to scope out the square, she found Bubba back beside her.

"Did you get it?"

He looked sincerely hurt. "You thought maybe Ah couldn't?" There was no time for verbal sparring. "Take over here."

She hurried to the truck and climbed in.

Surprisingly, the glove compartment actually contained a pair of Isotoner gloves. She removed them and began sorting through the other contents—some maps, a yellow receipt for an oil change, a page torn from a list of motel phone numbers, a couple of packs of Kleenex, and a small spiral pad with nothing in it. That was all.

Very disappointing.

She put all the papers back and was about to do the same with the gloves when she noticed the edge of a white envelope mixed in with the maps. She extracted a plain number ten envelope with no addresses on it. The flap was tucked in, not sealed.

Inside was a candid head-and-shoulders snapshot of a man partially framed by a doorway trimmed in cut stone. He was square-jawed, but with a face far from sculpted. His curly brown hair covered his ears and he wore Clark Kent glasses. Noting shadows of writing on the back, she turned the picture over, where she saw in neat block printing the name Anthony Hunter. Under that was a street address: Peyton Road, Coldwater, Miss. Below that: University of Tenn., Dept. of Physiol.

Thinking that there might be some connection between this man and the body stolen from the morgue, Kit placed the envelope in her lap, put the Isotoners back, and closed the glove compartment. She slid out and relocked the truck, the fear of being caught already lifting.

Even before she hit the sidewalk, she was telling Bubba, "Go . . . go."

The contraband white envelope felt hot in her hand, as though it were glowing, telling everyone they passed that she'd filched it. She shoved it into the pocket of her slacks, leaving her hand in there with it so her arm would hide the part still visible.

When they were safely in the car, she gave Bubba the envelope and her handbag. "I'm going around the square. When we pass that pickup, write down the license number. There's a pen in my bag."

"Ah already memorized it. Can we please go?"

"Okay. Write the number on the envelope for me."

All the way back to the road where they'd turned off to follow the pickup, Kit kept one eye on the rearview mirror, but she saw nothing to indicate they were being pursued.

"We did it," she said, turning the car toward home.

"Did what?"

"Got away clean."

"What with?"

"I'm not exactly sure. . . . I mean, I know it's a picture of a man . . . who I think lives in Coldwater, Mississippi, and works at the University of Tennessee in Memphis."

"An' dat'll lead to da body snatchers?"

"You ask too many questions."

A few miles later, Bubba said, "Uh-oh."

She glanced at him to see what was wrong. He was looking at the side mirror.

Checking behind them, Kit saw an oscillating blue light atop a police car.

9

Kit fanned her hand at Bubba. "Put the envelope under the seat."

"Ah can't be arrested. Ah'm goin' fishin' tomorrow night with Bobbie Dupree," Bubba said as he hid the envelope.

Kit pulled onto the shoulder, her mind chockablock with half-baked explanations of why they'd broken into the pickup.

The patrol car eased off the road and stopped. Heath Hubly got out and walked toward them. Still unprepared, Kit rolled down the window.

"Dr. Franklyn, what brings you back to town?" Hubly asked, his face filling the window opening.

"A meeting with my insurance company's claims adjuster to settle on my car."

Hubly looked around her at Bubba.

"That's my friend Bubba Oustellette. He's also my mechanic. He helped negotiate the final figure for my claim. The car was a total loss."

Hubly's eyes roamed over the car's interior.

Guilt whispered in Kit's ear: He knows . . . he knows.

"Did I say my car was a total loss?"

"I believe you did."

That was smart, Kit thought. Get a grip. . . . "Is this a social stop, or did we break a traffic law?"

He studied her without speaking, probably preparing to recite the section of the Courville legal code for breaking and entering.

"Didn't break any law," he said finally. "Just repaid the kindness I showed you the other night by conspirin' against me with my wife."

"I'm not following you." It was true; she didn't know what he meant.

"You called her last week and advised her to leave me."

Of course . . . "You have no right to hit her . . . none at all. And she doesn't have to take it."

"Well, that's none of your business, is it? I'm gonna get in my car and see you to the edge of town. And when you're gone, don't come back." He shoved a nightstick and his arm past Kit's nose and pushed on Bubba's shoulder. "That goes for you, too, little man. Now leave."

He stood there while Kit started the engine and pulled back onto the road. He then returned to his patrol car and tailed them to the city limits.

As they put distance between themselves and Hubly, Bubba said, "Dat 'little man' remark makes me want to come back. You gonna take his advice?"

"I'm not sure."

Kit heavy-footed it all the way back to New Orleans, eager to get with Broussard and discuss what she'd found. She dropped Bubba off at the impoundment lot at 4:40 and was knocking on Broussard's door fifteen minutes later. Happily, he was in, sitting at his desk. "Kit . . . I sure wasn't expectin' to see you."

"I suppose it's too soon to have heard anything from the prison board."

"Actually, I called 'em late yesterday."

"And?"

"Nothin' out of order at the prison. End of investigation."

"That's nuts. How long's it been?" She thought a moment. "Six days, including a weekend. It'd take that long to get the authorization paperwork down. What kind of investigation can you conduct in four business days?

"Same reaction I had."

"Well, I did a little investigating on my own today." She explained why she and Bubba had gone to Courville, then told him about her conversation with the waitress in Beano's.

"I remarked that prisons were dangerous places and she said something like, 'This one more than most, and the other inmates aren't the only ones you have to worry about.' When I asked her what she meant, she seemed afraid to say any more . . . worried, I think, about her husband, who's still in there."

"She must have meant the guards are dangerous, too."

"That doesn't seem like something you'd be afraid to talk about. Of course guards are dangerous—they have guns. But I have the feeling it was more than that. And I found this." She reached in her bag and pulled out the white envelope. She gave Broussard the picture and explained how she'd acquired it. "Think it means anything?"

"Can't say yet. Did you get the license number of the truck?"

"It's right here." She handed him the envelope.

"You're gonna get tired, you keep standin'."

While Kit pulled one of the two wooden chairs for visitors closer, Broussard reached for the phone. He entered the number for Homicide and had them run the plate number. After a brief wait, he nodded and expressed his thanks.

"Guess who owns the truck?"

Kit shrugged.

"Trip Guillory."

Broussard picked up the receiver again and punched in the number for information. "Memphis . . . the University of Tennessee, Department of Physiology." He wrote down the number and called it. "It's five o'clock. Hope somebody's still there."

Someone was. "May I speak to Anthony Hunter please." He listened, his head nodding slightly. "I wasn't aware of that. Do you know what the circumstances were? . . . I see. What did he do there? . . . Was he a member of the department long? . . . Yes, it is. . . . I'd rather not say, but I appreciate the information."

He hung up and stared at the phone, ignoring Kit until she rapped on the desk to remind him she was there.

"Anthony Hunter is dead. He died two days ago while joggin'. They found him by the road, half a mile from his home. The woman I talked to said he had a heart attack."

"You believe that?"

"Somebody does. I don't have enough information to judge."

"Come on, admit it. This can't be a coincidence."

"No, probably not. But there are two possible explanations. You'd like to believe he's dead because his picture was in the truck. Could be his picture was in the truck because he's dead."

"I don't get it."

"Suppose Hunter once lived in Courville and the local paper wanted to do an obit. That picture could be the one sent to Guillory so he could take it over there."

"I'll give it a one, and that's generous."

"I'm not sayin' that's the actual explanation. It's merely an example."

"All right, you've paid homage to the god of reason; now pick . . . door one or door two."

"I can't."

Kit blew air through her lips in exasperation. "Okay, let's put Hunter in context. Who was he?"

"Tenured associate professor of physiology. Ten years in the department. That's as much context as I got. Hardly enough to help us decide anything."

"Well, I think it's door one. What are we going to do about it?"

"Yesterday, when I heard the prison board had white-washed the investigation, I called the governor and told him what was going on."

"The governor himself or an aide?"

"Himself. Before he was elected, we served on a hospital board together. He was mad as a cornered cottonmouth when he heard my story. Said he'd personally look into the problem. I'll call him again and tell him what you've turned up. How's that?"

"Sounds pretty good . . . for now."

The door was barely shut behind Kit when Broussard made his call. Learning that the governor would be in a meeting for at least another thirty minutes, he left his number, then plucked a lemon ball from the bowl on his desk and tucked it in his cheek. From a side drawer, he took out Nick Lawson's article on the stolen body and read it again, his face glowing with as much irritation as the first time he'd seen it.

That night, Kit slept fitfully, dreaming that Lucky some-how wandered into a pit of alligators and she had to jump in and rescue him. When she woke, he was sleeping peacefully under her arm.

At odd times throughout the next morning, while she worked in the photo gallery, snatches of her first trip to Courville flashed into her head: the bright lights suddenly appearing behind her, the sickening feeling of her car rolling over, fighting for her life in the inky water, her foot caught, fear clotting in her throat. Running in and out between those memories were little gnomes with their names stitched on their shirts: Relief, Gratitude, Horror, Sorrow, Disbelief. . . . But the busiest gnome of all was Anger. She'd nearly been killed. Her life obviously meant nothing to the Guillorys and Hubly. She'd been manipulated and put at risk, as if she didn't matter.

"Kit, are you all right?"

She turned and looked at Nolen.

"Why do you ask?"

"You haven't moved for three minutes."

"Daydreaming, I guess."

"I wanted to tell you I had a temporary fix made this mornin' on that crack in your ceilin' so the loose piece wouldn't fall. We're tryin' to get some plaster washers so we can screw it to the lath, but it'll be a few days before they get here. Meanwhile, what we did is just temporary, so don't think it's gonna stay that way."

"I can't wait to see it."

"Temporary—keep sayin' that to yourself. I'm goin' out for a hot dog. Want one . . . my treat?"

"No thanks, but you can get one for Lucky."

"How's he take it?"

"Real plain . . . no bun."

"Be right back."

Three minutes later, Broussard called.

"Can you come over here today, at three o'clock?"

"I don't know. What for?"

"Somebody wants to talk to you."

"Who?"

"They asked me not to say."

"What's it about?"

"I don't know. But considerin' who it is, I think you should come."

Having complete trust in the old pathologist's judgment, she agreed.

When Nolen returned, she negotiated the time off, then took Lucky his hot dog, which he consumed with nearly as much enjoyment as Nolen had shown eating his.

Going upstairs to make lunch, she opened her front door and saw that the temporary "fix" Nolen had arranged for the ceiling was a two-by-four T brace, just the decorating touch the place needed. Feeling very depressed about her life, she heated some canned soup and toasted a bagel for lunch. As she ate, curiosity about who it was that wanted to talk to her nibbled at the edges of her depression until that dark state became a tattered remnant without influence.

Kit knocked and was invited in.

She found Broussard behind his desk and two other men in the visitors' chairs in front of it. They both got up and turned to look at her. She was shocked at who one of them was. She didn't recognize the other.

The familiar man came toward her, hands outstretched, his famous smile working.

"Dr. Franklyn, how good it is to meet you at last." He took her hand in both of his. "I'm Earl Bellair. The fine citizens of this state generously allow me to live in the governor's mansion."

"Yes, sir. I recognized you."

Bellair was in his early fifties, but his hair was already pure white, a contradiction to a face that looked far younger than his real age. He wore glasses with oversized lenses, which allowed an unobstructed view of hazel eyes so open and deep, it seemed you could see all the way to his heart. It wasn't his face, though, that had earned him Kit's vote two years earlier, but his strong position on preservation of the coastal ecology and his indignation at the state's long history of corruption in its public officials.

A lot of people in Louisiana distrust men in suits. Bellair was dressed in the outfit that had become his trademark during the campaign—khaki pants and a velour pullover, the two buttons at the neck open. Despite his casual dress, Kit wished she'd worn a dress instead of a blouse and slacks.

Bellair released her hand and gestured to the other man. "This is Brian Tabor, my personal aide. Brian was with the Army Intelligence Corps for eight years and the Baton Rouge Police Department for twelve, six of those in the Narcotics Unit."

Tabor was not an unattractive man. He was trim and she kind of liked his mustache. But he sure didn't look like a man with his record. Probably in his late forties, he was of average height, had major hair loss, and soft features that made him look like a pharmacist. He was dressed as casually as the governor, in slacks and an Izod pullover.

"Dr. Franklyn . . ."

Tabor offered a warm hand and Kit took it. His movements were confident and economical. Looking into his eyes, she saw sharp intelligence and felt him evaluating her.

"Dr. Franklyn, please . . ." Bellair turned his chair toward her and motioned her into it. Tabor arranged the other chair for the governor so it faced hers, then retreated to the table holding Broussard's microscope, where he perched on the corner.

"Kit . . . may I call you that?" the governor said, sitting.

"Of course."

"It's only fair, then, that you call me Earl." He leaned back and crossed one leg over the other. "Andy has told me everything that happened to you in Courville and about the confusion regarding the convict at Angola. I've also discussed this with the head of the prison board. And I have to say, I'm unhappy about everything I've heard. Brian's looked into the matter and has turned up some disturbing things. I won't burden you with what they are, but I'm convinced something very wrong is going on at the prison. I'm afraid, too, that its tentacles reach far into my administration. And I'm not going to stand for it."

"What will you do?"

"To a degree, that depends on you."

"Why me?"

Bellair looked over his shoulder. "Brian . . ."

Tabor left his perch and pulled a rolling chair over to join them. "Fifty miles west of here, in Thibodaux, there's a small research institute called Agrilabs. Supposedly, they're working on ways to increase meat production in cattle and pigs, but I can't find any evidence they've ever bought a single calf or own one pig."

Kit was confused. "What does that have to do with me?"

"I can't tell you the details, but I've found a paper connection between Agrilabs and the funeral home in Courville. I've gone as far as I can, though, by myself. Now, I need help. That's where you come in. The institute is looking for a research assistant with experience in gel electrophoresis and column chromatography. I believe that during your training at Tulane, you worked part-time in a lab where that's exactly what you did."

"You've been investigating *me?*"

"It's my job, nothing personal."

"And you want to send me into that institute as what . . . a spy?"

"That's as good a word as any, I guess," Tabor said.

Kit stared at Tabor, then at Bellair, then at Broussard, her mouth open in disbelief.

"We know they've been looking for someone to fill this position for months," Tabor said. "Thibodaux is small and doesn't have many people with laboratory skills. With your background, we believe they'd hire you on the spot."

Kit's head was swimming from the absurdity of their suggestion.

"You think they're dealing drugs?"

"We're pretty sure it's not that," Tabor said.

"I know we're asking a lot," Bellair said. "But considering what they did to you, we thought you might appreciate a chance to even things up."

Broussard could tell Bellair's words had found a home. Therefore, he was not surprised when Kit set her jaw and said, "I'm listening."

10

"We don't think anyone from Courville ever visits the institute," Tabor said. "So the risk of you being recognized from that direction is remote." He got up and retrieved a briefcase from behind Kit's chair and sat back down with it in his lap. He snapped it open and took out a piece of paper. "Do you recognize any of these names?"

Kit took the list and read the twenty names on it.

"I don't know any of these people," she said, handing the list back.

"Good. Those are the institute employees. None of them lives in New Orleans, so there's no chance they'd know you, either."

He put the list back in his briefcase and took out a manila envelope. "This contains a copy of your new résumé, a new Social Security card, and a new driver's license."

Kit opened the envelope and looked at the résumé. "Kate Martin?"

"That's who you'll be if you decide to do this. The phone

numbers listed for your references will be answered by our people."

"And this will work?"

"Most employers these days don't even bother to check references. And these people will be so glad to see you, they probably won't care where you worked previously."

"What, exactly, do you want me to do?"

"We want you to tap the director's phone." When he said "phone," his hand went to his ear and he made a telephone with his thumb and little finger.

"I don't know anything about—"

He dipped again into his briefcase and withdrew a zip-top plastic bag containing some equipment. "There's practically nothing to know." He opened the plastic bag and withdrew a plug. "This is a duplex phone jack. You'll simply unplug the existing phone line, plug the duplex into the existing jack, and reconnect the phone line to one of the two openings in the duplex—it doesn't matter which one." He put the duplex down and got out a small putty-colored box and a loose wire with a phone jack on one end and a round metal connector on the other. "This is a voice-activated tape recorder. The round end of this wire goes into the recorder here. It's just a push-pull connection. When it's in place, the recorder is ready to function. The opposite end of the wire goes into the free opening in the duplex. You'll mount the recorder on the underside of the low table the phone sits on by removing this protective strip, which covers an adhesive."

"Isn't that terribly obvious?" Kit asked. "I mean, all anybody has to do is look at the phone jack to see there's an extra wire coming out of it."

"The jack is fairly high on the wall behind the table holding the phone. The only way anyone could see the extra wire is if they got down on their hands and knees and looked under the table."

"Suppose they move the table?"

"Then the plan fails. There's a small amount of slippage in every endeavor."

"How do you know so much about the arrangement of furniture in the director's office?"

"We've had a man in there posing as a phone repairman." He repeated the telephone gesture he'd made earlier.

"Why didn't *he* do this?"

"There was someone watching everything he did. Then, too, there's the problem of tape retrieval."

"Retrieval?"

"This is a self-contained unit. The conversations recorded aren't relayed anywhere. They're stored on the tape inside."

"So periodically, someone has to get the tape and put in a fresh one."

"Right. Hence the need for that person to be an employee." Tabor reached into the bag again and brought out another recorder. "The adhesive strip is Velcro-coated on the outside. There's a matching strip on the recorders. You just pull one recorder off and put the other on. The recorders themselves"—he pressed the play button and they all heard the tinny sounds of "Stayin' Alive" by the Bee Gees—"are dual units. If anyone was to examine them—if, say, you were caught with one, it appears to be an ordinary tape player with one of your favorite songs on it."

Kit rolled her eyes. "Puh-lease."

Tabor grinned and shut off the tape. "Okay, then . . . one of Kate Martin's favorite songs. The recorded conversations will be on a different tape that can be accessed only by a special player. That way, the recorders can't be used to incriminate you."

"Why don't you just break in at night and do all this?"

"We've accessed the building but have been thwarted by the security door on the director's lab. To make this work, we can't be leaving evidence we've broken in. And so far, we haven't found a way to do that."

"And you can't tap the line outside the building?"

"No."

"Would I need to change my appearance?"

"You could put your hair up and maybe use a little makeup just to minimize your individual visual cues on the off chance someone who's seen you before might pass through the room. That's about it."

"This résumé you gave me says I live in Thibodaux."

"We've rented a house there for you."

"What made you so sure I'd agree to help?"

Tabor shrugged. "We had to have a local address for the résumé."

"Would I have to live in Thibodaux? Couldn't I stay in my New Orleans apartment?"

Tabor considered the question, then said, "I think that'd be all right."

Now Bellair spoke. "Kit, you should understand that because we don't know what these people are doing, we have no idea how high the stakes are. They could be high enough that they would do almost anything to protect themselves."

"Which is why you'd have to agree to wear this," Tabor said. He put the bag of recording equipment back in his briefcase and brought out a holstered pistol. "This is designed to be worn above your ankle under slacks like those you've got on. There's padding that permits air circulation on the part that rides against your skin, so it won't be an irritant. The gun itself"—he loosened a Velcro strap and slipped a sleek chrome revolver from the holster—"is a thirty-eight-caliber Ladysmith. Small, lightweight, and reliable. Capacity, six rounds."

He slid the gun back into the holster. "After an hour or so, you won't even know it's there. If you agree to help, I'll take you out to a firing range and show you how to use it. It's very simple."

Now this was really getting serious. "Couldn't I wear a

radio or something? I mean *if* I do it.... I'm not a gun person."

"A radio wouldn't be practical," Tabor said. "If you get in a jam, by the time anyone could get to you, it might be too late. I'm not going to honey-coat this. You'll have to be prepared to take care of yourself."

This was too much ... too bizarre. Going undercover wearing a gun ... She was a clerk in a photo gallery, for God's sake. She looked at Broussard, who'd said nothing. "What do you think?"

"Frankly, I wish you wouldn't do it."

She turned to Bellair. "Suppose I say no."

"I wouldn't think any the less of you. It could mean, though, that we'll never get to the bottom of this."

Kit sat there with three pairs of eyes watching her intently. A .38 ... like some goofy TV show. Jesus ... Forget it....

But then the water of Snake Bayou began dripping over her misgivings.

They'd totaled her car and almost killed her.

The water came faster....

She heard Hubly's hand strike his wife. Women, it seemed, weren't people to these cretins.

The water was gushing now in spurts that scoured at the foundation of her reluctance.

Smug, self-satisfied bottom-feeders ... wife-beaters ...

The footings under her reservations shifted.

Well, they'd picked on the wrong woman this time.

Chin raised, she looked at Tabor, then at Bellair. "I'm in."

"Are you also looking into the death of the Tennessee professor?" Broussard asked.

"That's beyond my geographical concern," Bellair replied. "Besides, wasn't that ruled a heart attack?"

"So I was told, but whoever made that call could have missed something."

"We've got our hands full with difficulties in Louisiana. I

don't feel much like taking on Mississippi and Tennessee problems, too."

Broussard pressed the point. "It *is* a related event, possibly a significant one."

Bellair's eyes narrowed. "What are you getting at?"

"The *Picayune* has given me a good roastin' over the loss of that body, so I'm personally involved in this, too."

Bellair looked at him for a long minute, then said, "When does your plane leave?"

"Monday mornin'. Phil Gatlin has arranged for someone he knows in the Memphis Homicide Division to give me a hand."

"Since you're already going up there"—Tabor reached again into his briefcase and gave Broussard his business card—"I'd appreciate being kept informed of what you learn. That's my pager number. When you hear two tones, enter the number you're calling from, including the area code if you're out of five-oh-four. I'll usually return your call within fifteen minutes." He turned and gave a card to Kit.

Broussard looked briefly at his card and put it on the desk. "I'll do that."

"Kit, it's essential you tell no one what you're doing for us," Bellair said. "Not your boyfriend, not your parents . . . no one. That goes for you, too, Andy."

"Gonna be kind of hard to keep my Memphis homicide detective in the dark."

"Do the best you can. If he presses you hard, refer him to Brian. Are we all agreed?"

Broussard nodded. When Kit did the same, Bellair sealed the bargain with another big smile.

"If you're free, we can go out to the firing range right now," Tabor suggested.

Reluctantly, Kit agreed to that, too, and the meeting was over.

Broussard saw them all out, then returned to his chair,

where he popped a lemon ball into his mouth and lapsed into thought, idly tapping Tabor's business card on the desk while he pictured all the trouble Kit could get into. If he had the power, he'd have probably forbidden her to help them. Though she didn't believe it herself, she was about as resourceful a person as he'd ever known. But this could turn into more than she could handle.

It was tough, this caring for people.

Needing to get his mind back on morgue business and the loose ends he had to tie up before leaving for Memphis, he reached for his wallet to put Tabor's card away. As he did, he saw that Tabor had mistakenly given him a card with someone else's name and phone number written on the back, someone named P. Bates. But it was too late now to catch him. He'd mention it next time they spoke.

Tabor and the governor had come down from Baton Rouge in separate cars. Surprisingly, Bellair had driven himself, an unpretentious act that made Kit respect him even more than before they'd met. Before Bellair left to go back to the capital, he again shook Kit's hand warmly and thanked her for helping. He promised to have her to the mansion for dinner when this was all over.

Kit was afraid the lot where she'd parked would be closed when they got back from the firing range, so before they left, they dropped her rental car off at Nolen's garage.

As they finally got under way, Tabor asked, "Have you ever shot a pistol of any kind?"

"My boyfriend taught me how to use his. It's a twenty-two-caliber revolver."

"You'll find that a thirty-eight has a good bit more kick."

"Couldn't I have a twenty-two?"

"They don't have enough stopping power." He took his eyes off the road and glanced at her. "I have to say, I admire your courage."

"I'm not courageous so much as easily outraged. I don't like to be manipulated and I'm not good at turning the other cheek. I suppose it's a character flaw."

"Not to me. What does your boyfriend do?"

"He's an alligator farmer in Bayou Coteau, a little town about sixty miles from Baton Rouge."

"Long-distance relationship, huh?"

"We're together mostly on weekends. I know that seems odd, but it has its advantages."

"So you'll see him tomorrow?" As he said the word *tomorrow,* he made a thumbs-up gesture by his cheek and twitched his thumb toward his ear.

"He'll be here by breakfast," Kit said.

"You're probably going to feel guilty about keeping this from him."

"I know."

"He'll be here the whole weekend?"

"He usually leaves Monday morning."

"What time? We'll need to get you to Agrilabs Monday to apply for that job, and I have to show you where your résumé says you live."

"He's always gone by six."

"How about I come by at eight, then?"

"All right."

"We'll be going in separate cars."

"I assumed as much."

Tabor checked the rearview mirror and changed lanes to pass a car whose left-rear tire was wobbling as if it were about to come off. "What's your boyfriend's name?"

"Teddy LaBiche."

"I'll bet the fact we're even talking about hiding this from Ted bothers you."

"I don't deny it."

"By Sunday night, the temptation to tell him will likely be unbearable."

"You're suggesting I won't keep my word?"

"I simply want you to be prepared for that moment. Also, since by your own admission you're not a gun person, it could be very awkward for you if he should find the one I'm going to give you."

"Do you own a lot of tools?"

"A fair number, why?"

"I'll bet most of them are hanging on a Peg-Board with their outlines drawn behind them."

He looked at Kit and grinned. "Did I enjoy being in the army?"

"The order appealed to you, but there were a lot of procedures you felt were poorly thought out."

"You make me feel like I've got a little window in my skull."

"We all do. It's just a matter of recognizing what can be seen through it."

The firing range was thirty minutes from the heart of New Orleans, at the end of a rudimentary road that, had Kit not heard the sound of gunfire ahead, would have had her believing Tabor had lost his way. Eventually, they emerged from the scrub into a clearing that contained, to their right, a small lake surrounded by cattails. Three armed men facing the lake across a stretch of grass were knocking skeet from the sky. Straight ahead, under a long, low roof, a dozen people with their backs to the road were peppering targets with their weapons.

Tabor parked next to a purple Silverado that blocked Kit's view of the skeet shooters. He shut off the engine. "It'll be noisy out there, so before we go, I'll tell you how the range operates. It functions in cycles. You shoot for fifteen minutes; then the range supervisor shuts it down so everybody can go and check their targets. When it's shut down, all weapons are unloaded and all revolver cylinders are left open and the clips of automatics removed so the range attendant can verify that. Everybody then steps behind the yellow line that runs the length of the place. The gate to the target area is then opened. During shutdown, no one is allowed to cross the yellow line. After a sufficient time to examine and adjust targets, a one-minute warning is issued. When everybody is out of the target area, the line is once again declared hot. Okay?"

Kit nodded.

"I notice you're right-handed. Is that also your dominant eye?"

"I don't know."

"Let's get out and see."

She joined him at the trunk of the car, where he told her to stand facing him. "Now, make a triangle with your two hands and your thumbs like this and then look at me through it."

Kit did that.

"Now, move the triangle close to your face. . . . Keep watching me. . . . Ah, you're cross-dominant."

She had brought the triangle to her left eye.

"Is that bad?"

"No, it just means we have to adjust for that in your stance."

Tabor unlocked the trunk and opened his briefcase. He transferred the Ladysmith into a gym bag, then hauled the bag out and locked the trunk. "C'mon."

She followed him to a small office situated between the left and right wings of the range. Windows on three sides gave the man occupying it full visibility of the firing positions and the targets downrange.

"I need to stop in here and pay the fee." He put the gym bag down and went into the office. When he returned, he reached in the bag and brought out two objects that looked like radio announcer headsets. He offered her one of them. "Put this on. It'll protect your hearing."

He didn't have as much hair as she did, so he got his on first.

"Can you hear me?"

It wasn't great, but she could make out what he'd said, so she nodded.

"Good. Bring the bag."

He went to some bins containing targets on legs, chose one with four separate sets of concentric rings on it, and carried it to the firing line entrance, where he showed his receipt to an attendant wearing an orange vest over blue work clothes. Satisfied they weren't trying to sneak in, the attendant pointed to an open cubicle four down on the left. Over a loudspeaker, a voice said, "ONE MINUTE."

Reaching the assigned spot, Tabor got out the Ladysmith, along with one blue and one yellow plastic box, each containing about fifty rounds of ammunition, and put them on the carpet-covered work surface in front of him. Around them, the air was filled with pregnant explosions whose issue ripped into the paper targets downrange and kicked up dirt behind them. Beyond the farthest target, an earthen berm as tall as a house ensured that no flying slug found its way into a passerby.

In the cubicle next to theirs, a guy wearing a leather glove with no fingers was firing from a sitting position on an upturned bucket, his pistol resting on a sandbag. The expression on his face was positively orgasmic. Kit was searching her mind for any studies she'd read to corroborate her intuitive belief that there was likely an inverse relationship between penis length and the size of a man's favorite handgun when the loudspeaker announced, "THE RANGE IS NOW CLOSED."

Tabor motioned her to the bench behind the yellow line, where they removed their ear protection and waited for the other shooters to unload and step back. When the attendant had verified that cylinders were empty and clips removed, he opened the gate to the target area.

"No need for you to come," Tabor said. He took the target he'd picked out earlier to a spot about seven yards in front of their cubicle and threaded its legs into two plastic pipes in the ground. He then came back and sat down.

With nothing else to do, Kit broached a subject she'd been curious about since they'd first met. "I was wondering—a couple of times in Andy's office when you mentioned phones, you made a gesture like a telephone next to your ear. And talking on the way over here, you did a little thing next to your cheek. Why?"

Tabor reached in his back pocket, took out his wallet, and showed her a picture of a pretty little girl. "That's Ellie."

"Your daughter?"

"Yeah. She's ten. She was born with a heart defect and an absence of the apparatus in her ears that receives sound. The doctors think her mother may have had a mild case of German measles we didn't notice during the first part of her pregnancy. That's when the heart and ears are most suscep-. tible. They were able to repair her heart, but they couldn't do anything for her hearing. I'm so used to signing with her, I sometimes do it in normal conversation."

"She's a beautiful girl."

"And despite all she's gone through, she's happy all the time. I wouldn't trade her for any other kid in the world. They say you don't become part of the human race until you've had kids. I never knew what that meant until Ellie came along." A flicker of recognition that he was talking to someone who didn't have kids crossed his face. "I'm sorry, I didn't mean to . . . gloat."

"No apologies needed. You've got every right to be proud."

"THE LINE IS NOW HOT."

They donned their ear protection and returned to their firing position, where Tabor closed the empty cylinder on the

Ladysmith. "We'll start with stance and some dry firing. Since you're cross-dominant, you'll want your left leg slightly forward, right hand around the grip, left hand supporting it like this, thumbs out of the way." He raised the gun and sighted along it with his left eye. "Elbows slightly bent. Here, you try."

Kit took the gun and assumed the stance he'd demonstrated.

"Good. Now, you know about sighting?"

"Front sight centered and its top level with the top of the rear sight. Top of front sight centered on the target."

"Very good. Let's see your trigger work."

She squeezed the trigger three times.

"Excellent. Let's try the real thing."

He took the gun and loaded it from the blue plastic box, then handed it back. "Start with the target on the upper left."

Her first shot was wide of the outer ring of the target by a good two inches and the kick threw her hands up. "Wow, that's powerful," she exclaimed.

"Try again."

The next shot nicked the outer ring, but again it kicked her hands up.

"You'll get it."

She emptied the gun at the target, getting close to the bull's-eye and controlling the kick better with each round. Tabor removed the spent shells from the cylinder, reloaded from the blue box, and handed the gun back. This time, she put one round dead center and five in a tight cluster around the bull's-eye.

"Damned if you haven't got a shooter's eye," Tabor said.

It was better than she'd ever shot with Teddy's .22, maybe because he'd never realized she was cross-dominant.

"Wasn't that fun?" Tabor said.

"Not particularly."

She handed him the gun and he reloaded it from the blue

box. "Now, I want you to imagine the target is an armed man . . . and the bull's-eye is the center of his chest—that's where you aim, not the head. I want you to fire each round as quickly as you can and still be accurate."

"New target?"

"Upper right."

She took the gun, quickly lined up the target, and fired the six rounds in rapid succession, most of the time between shots being consumed by resighting after the kick. The result was only slightly inferior in accuracy to the previous six rounds.

"Good placement, speed a little slow," Tabor said, holding his hand out for the gun.

"Can we go?"

He loaded the gun again and put the blue box in the gym bag. "Six more rounds and we'll leave," he said, handing her the gun. "Control that kick now. Lower-left target."

Her final six rounds were the fastest yet and were crowded around dead center. Tabor shook his head in admiration. "Best teaching job I ever did."

She gave him the gun, happy to be rid of it, and watched while he reloaded all six chambers from the remaining box of cartridges. He then slipped the gun into the holster and put everything in the bag.

"Aren't you supposed to leave the chamber under the hammer empty to keep the gun from firing accidentally?" Kit asked.

"Not with modern revolvers."

Following Tabor's lead, Kit left her ear protection on until they reached the car, where Tabor put both headsets in the trunk along with the bag. Before closing the trunk, he again got out the holstered Ladysmith. "I want to show you how to wear this. Put your foot on the bumper and pull your pant leg up to the knee."

She did as he said and he strapped the holster to her leg about four inches above her ankle, one Velcro strap encircling her calf at holster level, another that stabilized it above the first, four inches below her knee. He then pulled her pant leg down.

"How's that feel?" Coincident with the word *feel,* his middle finger went to his chest and he flicked it upward in another gesture he'd learned for his daughter.

Kit put her foot on the ground and took a few steps.

"Uncomfortable."

"You'll get used to it. You may need to adjust the tension on the straps. It looks good."

"I feel like I should get a tattoo or buy some cigars."

"C'mon. I'll take you home."

Before leaving the parking lot, Tabor gave her another pointer. "If the time comes when you need to use the gun, fire twice before checking to see what you've accomplished. That way, you'll still have a few rounds left for dealing with any unexpected circumstances or to finish off your primary target. Now, there's one other issue. I'm convinced you've got the technical skills to protect yourself and you've got the tactical know-how. But have you got the character?"

"You think I lack character?"

"I'm not talking about it in the usual sense. Before I let you go into that institute, I've got to know you have the strength to use deadly force against another human being."

"If it means saving my life, count on it."

Tabor looked deeply into Kit's eyes, searching for affirmation of the resolve she'd expressed. Apparently finding it, he said, "I believe you."

Thirty minutes later, as she was getting out of the car in front of the photo gallery, he stopped her. "Wait, you forgot these." He pulled the briefcase onto the front seat and got out the Baggie containing the recording equipment and handed it to her.

"Isn't this premature?" she asked. "What if they don't hire me?"

"They will. Don't bother bringing a recorder on Monday.

It's not likely you'll get a crack at rigging it that soon. And even if you see what appears to be an opportunity, your unfamiliarity with the routines of the place will make you unqualified to judge. Don't forget the gun. You should spend some time between now and Monday studying your résumé—not in front of your boyfriend, of course."

"Of course."

Watching him drive away, the Bee Gees began playing in her head. Stayin' alive . . . stayin' alive.

Good God. What had she gotten herself into?

11

Tabor picked Kit up at eight Monday morning as planned and they headed for Nolen's garage.

"I've been thinking," Kit said. "If I've got all this great technical ability, why have I suddenly appeared in this town where there's probably only one possible place I could be employed to use it?"

"Your family lived there when you were a child. But your father moved you all to New York State, where he operated a small hardware store until the big chains drove him out of business. He retired after that and died last year. As so often happens when one member of a couple passes on, your mother followed him two months ago. Then the long-term relationship you'd been in deteriorated and suddenly you were all alone. Needing time to think, and remembering the happy times when you all lived in Louisiana, you decided to come home for a while."

"Do I have any relatives nearby?"

"Your mother's sister lived in Sorrento, but she's gone now, too."

"Isn't that a dangerous story? Suppose I meet someone at the institute whose family has lived in the area forever and they start asking me questions about when I lived there?"

"You were old enough to remember being happy, but not old enough to recollect anything else."

"When did you prepare all this?"

"A few minutes before I picked you up. The same question you just asked occurred to me, too."

"So you made it up in two minutes."

"More or less."

"You're very good."

"I should have thought of it before we ever talked the first time so I could have had it written out for you to study."

"Now I'm getting worried. I was thinking you had this totally planned and were in full control."

Tabor glanced at her, his face deadly serious. "In an operation like this, you never have full control. That's why I gave you the Ladysmith. You *are* wearing it?"

"I have it."

"Ultimately, you're the one you'll have to depend on, not me. I thought I'd made that clear. If I didn't, and you want to back out, now's the time."

"I don't want out. It was just a comment."

"Just so you fully understand. . . ."

Before letting her out at the garage, Tabor had some final words for her. "I'll take you first to the house we've rented for you so you'll know what it looks like and where it's located. We'll leave your car there and I'll show you the institute. Then I'll take you back to the house and you'll return to the institute alone and apply for that job. Don't be surprised if they want you to start immediately. You've cleared your time?"

Kit nodded.

He waited until she'd maneuvered her car out of the

garage and relocked the sliding garage door. She then followed him out of the Quarter.

She'd cleared her time all right, but Nolen hadn't been happy about it. He'd been able to get his perpetually unemployed half brother to fill in for the next week, but he told her she needed to decide whether she was working for him or not.

An hour later, Tabor pulled to a stop in front of a small gray clapboard cottage with dark red shutters and white trim. He motioned for her to go into the dirt driveway first.

As she got out of the car, a mockingbird perched in the boughs of a nearby live oak welcomed her with a dazzling display of trills and runs. The large lot on which the cottage sat was screened on three sides by thick stands of bamboo that gave the place the kind of privacy she had always prized and which, in her present living arrangement, was distinctly lacking.

She thought Tabor might show her the inside of the cottage, but when she looked at his car, which was still running, he beckoned. She walked around to the passenger side and got in.

"Don't I even get a house tour?"

"You're not planning on staying here, so why bother?"

"What about the answering machine you were going to set up?"

He raised his open hand, thumb up, and flicked the air. "Already done."

"Whose voice is on it?"

"Yours."

"How did—"

"I called your apartment in New Orleans while you were out and recorded the message you've got on that machine."

"Aren't *you* resourceful."

"I try. Ready to see the institute?"

"I guess."

Agrilabs, Inc., was exactly two and three-tenths miles from the cottage. It was three stories of white cut stone inset with long narrow silver strips that Kit guessed were the windows. The institute name along with the motto, "Toward a world without hunger," were lettered on all four sides of a big white box on the roof.

"Looks like a big birthday cake," Kit said.

"Don't let appearances fool you," Tabor replied. "John Wayne Gacy used to dress up like a clown."

They returned to the cottage, where Tabor shut off the engine and turned to face her. "What's the address of this house?"

Without looking, Kit correctly recited the black numbers beside the front door.

"What's the name of the street?"

She also got that right.

"Spell it."

She rattled off the correct spelling.

"What's your Thibodaux phone number?"

In this, too, she was perfect.

Tabor reached in his shirt pocket for a plastic card. "Here, this tells you how to access the answering machine inside from your phone in New Orleans so you can check on any messages the institute might leave for you." He plucked two keys from the change box near the gearshift and gave one to her. "In case you want to get in this house for any reason. This one"—he gave her the other key—"is for a car we've provided for you. It's parked behind the house."

"Why do I need another car?"

"We don't want them learning your identity by tracking your license plates."

"I'm driving a rental car."

"What name did you use when you rented it?"

"I see your point."

"Always leave your car behind the house and take ours to

the institute." He reached again into his shirt pocket. "Here's the registration."

Kit looked at the form he gave her and saw that the owner of the car in question was Kate Martin.

"It's new, so try not to hit anything," Tabor said.

"Glad you mentioned that. I was planning on running into a couple of mailboxes on the way over."

Tabor grinned. "You've got my pager number?"

She nodded.

"When you get home, call me and leave your number. I'll—"

"I know. You'll get back to me within fifteen minutes."

"One final point. If you encounter the slightest hint of trouble at Agrilabs, clear out. Any questions?"

"None come to mind."

"Then it's time to go."

Kit tingled all over and her heart bobbed against the roof of her chest. She felt like a character in a Dick Tracy comic with an arrow over her head labeled "Fraud". But it was too late to back out now. She took a deep breath and went in.

The door opened onto a carpeted foyer in which she found a tendinous woman who could have begun drawing her IRA tomorrow with no penalty seated at a wooden desk large and fine enough for the CEO of Chrysler. Her black hair was obviously a wig. Behind her sat a large fish tank beautifully decorated with a bank of shale and luxurious green plants that, unlike the woman's hair, were real. The two dozen fish in the tank looked in perfect health. If the fish tank was any indicator, Agrilabs certainly knew how to manage plants and animals.

"Good morning. I'm here to apply for the opening you have for a lab tech." Suddenly, the gun on Kit's ankle felt as big as a cannon. Already so close to the desk that the woman behind it couldn't have seen the gun if it were on the *outside* of her slacks, Kit still took another step forward.

"How nice," the woman said. "I had a feeling we might find someone today. Don't you sometimes have an intuition things are about to happen and then they do?"

"I think everybody does," Kit said, unable at the moment to remember a time she did.

"You brought a résumé?"

Kit got the fake résumé Tabor had prepared for her from her bag and offered it to the woman.

"Rose is the one who needs to see that."

"Rose?"

"She's in charge of all the techs. I'll tell her you're here."

She called for Rose Lewis on the intercom. "There's a sofa if you'd like to sit."

Afraid that if she sat, the Ladysmith might show, Kit said she'd prefer to stand. A few minutes later, through the glass doors to the rest of the first floor, Kit saw a short, stocky man with a florid complexion step into the hall and head for the foyer. He came through the door and looked at her. "So you want work?"

With a shock, Kit realized it was a woman—one whose picture wouldn't look out of place in a text on endocrinology disorders.

"I'd love to work here."

"Is that your résumé?"

Kit stepped forward and was in the act of handing it to her when the woman said, "I asked you a question."

"Yes. It's my résumé. I was about to give it to you."

"Well, *do* it."

Kit handed her the phony document. To keep from worrying about the lies on it, she busied herself thinking of all the ways the troll reading it could lose the chin whiskers.

After a few minutes, Lewis gave her a hard look and said, "I guess you wouldn't mind waiting out here while I make a few phone calls. . . ."

"Not at all."

Kit watched Lewis as she walked back to the room where she'd been before coming to the front. Obviously, she was planning to check the references in the bogus résumé. No reason to be nervous—Tabor had said that was covered.

A quarter of an hour later, when Lewis hadn't returned, Kit was convinced something was wrong. Maybe instead of calling the numbers on the résumé, she had checked with some security database that had flagged Kate Martin as a fraud. Kit had almost decided to get out of there when she saw Lewis coming back.

Was it good news or bad? You certainly couldn't tell from the expression on the woman's face. She came through the glass doors and walked over to Kit.

"According to your former employers, we shouldn't hire you; we should build you a shrine and worship at your feet. Let's get a few things straight on the front end. I'm Rose Lewis, senior research associate and tech coordinator. If you're hired, you'll be assigned to one of the staff scientists, who will direct your daily activities. But ultimately, you're accountable to me. So I'll be watching your performance closely to see that it measures up. One complaint about you and you get a reprimand. Two complaints and you're gone. Your résumé says you're single. That doesn't mean divorced, does it?"

"No." Lord, they were going to give her the job right this minute, just as Tabor had predicted.

"Good. If we need you beyond five o'clock, there'll be no kids to worry about, and no former husbands making trouble. On the other hand, being single suggests you're not a good risk for long-term employment." She leaned forward and fixed Kit with an unblinking stare. "We would be very unhappy if after we've trained you, you get married and quit."

It was difficult for Kit to keep quiet and not respond to this insufferable ranting. The single most consoling fact allowing her to retain her composure was the knowledge that she was armed and dangerous.

"Your workday starts at eight o'clock, not two minutes after, or one minute after. You'll be given a fifteen-minute break in the morning and another in the afternoon. You get an hour for lunch. This is a salaried position budgeted at nineteen hundred a month. If you're needed beyond five P.M., you won't be paid for the additional time. We don't allow visitors, so you'll have to meet your boyfriends outside."

She called up a facial expression one might use after finding a condom in the orange juice. "I suppose men find you attractive. I don't want you flirting with any of the doctors and disrupting the activities here. These men have serious work to do and you're not to be diverting their attention. Any report you have encouraged them will result in immediate dismissal. Are these conditions acceptable?"

"I can live with them."

"Any reason you can't begin immediately?"

"None."

Lewis turned to the woman at the desk. "Get her through the necessary paperwork, will you? Give her a key to the side door and to Dr. Mudi's lab; then call me."

When Lewis was out of earshot behind the glass doors, the woman at the desk said, "Don't mind Rose. Her bark is worse than her bite. Well, a little worse."

Tempting as it was, Kit suppressed the impulse to comment on how well the bark analogy fit. She thought about asking if Mudi was the director, but decided not to do that, either, as it might seem an odd question.

On the initial form she filled out, she wrote her first name as Kit before catching herself. Changing it was an easy matter, and she suspected Tabor had purposely chosen Kate as her fictitious identity for just that purpose.

A flurry of paper later, Lewis returned and showed Kit to a locker that would be her very own. After a quick lesson on how to custom-set the combination, they went to a lab on the second floor, where they found a dark, bearded man and an Oriental girl standing over an illuminated view box.

"Dr. Mudi, this is Kate Martin, your new tech. I hope you find her work satisfactory. If not, I want to know it."

The tone of Lewis's remark to Mudi strongly suggested he was not the director.

Mudi bowed faintly as Lewis turned and stalked out. "Do not trouble yourself over that woman," he said in an Indian accent. "I wouldn't tell her if she was about to step on a crocodile. This is Jenny Ling. You will like her tremendously."

The girl beside him had a face that belonged in *Vogue*. She had shiny black hair, flawless skin, and a tiny heart-shaped mouth. She wore a lot of makeup but did it well.

"Welcome to Buchenwald," she said. "Delousing begins in fifteen minutes."

Obviously, American-born.

"What are you looking at?" Kit asked.

"I trust you are familiar with gel electrophoresis?" Mudi said.

He was referring to the process in which a mixture of proteins was loaded into slots at one end of a thin gel cast on a solid plastic support and the individual proteins were segregated into different regions of the gel by an electric current. "I've run my share," Kit said.

"What we are doing is this," Mudi explained. "We have supplemented the culture medium of immature bovine muscle cells with growth hormone and I now want to compare the protein profiles of treated and untreated cells to see what effect this had. But we are getting no patterns at all."

After what Tabor had said about the place, Kit was surprised to hear Mudi was working on such a mundane project—one clearly within the stated purpose of the facility. She stepped to the view box and looked at the gel. Instead of a series of thin blue lines indicating separate proteins, the gel was a smear of blue from top to bottom. She looked at Mudi. "Did you put an enzyme inhibitor in the extraction buffer?"

"We did not."

"That's likely the problem. When you broke the cells open, their endogenous enzymes digested the other proteins, breaking them down into a hodgepodge of fragments that caused the smear. Try adding an inhibitor like PMSF next time."

"Hodgepodge," Mudi said. "What a lovely word. It means . . . heterogeneous mixture, yes?"

"Exactly."

"'Hodgepodge.' It sounds like something sticky to eat."'

"It does at that," Kit said, smiling.

"Now you must have a tour. Then, after Jenny shows you around, I want you both to prepare more samples . . . with enzyme inhibitor. Kate, I'm liking you already."

When they were out in the hall, Kit said, "Mudi seems pretty easygoing."

"He's a sweetheart."

Jenny took Kit on a brief tour of the place and introduced her to some of the other technicians, whose projects all seemed as appropriate and straightforward as Mudi's. She found the facilities superb and all the instrumentation state-of-the-art.

"And this is our walk-in freezer," Jenny said, leading Kit into a small room largely filled by a white metal box. "It's wired so if the temperature goes up even a few degrees, a buzzer will sound. If you ever hear a noise so loud it makes you want to spit nickels, that's probably what it'll be." She pointed to a card taped on the door. "These are the phone numbers for the refrigeration man. If you're here alone and it goes off, call him and report it."

"How come there's so much junk in here?" Kit said, looking at the piles of equipment lining the wall opposite the freezer.

"It's a mess, isn't it? We've been replacing a lot of our old equipment with newer models and the discards end up here. I don't know why—maybe they're waiting to have it all hauled away at once. Anyway, that's about what there is to see."

On the way back to Mudi's lab, they passed a door marked AUTHORIZED PERSONNEL ONLY.

"What's in there?"

"That's Dr. Woodley's area. He's the director. Only he, Lewis, and Tom Ward are allowed inside."

"Who's Ward?"

Jenny's beautiful face twisted into a grimace. "He's sort of a handyman. If I were you, I'd stay away from him. He's said some obnoxious things to me and a few of the other women, and I think he's dangerous."

"Why?"

"About two months ago, he and a deliveryman got into it— over what, I don't know—and they began shoving each other. When Ward started to get the worst of it, he pulled a knife."

"So why is he still around?"

"You tell *me*."

"What's Woodley like?"

"I don't have much contact with him, but he seems like a nice man, very regimented, though. They say he brings the same thing in his lunch every day—two cheese sandwiches on rye and a bottle of Evian."

"Pretty Spartan meal."

"And if it's not raining, he and Rose Lewis will be sitting next to the bayou out back on folding chairs set up under the big tupelo gum from twelve-thirty to one-thirty every day of the week."

"Are you saying they're . . . involved?"

"Heavens no. I don't think Rose likes men, if you know what I mean."

"She sure didn't cut *me* any slack."

"Maybe you're not her type." Shocked at her own words, Jenny's eyes widened. *"Shame* on me."

As they walked back to Mudi's lab, Kit mulled over what she'd learned. Clearly, the director's office and lab held whatever secrets the place harbored. But how the devil was she going to get in there?

12

Broussard always flew first class, certainly not for the food, which even in that favored nation was a gruesome experience, second only to losing all power in the aircraft and plummeting to the ground. Rather, he went first class because he couldn't fit in the other seats.

In any event, the food wasn't an issue on this flight because the plane covered what would have been an all-day car trip in less than an hour, seemingly starting its approach to the Memphis airport practically as soon as it had reached cruising altitude.

Broussard wanted to get his inquiry under way before Hunter was buried. Fortunately, the funeral had been delayed until three o'clock today to accommodate Hunter's brother, who was flying in from New Zealand. That had allowed Broussard to avoid coming up here on the weekend, when nobody would have been where they were supposed to be. Still, that decision had left him with a small window of opportunity.

As soon as they reached the gate and the seat belt light flicked off, he claimed his forensic satchel and flight bag from the overhead and made for the terminal.

Inside, he scanned the few people obviously waiting to greet arrivals, looking for a man who fit Gatlin's description of his friend in Homicide.

To his right was a couple in their eighties. On his left, two teenage girls stood distinctly apart from a young man clutching a bouquet of spring flowers. A Rubenesque woman nicely dressed in a black jersey pullover under a gray plaid blazer with matching slacks waited by the newspaper racks. No homicide detective.

Thinking he ought at least to stay by the gate a few minutes before concluding his contact wasn't coming, he headed for a spot where he'd be out of the way.

"Are you Dr. Broussard?"

Turning, he saw that it was the woman in the plaid outfit. He acknowledged his identity.

"I'm Sergeant Noell, Memphis Homicide." She offered no hand. "Lieutenant Garza intended to meet you, but something important has come up, so I'm to be your liaison while you're here."

"Appreciate that."

"Maybe you shouldn't. As the only woman in the squad, I generally get the details no one else wants. To put it in terms my male colleagues might, you've been lateraled off. They're big on football analogies. Are those your only bags?"

"Yes."

"Good. It takes forever for luggage to get to the claims area. Come on."

Broussard was not in the market for a woman. He didn't window-shop for them or engage in fantasies about those he saw on the street. He was a self-contained man who found all the satisfaction he needed in good food, fine wine, old master oil paintings, Louis L'Amour novels, shoes that didn't make his feet sweat, and making sense out of death. Women were not part of his life. But when he'd first seen Noell by the newspapers, he'd felt a puff of interest against his sails. Hearing her sharp tongue, that little breath moved on.

She was a fast walker, and when they got to her car, Broussard was puffing. He dumped his bags in the trunk.

"Where are you staying?" she asked.

"The Peabody."

"Hope you like ducks." She got into the car and unlocked his door.

When he was inside and settled, she said, "Garza gave me a little background on what you want to do while you're here. You understand we don't have any file on this death, don't you?"

"Since it was ruled natural causes, I didn't think you would. And I believe he lived and died in Mississippi, which means it's out of your jurisdiction, anyway."

"That's where my remarks were headed. Just so you realize we can't demand anything over there. We can ask and that's all."

"Believe me, I know what you mean."

"This guy lived in Coldwater, which is about twenty-five miles south. Your hotel is ten miles north. You want to see where the body was found before you check in?"

"I'd like to talk to the coroner who handled the case."

Noell shook her head. "Can't . . . at least not face-to-face. He had to go down to Belzoni to check on construction of some new ponds for his catfish farm. Thought he'd be back late tomorrow. But I talked to him before he left and he filled me in. I would have gotten you a copy of his death report, but he hadn't written it yet."

"You're very efficient."

"For a woman you mean?"

"I've found that, like ineptitude, neither sex has a monopoly on competence."

"You're a man ahead of his time. Death scene or hotel?"

"Death scene."

She started the engine and backed out of the parking space. At the collection booth, she shook off the five he offered and they were soon on the expressway, headed for Coldwater.

Accustomed to living below sea level and being surrounded by swamp, Broussard found the Tennessee and Mississippi countrysides dry and dull. And without Spanish moss in them, the trees here looked incomplete. He suspected that to get crawfish on the dinner table, they had to be imported.

Shortly before they reached Coldwater, his opinion of the area rose as they passed a stretch of swamp that bordered both sides of the highway. There were even some cypress trees in it, though they bore no moss.

But the swamp didn't last and the highway again was flanked by cornfields and pasture. Noell left the highway at an exit marked by a stand of fine old pine trees and continued on a two-lane country road. After a mile or so, they turned onto an even more rural road, which wound through a sparsely populated area of hills and valleys that harbored hobby farms with a few horses and occasionally some cows. The only water here was in ponds formed by damming the outlet of a valley, resulting in muddy little pools reliant on runoff to keep them filled. Their numbers showed that even people who don't live in Louisiana long for the water. Not many vehicles passed, but whenever one did, the occupants waved.

A small wood came up on their left. "The house where the deceased lived is just beyond these trees," Noell said.

When they cleared the woods, Broussard saw quite a different setting from the rugged rural simplicity enjoyed by Hunter's neighbors. For at least a quarter of a mile ahead and a couple hundred yards deep, the road was flanked by what looked like a park. Sitting royally in the center of this verdant oasis, like a pearl on a velvet cushion, was a large-columned antebellum home.

"Looks like professors do all right here," Broussard said.

"I hear his wife's an investment banker. That's probably where the house came from. It's the oldest in the county. The columns are hexagons. The story is that when the Union army came through here, the owner hid in one of them for three days."

"Good thing they weren't Sherman's troops."

"I hate Sherman for what he did to southern architecture. It's a damn disgrace."

Because her views on this subject paralleled his own, Broussard moved her to a higher position on the multiphasic personality profile he was constructing of her.

There were four late-model cars in the home's circular driveway, all freshly washed—friends and relatives gathering to say good-bye to Anthony Hunter and comfort his wife.

Once they'd passed the house, Noell gave the car a little more juice. They drove only for another minute, that time taking them beyond the far border of Hunter park and into unkempt terrain.

She pulled off the road onto the weedy shoulder. "He was found right here—facedown, stiff as a carp, one leg in the road."

"What time did this happen?"

"A little after six A.M. He ran two miles every morning before breakfast."

"So he'd come directly from home?"

"That's my understanding. He'd been gone about thirty minutes when his wife got a knock on the door from a neighbor who'd found him."

Broussard's brow furrowed. "You said 'stiff as a carp.' Is that right? He was in rigor?"

"Well, I don't actually know if he was when the neighbor found him, but the coroner said he was when he got there around seven-thirty. I know that seems kind of quick for rigor to begin, but didn't I hear somewhere that physical exertion immediately before death hastens its onset?"

"That's true. How was he dressed?"

"Jogging shorts, sweatshirt, running shoes."

"How'd this fish farmer coroner decide it was a heart attack?"

"He didn't see any gunshot or stab wounds, so he figured, guy drops dead jogging. What do you think?"

"Did he make this decision on the spot? I mean, did he take the body anywhere and examine it unclothed or get medical input?"

"Decided right here."

"Makin' a judgment like that by lookin' over your thumb leaves room for mistakes. Do you know what funeral home has the body?"

"It's in Memphis."

"Mind takin' me over there?"

"You're what I'm doing today."

Thirty-five minutes later, they were waiting for someone to answer the bell at the back door of a sprawling white building accented with a lot of Chinese Chippendale fretwork. After a short delay, the door was opened by a bearded young man in a blue scrub suit.

Noell flashed her shield. "I'm Sergeant Noell, Memphis Homicide, and this is Dr. Broussard, the New Orleans medical examiner. We'd like to talk to you about the body of Anthony Hunter."

"You don't want to talk to me," the guy said. "You want Janie. Come on."

Broussard and Noell followed him through a cold-looking room whose walls and floor were covered with pale green ceramic tile and then into a carpeted hallway. After running a rat maze that allowed them some quick looks at the public part of the funeral home, they were led through a door into a restricted area marked FUNERAL HOME ASSOCIATES ONLY.

Here, the world was gray, and except for the hum of a small pump and the voice of a woman who seemed to be on the phone, the room was underlain by a cottony hush.

Their guide ducked his head into an open doorway to the right. "Janie, when you're finished, there are some people out here to see you." Then to Broussard and Noell, he said, "She'll be with you in a minute. Sorry we don't have any chairs. Most people who end up back here can't sit. If you'll excuse me, I've got some work to do."

He went to a nearby gurney and began dressing the corpse of a slim white man whose lower torso and legs were in such a state of decomposition, it had been necessary to outfit him with a pair of plastic pants and booties to make sure leaking fluid wouldn't soil his clothing. In contrast to his damaged body, the cadaver's face looked healthier than most living men his age.

Just beyond Janie's office was a large room with a wide doorway, through which Broussard could see another man in blue scrubs working at a porcelain table. He was using a long trochar to probe the body cavities of an obese white male. As the probe found the various liquid-filled viscera and punctured them, their contents went down the drain via a large transparent plastic container holding four inches of red fluid topped by a pink froth.

Meanwhile, the fellow dressing the body slipped a pair of socks over the plastic covering the cadaver's feet. He then slit a pair of pants from the waist to the crotch and threaded them over the legs. He cut a T-shirt up the back and down the arms and placed it over the chest. Noticing a weeping abrasion on the cadaver's neck, he removed the T-shirt and sprayed the spot with a liquid adhesive. He briefly fanned the abrasion with a piece of cardboard, then, satisfied with the result, resumed his duties as valet to the dead.

Beyond the cadaver being dressed lay four more, partially under sheets, their gray-haired heads facing the far wall, blocks under their necks. To their right, on a gurney turned sideways, another cadaver was all dressed and ready to go. Instead of a sedate dark suit befitting the sad occasion, he was wearing a yellow shirt, a bright green sport coat, brown pants, and white shoes. He hadn't yet been posed for viewing, so his feet were widely parted and his arms were spread at his sides. The total effect was so surreal and unexpected that before the thought could be screened, Broussard pictured him as a huge St. Patrick's Day balloon. It was such a disrespectful, uncharacteristic thing to have done, it made Broussard ashamed of himself.

As he was dealing with this, Janie finished her phone call and came out to meet them.

Broussard had expected an older woman whose skin had been pickled by all the fixatives she had to work around. But she was young and pretty, with a soft complexion that couldn't be produced by even the skill of those who could make the dead appear to be merely resting. It was apparent from Noell's introductory remarks to Janie that they hadn't previously met. After telling her who Broussard was, Noell let him take over.

"Janie, I understand you have the body of a man named Anthony Hunter."

"He's upstairs."

"I realize this man's death certificate says he died of natural causes, but some facts have come to light in New Orleans to make me think that judgment may be wrong. Would it be possible for me to examine the body?"

"You don't mean just step up and look at it."

"No. I was hopin' I could see it unclothed."

"Well, that's just not possible. I've got the family and friends coming in here this afternoon, and he's already up there waiting for them. And I've got more to do here than I can handle. I just can't help you."

"It's possible this man was murdered," Noell said. "Do you want a murderer to go unpunished?"

"It happens all the time," Janie said, "for one reason or another. You want to examine him, dig him up." She turned to

Broussard. "I don't even know you. You don't have any juris-diction here. Show me a legal paper."

"Could I at least see the embalmin' report?" Broussard asked.

Janie thought about this for a moment, then turned and went back into her office.

Broussard looked at Noell to see if she knew what this meant, but she merely shrugged. Before they had to make any decision about it, Janie came back out of the office and handed Broussard the report he'd requested.

The entry that interested him, a description of any wounds on the body, was near the top. But it listed only some small stone punctures on the forehead and a scrape on the left knee, all of which were surely acquired as Hunter fell. He glanced over the rest of the form, then looked at Janie. "The only wounds you've listed were on the forehead and one knee. Was that all you saw?"

"If that's what I wrote down, that's it."

Broussard was not sure what to do now. He hadn't wanted to talk to Hunter's wife without at least one fact to support his suspicion that Hunter's death had been engineered. He obviously wasn't going to find that here.

He handed the report back to Janie with his thanks and added, "I'm not sure we can find our way out."

The fellow with the beard volunteered to help and the three of them filed back into the hall. Before they'd gone ten feet, the door to the embalming area opened and Janie stepped into the hall, her face flushed.

"I . . . I just remembered. There *was* a wound I didn't write on the report. Don't know how I could have forgotten."

Eagerly, Broussard went back to hear what she had to say. The others followed.

"After I took off his right shoe and his sock, I found a ban-dage on the sole of his foot. It covered a small skin punc-ture."

"Was the gauze on the bandage bloodstained?" Broussard asked, trying to ascertain how deep the wound went.

"A little."

"Exactly where on the sole was this wound?"

"Just behind the middle two toes."

"Do you still have the shoes he was wearin'?"

"We gave them to his wife when she came in last night for a private viewing."

Broussard thanked her again and he and Noell followed their guide to the back door.

On the way to the car, Noell said, "Coldwater again, right?"

"Afraid so."

When they were under way, Noell said, "It's funny, I've been in Homicide six years and have seen over a hundred dead bodies. But the first time it *really* sank in that we're all headed that way was last summer on a tour I took of England. We stopped at the cemetery where Winston Churchill is buried. He's not in Westminster Abbey like you'd think, but in a little churchyard in a sleepy out-of-the way village where they mow the grass with a hand mower. He doesn't have a big fancy monument, just a minimal little marker in the grass. The inscription doesn't even mention he was prime minister. There was something about that simplicity that hammered me. He was a historical figure, yet there he was under our feet, his stone saying little more than that he lived and he died. I thought about it for weeks, trying to figure out why the deaths I see in my job don't affect me like that."

"What did you decide?"

"That I've been hardened. I can't even remember my first case or how I felt about it. You'd have to be a prime minister now before your death would affect me. I don't like that."

Remembering his own reaction to the corpse in the green jacket, Broussard said, "I'm havin' the same trouble."

13

A dark-haired woman in a black silk dress opened the door. She phoned in a smile and waited for an explanation.

Noell repeated the routine she'd given Janie at the funeral home, and then it was Broussard's turn.

"We're lookin' for Mrs. Hunter."

"I'm Val Hunter." Her smile wavered.

"Mrs. Hunter, I know this is a bad time for you, but there are some questions about your husband's death. . . ."

"What kind of questions?"

From behind her, a female voice said, "Val, Dad's blood sugar is low and he's getting the shakes. He needs to eat."

Val looked over her shoulder. "There's all kinds of food in the kitchen from the neighbors. You all go on and help yourselves. I'll be there in a minute."

When she looked back at Broussard, he attempted to answer her question. "There's a chance your husband's death wasn't natural."

"Not natural," Val repeated. She shook her head. "I don't understand."

"Someone may have caused it."

"How do you cause a heart attack?"

"It may not have been a heart attack."

"Could you please get to the point. I'm not up for this."

"I'm sorry, I don't mean to be so vague, but I don't know exactly what happened. It's possible I'd know more if I could see the shoes your husband was wearin' when he—that mornin'."

"His shoes . . . God . . . His shoes?"

"If we could."

Apparently resigned that she'd have to give them what they wanted, she stepped out of the way and Noell and Broussard went inside, where Broussard's own heart nearly stopped.

It was like the old adage from the Pogo comic strip, "We have met the enemy and he is us." The house might not have been burned by Sherman, but the Hunters had destroyed it almost as effectively.

All the heavy molding the original builders had surely put in the house was gone, replaced with simple modern equivalents. There was no plantation mural or elegant French paper on the walls. Instead, almost the entire foyer was painted beige, with black portholes of recessed lighting pockmarking the ceiling. On the wall to the right hung a big cartoonish black-and-beige wooden artwork that had been cut out on a band saw. At the far end of the foyer, the wall was covered in mirrors that made the one life-sized chrome android sculpture in front of it appear to be two. And the poor staircase—they'd ripped out its newel posts and lovely turned rails and banister, replacing them with four curving horizontal tubular rods, each in a different primary color.

Val gestured to a room on the left. "Have a seat and I'll get Tony's shoes."

A seat was just what Broussard needed, for what the

Hunters had done to their house made him weak in the knees.

Rocked as he was by what he'd seen, it was doubtful that he could have rallied even if the sitting room had been furnished in impeccably correct Louis XIV. But it wasn't Louis the *anything*. It was two brown sofas and a chair, all of which resembled tufted sausages, grouped around a glass and chrome coffee table that, like the sausages, stood only eight inches high. On the wall was a massive painting consisting of five swatches of color against a beige ground that matched the walls and carpet.

The sausages were so low, Broussard was afraid if he sat on one, he might not be able to get up without help. Noell apparently didn't find the seating inviting, either, so when Val returned carrying a pair of Adidas running shoes, she found both of them still standing.

"I don't know why you want them," she said, crossing to where Broussard waited, "but here."

Broussard took the shoes from her and determined left from right. He put the left one down and examined the sole of the other through the bifocal part of his glasses.

Finding an area of interest, he rummaged in his leather bag for a metal probe, then placed its point against the shoe sole. A few twists of the probe sent the point into the rubber. He moved to the big painting, tilted the shoe in the beam from the track lighting overhead, and looked inside. Turning to Val, he said, "Could I see where your husband put on his joggin' clothes that mornin'?"

It was clearly not anything Val wanted to do, but she agreed, signaling that they should follow her. "You'll have to excuse the mess in our bedroom," she said, heading for the stairs. "I've been too busy to deal with it."

After becoming nearly beige-blind from the decor downstairs, Broussard's retinas were dazzled by the Hunters' bedroom, whose walls were adorned with massive tree boughs and huge flowers on a silver foil ground. Set into the circular wall opposite the door was a chrome-trimmed glass cabinet with built-in lighting that made the collection of citrine-colored glass inside glow with a rich fire. Underfoot, a sculpted forest green carpet pulled it all together so nicely, the clothing littering the bed and the chaise were hardly noticeable.

Never having found practical significance in the observation that some good can be found in even the most evil men, this discovery of one attractive room in the Hunter home didn't suddenly make Broussard a fan. He'd come up here looking for a specific item and had a good idea where it would be. In his quick appraisal of the room, though, he'd failed to spot it. An open door to what appeared to be the master bath pulled him that way.

In the bathroom, he went directly to the wastebasket and put on a rubber glove from his bag. He then began pulling out the wastebasket's contents and piling them on the floor: cotton balls with makeup on them, a wadded Kleenex. . . .

"Must you do that?" Val said from the bathroom doorway, her face flushed.

Broussard paused in his work. "It could be crucial."

Oh, do what you have to, then." She left the doorway and crossed to the bedroom windows, allowing Noell to take her place.

Continuing with his plundering of the wastebasket, Broussard removed a box for a tube of Gleem toothpaste and one for a Clairol hair-coloring kit. Then his own face grew rosy as he gingerly added a Lightdays sanitary napkin to the growing pile of detritus.

With the removal of that last item, the bottom of the wastebasket was now revealed. On it lay the object he sought. He obtained from his bag a small evidence envelope with a transparent window. From the doorway, Noell saw him pick something small out of the wastebasket and drop it in the envelope.

He put the envelope in his bag and cleaned up the mess he'd made. When he stood up to leave, he was breathing heavily from being so long in a position that compressed his belly. Noell gave ground and he returned to the bedroom. "Mrs. Hunter, I'm finished."

Val turned from the window. "Did you find what you were looking for?"

"I think so. I'll need to conduct some tests before I know."

"What is it?"

Crossing to the window, Broussard reached into his bag, removed the envelope, and handed it to her. "Have you ever seen this before?"

She held it up to the window.

Curious herself about what Broussard had found, Noell moved in for a look. But before she could get into position, Val returned the envelope to Broussard.

"It's not the kind of thing I'd notice."

"Val, something's bitten Mom on the leg," a voice said from the doorway to the hall.

It was a younger version of Val.

"She's got a red welt the size of a quarter. Do you have anything we can put on it?"

"I'll find something for her." Val looked at Broussard, her eyes saying, Please go.

"I can see you've got things to do," Broussard said. "And we're finished anyway."

Everybody trooped downstairs, where, after Broussard advised Val not to throw out her husband's jogging shoes, she smoothly turned him and Noell onto the front porch.

When the blue front door had been shut behind them, Noell said, "Bad enough she had to lose her husband; now she's gotta put up with a houseful of relatives. What was that you found in there?"

Broussard opened his bag and handed her the envelope. She shook it to get the object out of the crease in the bottom and pinned it up where she could examine it.

"It's a weird kind of nail," Broussard said, "with barbs on the shank."

"And you believe when Hunter put on his jogging shoes, this nail was sticking through the sole."

"The facts predicted its existence and suggested it'd be in the nearest wastebasket to where he dressed. And its shape is right. With those barbs holdin' it in place, it'd puncture the skin before bein' dislodged from the shoe."

"If you're right, then the nail must be—"

Falling into the long-standing habit he'd acquired in conversations with Phil Gatlin in which each of them tried to be the first to state the implications of the facts under discussion, Broussard said, "It must be poisoned."

When they were once more in the car, Noell said, "Where to now? Toxicology?"

"Before we get them involved, there's a test I want to conduct. So we need to stop at a pet store, then the regional forensic center."

The car was suddenly filled with a rumbling noise that for a moment made Noell think the transmission was going out. But then the noise came again and she realized it was Broussard's stomach.

"Sounds like you could use some food," she said. "So could I."

"No time now. I need to get this test done before Hunter's buried." He stiffened against the floorboard and fished some lemon balls out of his pocket. "Try a couple of these. They'll hold you."

Had she not been driving and been able to see the pocket lint and the curly brown hair among the candies, she might have refused. Without this advantage, she took one and put it in her mouth. Broussard popped two himself and they headed back to Memphis.

Forty-five minutes after leaving Coldwater, Noell parked behind Ruby Begonia's Pet Emporium.

"No need for you to come in," Broussard said, climbing out. "I'll only be a minute."

He disappeared through the pet store's open back door, returning five minutes later with one of those white containers that usually have Chinese food in them. Stomach still rumbling, he sat cradling the container in his lap as they headed for their next stop.

After a short drive, Noell turned into a supermarket parking lot and found a slot.

"I thought we were going to the forensic center," Broussard said.

"This time, *you* stay in the car."

The whole time she was gone, which actually wasn't very long, Broussard counted the minutes, afraid he would lose Hunter's body to the earth before he could determine if he was right about that nail.

When Noell came back to the car, she was carrying a plastic sack, which she handed across to him before getting in.

"The time it'll take us to eat this isn't going to make any difference in what you need to do. Dig in."

"Diggin' is just what I'm worried about."

"Eat."

She'd bought them each a grilled chicken sandwich, some potato salad, and a Snapple iced tea. To Broussard, the theoretical standard for gastronomic barbarity had always been eating in a car. The only food-related activity he rated lower was cooking on the car engine and eating that food in the car. Surprisingly, this, his first experience in automotive dining in thirty years, was not at all unpleasant. So as they pulled out of the parking lot after finishing, he didn't mind the time he'd lost.

The Shelby County Regional Forensic Center sits a hefty scalpel throw west of where I-240 pours cars onto Madison Avenue, a situation that forced Noell to blend quickly with the efflux so she could make the right turn into the parking lot.

It was the first time Broussard had ever seen the place and he liked it immediately, mostly because it wasn't in a basement. All those windows . . . the light . . . four floors, all for forensics—scandalous and marvelous.

The parking lot was nearly full and included two patrol cars.

"Looks like business is booming," Broussard said.

"Lucky we got in when the price was low."

They parked, got out, and Broussard followed Noell up a short flight of steps to a single-story annex of the main building. She put her finger on a bell by the reflective glass door.

Broussard had already spent far too much of his day standing outside a place he wanted to enter. One thing about working with the dead, they never keep you waiting.

The door squalled open and a face from hell said, "Sergeant Noell, I wasn't expecting you. Come on in."

Noell stepped inside and Broussard followed.

"Wasn't expecting to be here myself," Noell said. "But that's what makes life so damn interesting. This is Dr. Broussard, the New Orleans ME. You'll have to ask him why we're here. Andy, this is Buddy Harper."

Buddy examined his own hand, then trolled for a handshake.

Broussard found his mitt warm and moist.

Buddy, of course, had not come from hell, but he had obviously been through it, for the left side of his face and most of his neck were stretched and raw with the aftereffects of burns that had surely been deep enough to expose the fat in his subcutaneous tissue. To his credit, he seemed outgoing and cheerful.

"Buddy, I'm here in Memphis investigatin' a possible murder. To do that, I have to carry out a little experiment, for which I'll need a benchtop and a few disposable supplies. Can you help me?"

"Question is, is it okay with Doc Graham? I'll need to check."

"Absolutely. You call him and give me the phone."

Buddy punched Graham's extension into a nearby wall phone and once again Broussard found himself standing around doing nothing while Hunter's funeral inched closer.

"Dr. Graham ... Buddy. There's a Dr. Broussard from New Orleans here. Wants to speak with you. Here he is."

Broussard took the receiver. "Gene ... Why have you never told me what a nice place you have here?"

"Didn't want you gettin' jealous. What are you doin' in Memphis?"

"I'm checkin' out a Tate County, Mississippi, case that may reach into my backyard."

"I've got a couple of detectives with me at the moment, but I should be finished in ten minutes. We can talk then."

"I'm kind of pressed for time. What I need right now is access to your facilities and a few dollars' worth of supplies to find out if I made the right decision comin' up here."

"Anybody who can learn if he did the right thing for a couple dollars ought to be helped, especially if okayin' it is all *I* have to do."

"The body in question is at a Memphis funeral home and they're gonna bury it today at three. If my hunch is right, I'm gonna want to get some samples from that body before the funeral. I've already been over there and found that the person in charge doesn't find me as charmin' as most folks do. So I'll need somebody with me who can get 'em to cooperate."

"And I suppose that somebody is me."

"Nice of you to offer."

"I hope you're wrong. Put Buddy back on."

Hearing that Graham gave Broussard's project his blessing, Buddy nodded and hung up. Motioning for Broussard and Noell to follow him down the hall, he said, "What are you gonna need?"

"A disposable two-cc syringe, the smallest needle you can

find, a two-milliliter test tube with a screw top, a rack to hold it, and some saline. Can you do that?"

"I think so."

Buddy led them to a room with a morgue green cement floor and lined with cabinets and benches, where he pulled out drawers and prowled through rows of bottles until he'd gathered up everything Broussard wanted. Then he and Noell watched to see what Broussard had in mind.

After donning a pair of rubber gloves from his bag, Broussard withdrew a small amount of saline from its rubber-stoppered bottle using the syringe and needle he'd requested. He discharged the saline into the small test tube, then dropped the nail from Hunter's wastebasket, point-first, into the test tube so about half of it was immersed. He capped the tube and shook it for about thirty seconds. He unscrewed the cap, drew the saline into the syringe, and laid it on the test tube rack so it wouldn't roll off.

From the Chinese food container, he produced, as Noell guessed he would, a mouse. More dexterously than she would have predicted, considering how short and thick his fingers were, he immobilized the mouse, belly out, in his left hand. With his right, he injected the contents of the syringe into the animal's peritoneal cavity. He put the animal on the bench and joined Buddy and Noell in watching every move it made.

At first, it mostly sniffed the benchtop, whiskers twitching. Then it stood on its hind legs and took a look around. Dropping again to all fours, it began an erratic tour of the benchtop, nose to the metal. Eventually, it traveled all the way to the end of the bench and Broussard had to reposition it. So far, it was showing no signs of distress.

This time, it went in the other direction. About halfway to that end of the bench, it took a ninety-degree turn, which brought it to the front edge. With Broussard close by in case it decided to jump, it sniffed along the edge.

"Doesn't look like it's having any problems," Noell remarked.

The mouse stood up again and stared across the room. It remained that way for several seconds, then, immobile as a rodent statue, toppled off the bench into Broussard's cupped hands.

He rolled it from side to side in one palm, which elicited no response. He probed it with his fingers and pushed on its legs.

"Is it dead?" Noell asked.

Broussard nodded. "And in full rigor."

"You haven't got enough murders in New Orleans, you gotta drum up some in other cities?" Gene Graham said. He was a large, imposing figure with silver hair that crested on his low forehead in a wavy pompadour. An aficionado of string ties like the one he was now wearing, he distrusted all men who wore more traditional neckwear. Broussard's penchant for bow ties united them in a small but select brotherhood.

"Whatever that poison is," Broussard said, "it seems to put skeletal muscle in a state of permanent contraction."

"Question is, is that a primary effect or a secondary result from attack on the central nervous system?" Graham said.

"So you've never seen anything like this, either?"

"I have not. And that annoys me. I have to tell you, I'm not comfortable with takin' samples from the deceased before I've got written authorization from his wife."

Had Hunter's death occurred in Graham's jurisdiction, Mrs. Hunter's permission wouldn't be needed. Under the circumstances, Graham's concerns were appropriate.

"I understand that," Broussard said. "But as I told you on the phone, she said if we'd leave the papers at the funeral home, she'd sign them when she arrives today."

"Which is when?"

Broussard looked at his watch. "In about an hour."

Graham lapsed into thought. "If we wait until she shows up, we'll disrupt the funeral. I don't want to do that." He looked at Buddy. "Would you get me what I'll need to draw vitreous and spinal fluid from this case. I'll want a bottle for the spinal fluid."

When looking for an exotic poison in a fluid sample, it may require many tests to identify the toxin. It's therefore important to get as much sample as possible. Had Broussard been in charge, he, too, would have asked for a bottle instead of a test tube.

While Buddy gathered up the necessary items, Graham looked at Broussard. "Just for the record, if the state of Mississippi won't cover the cost of the tox analysis, who am I gonna bill?"

"Send it to me."

"Anybody audits expenditures for your office, they're gonna wonder. . . ."

"I'll pay for this one myself."

14

Whatever Gene Graham wanted, funeral home Janie was ready to provide, so that minutes after their arrival, the body of Anthony Hunter was back in the embalming room on a gurney, his split suit coat and his tie off, the toothed plastic caps that held his lids in place and ensured his dead eyes had the proper contour removed.

Graham withdrew as much fluid as he could from the globe of each eye, a process that usually led to ocular collapse. Having been exposed to the firming influence of embalming chemicals, Hunter's eyes retained their shape fairly well.

Janie and her bearded assistant carefully rolled the body onto its side so Graham could slip a syringe between the lumbar vertebrae into the subarachnoid space. He withdrew a syringeful of clear liquid and discharged it into the plastic bottle he'd brought. He then went back for more, this time getting less than before.

They left the authorization for Hunter's wife with Janie,

and Noell and Broussard took Graham back to the forensic center.

"I'll get these samples to Toxicology right away," Graham said, standing by the car and talking to Broussard through the open window. "Obviously, I can't say how long it'll take for results"—he raised his eyebrows—"or how much it might cost."

"They find that toxin in Hunter, he'll have to be exhumed and a full autopsy done," Broussard said.

"Well . . . it's always somethin'. When are you goin' home?"

"I left it open. Now that it's pretty certain Hunter was murdered, I'd like to know more about him—what kind of research he did, for one thing. So I'm gonna stick around awhile."

"The wife and I are goin' out tonight to celebrate our fortieth anniversary. Want to come along?"

"I don't think she'd appreciate the company."

"Might not at that. You'd think after forty years she'd be used to me, but I seem to get on her nerves now more than ever. Tomorrow night, then, you and I will go somewhere. *If* you're still here. Let me know. . . . He bent down and looked at Noell. "Sergeant, you come back again now."

Noell drove Broussard to the Peabody, where she parked near the back entrance near a flower bed overflowing with purple and white petunias. "What's the schedule?"

"I'm gonna register, then check on the hours at the medical center library. I want to read some of Hunter's research papers and see what biographical information is available on him."

"I can stick around and take you."

"No need. If I go, I'll catch a cab."

"What about tomorrow?"

"I'd like to visit the Physiology Department at the medical center and talk to the people who knew Hunter. That'll probably go better if you're there, too."

"*I'd* start with the wife."

"I know that's the usual way to go, but this isn't a typical case."

Noell waited for him to say more.

"I wish I could, but I can't discuss it in any more detail."

"Good thing for you he was killed in Mississippi. Otherwise, we'd have a problem. As it is, I'm only a tour guide."

"I appreciate your understandin'."

"You want to start at UT, that's what we'll do. I'll pick you up right here, then, at . . . nine?"

"I'll be waitin'."

They went around to the trunk to get Broussard's bags.

From a few blocks over on Beale Street, they could hear a funky electric guitar in the hands of a real bluesman, making Broussard feel as though he wasn't as far from the French Quarter as he thought. His flight bag had tipped over and the paperback he'd stuffed in the side pocket had fallen onto the floor of the trunk. As he retrieved it, Noell said, "Crossfire Trail. I've read that. You're a Louis L'Amour fan?"

"Enough to have read fifty of 'em."

"I'm not far behind you. There's just something about the way that man tells a story . . . like he'd actually seen everything he writes about."

They stood there without speaking, Broussard wondering where to go with this newly discovered common ground. Throughout the day, he'd felt increasingly at ease with her and at one point had directed his attention to her left hand where it rested on the steering wheel, admiring her well-shaped fingers, he told himself, but also noting that she wore a wedding ring.

Why, then, did he hear himself saying, "Look, you bought lunch, so how about you and your husband joinin' me for dinner tonight in the hotel, as my guests?"

"My husband is a minor-league baseball umpire," Noell said. "Tonight, he's in Birmingham doing a Stallions game, or whatever that team is called."

"What would you think about comin' without him?"

He'd clothed his invitation as repayment for a favor, trying to hide its deeper significance even from himself. But a part of him saw through that, so when Noell hesitated, he felt as though everyone with rooms in the back of the hotel were watching and eavesdropping with parabolic listening devices.

Finally, she said, "What time?"

"Seven?"

"I'll meet you in the lobby."

At the hotel entrance, Broussard declined the bellhop's solicitation of his bags and went inside, mulling over what had just happened. Noell's hesitation meant she, too, thought there was some impropriety in the two of them having dinner without her husband. But she'd agreed anyway. Which meant . . . She liked Louis L'Amour enough to want to talk about his work with another fan over a nice meal. Surely that's what it was, nothing more. And really, wasn't that all *he* wanted?

Actually, he shouldn't be thinking about any of this, he reasoned. He needed to get to his room and let Kit and Tabor know Hunter had been murdered. With luck, Kit wouldn't already be in Thibodaux.

The hotel lobby was bedlam. There were kids running everywhere, carrying floating balloons. Thickets of people with name tags crowded the bar and stood chatting in small groups, most of them undoubtedly there for the Arnold's Beauty World convention, which was welcomed by a big red-and-white banner stretched across a line of booths on the mezzanine. At the end of the lobby opposite the bar, a piano with no one at the keyboard cranked out a jazz number, the music mingling with the sound of splashing water from a large fountain where camera flashes were recording the movements of the ducks that swam there.

He made his way to registration, checked in, and hurried to his room, where he called Kit. Getting only her answering machine, he left the news about Hunter and dialed Tabor's pager.

True to his word, Tabor returned the call a few minutes later.

"Brian . . . Andy Broussard. I've got news. Anthony Hunter *was* murdered." He recounted his visit to Hunter's home, his experiments with the mouse, and the trip to the funeral home to draw samples. He then asked where Kit was.

"Far as I know, she's working at the institute in Thibodaux."

"She needs to be told about Hunter."

"I agree. It's too risky, though, to call her at work and tell her. Someone may overhear. We'll have to wait until she gets home. It shouldn't be much longer."

"I already left a message on her machine about it. If that institute has anything to do with Hunter's death, it's too dangerous for her to be there."

"I'll talk to her tonight."

"And pull her out of there?"

"That could happen."

"I hope it does."

"When are you coming back to New Orleans?"

"I don't know. I want to scout around here some more."

"Okay. Keep me informed."

"I will."

At practically the same moment he hung up, Broussard remembered he'd forgotten to mention the phone number on the back of Tabor's card. No matter, he'd do it next time. He then called the UT medical library. Learning they were open until 10:00 P.M., he went downstairs and found a cab.

Broussard had heard that Memphis sat on a major earthquake fault. Apparently, the architects for the medical center library were unaware of this, for the building, a seven-story cement monolith, was perched on pillars like a bayou fishing shanty. As he went inside and rode the elevator up to the library, he felt he should read fast and get out.

From Hunter's entry in *American Men of Science,* he learned Hunter had been forty-two, had received his Ph.D. from Washington University in St. Louis, had been a three-time grantee from the National Heart, Lung, and Blood Institute, and had served on the editorial board of the *American Journal of Physiology.* His entry did not say why anyone would want him dead.

Reading over the abstracts of Hunter's work he found in the computer database for *Index Medicus,* he discovered that Hunter's research dealt with dietary influences on coronary artery disease. Hunter seemed particularly interested in the French paradox, the fact that the French cook with lots of butter and cream yet don't develop coronary artery disease like we do in this country. For a decade, Hunter had published at least four papers a year. Oddly, he'd published nothing last year or the year before. The index did not contain a list of his enemies.

Broussard returned to the Peabody at five o'clock, to find a large crowd arranged in two lines facing each other across an open space that ran from the lobby fountain to the elevators. Whatever was going on was taking place to the accompaniment of a Sousa march. Curious as to the meaning of this, he joined the nearest line and found a space he could peek through.

It was the fountain ducks, being leisurely herded down a red carpet to an open elevator. When they reached it, the ducks and their trainer got on, the doors closed, and the crowd melted away. Always a detail man, Broussard wondered as he waited for his own elevator what the trainer would have done if the ducks had soiled the red carpet.

Noell wasn't to arrive for another two hours. Broussard spent most of that time in his room reading *Crossfire Trail.* Around six, he thought about calling Kit, but didn't. As much as he wanted her out of harm's way, it wouldn't do to pressure her. Do that and she'd probably decide to take the opposite position. He'd passed along the critical information. It was up to her now. A few minutes before seven, he put the book down and changed into fresh clothes.

Noell walked into the lobby at exactly 7:00 P.M., wearing a black skirt and a sleeveless white jacket with a black orchid design. Her hair looked as soft and light as spun gold. She was, Broussard thought, an uncommonly fine detective.

Feeling awkward about commenting on her appearance, he greeted her by saying, "You're very punctual."

"It's my best feature."

"Would you like a drink before dinner?"

"Sounds nice."

They found a couple of unoccupied armchairs facing each other over a small table and gave their orders—a strawberry daiquiri for Broussard, a white Russian for Noell—to a young cocktail waitress in a short black dress. As the waitress left them, Noell said, "Did you find anything useful in the library?"

"Nothin' jumped out at me. But it's really too soon to expect that."

"I prefer to discover who the killer is right away."

"Does that happen often?"

"Sometimes he's still kicking the body when the first cop gets there."

"But then there's no challenge."

"I'd rather have a perfect solve rate than a lot of challenges."

The waitress soon appeared with their drinks and for the next few minutes they sat quietly, just enjoying the old hotel's ambience, which had improved greatly with the arrival of a real person to play the piano and the absence of the ducks and the cameras they attracted.

During this interlude, Broussard's mind drifted to the past

and he imagined himself as William Faulkner, drinking bourbon and sitting there with Faulkner's writing protégée and Memphis mistress, Joan Williams, the other guests whispering behind their hands about them.

Noell brought him back to the present. "Have you read Louis L'Amour's autobiography, *Education of a Wandering Man?*"

"I have indeed."

They spent the next few minutes talking about the kind of boy who would quit school at fifteen because it was "interfering with his education," and they speculated on the nature of parents who would let a son of such an age go on the road by himself.

They moved the discussion into Chez Phillip, the hotel's premier restaurant and one of the best in the city, where Noell deferred to Broussard's obviously greater knowledge and experience in these matters, allowing him to order for both of them, a gesture that pleasantly surprised him.

Over an appetizer of rabbit-leg confit with carrot crostini and coriander-flavored wasabi sauce, they both laughed at Broussard's observation that even as a boy, he couldn't have survived on one sandwich a day, as L'Amour had done while saving up for some books he wanted. As they savored a wonderful red onion bisque with homemade sausage, they discussed the battle of Doubtful Canyon, in which seven white men held off many hundreds of Apaches for three days, killing 150 Indians before most of the seven died of thirst and one killed himself with the last round of ammunition. Noell agreed with Cochise, who later said the seven were the bravest men he'd ever heard of. Broussard believed they merely did what they had to do.

Appropriately enough, Broussard had ordered for their entrée roasted venison loin à la Choctaw, with smoked sweet potatoes and wild hackberry sauce. During this portion of their dinner, the subject became the battle of Adobe Walls and Billy Dixon's famous long shot that knocked an Indian off his horse seven-eighths of a mile away.

Finishing with fig and Armagnac puff pastry with malt and anise ice cream, they speculated on whether the hand and footholds allowing access to the Anasazi cliff dwellings really were placed so if you began on the wrong foot, you became trapped partway up. The conversation ended with a debate over which was Louis L'Amour's best book, both now so satiated with food, neither could mount a very spirited defense of their choice.

To Broussard's disappointment, Noell insisted on paying for her own dinner, which, on a detective's salary, was not an insignificant sum.

Later, lying in his bed, Broussard remembered how, on three occasions, when Noell was impatient to speak, she touched his hand, letting it linger a bit longer than necessary.

Except for lunch, which they ate at a nearby restaurant called Thrifty Fifties, a place featuring ninety-nine-cent hamburgers and a jukebox full of vintage rock and roll, Kit and Jenny spent the rest of Kit's first day preparing fresh electrophoresis samples, finishing at 5:20.

Kit reached home an hour later, absolutely worn out, mostly from the strain of having spent the day as someone else and worrying that the gun on her ankle was going to come loose and slide onto the floor.

The first thing she did was listen to the message Broussard had left about Hunter. With that news and the rest of her day tumbling around in her head, she fed Lucky and shed the Ladysmith. She then called Tabor and left her number.

Ten minutes after she'd put a TV dinner in the oven, Tabor called back.

"They checked my references," she said.

"So I hear."

"Your people almost overdid it."

"So you got the job."

"Yeah, but I don't think I can do what you want."

"Because Anthony Hunter was murdered?"

"Andy told you?"

"Right after he left you the message. Is that why you don't want to continue? If it is, I can respect that."

"That's not why. I thought Hunter had been murdered when we first learned he was dead."

"Why then are you having second thoughts?"

"The director's lab and office are behind a door that doesn't even have hinges. It just slides in and out of the wall. And I'm working for someone who doesn't seem to have any connection with the director. . . . So how am I going to get access to his phone?"

"You've only been there one day. Don't be so impatient."

"What, exactly, do you think is going to happen to make this work?"

"If you stay, I think you'll study the situation and come up with a plan."

"Me? I thought you were the one with the plan."

"Like I told you before, there's always a certain amount of slippage. Give it a little time. Think about it and we'll come up with something together . . . *if* you decide to go back."

"I don't think I'm smart enough to do this."

"Kit, I know your record. Intelligence is not an issue. You're probably the smartest, most resourceful woman I've ever worked with."

"You can't know that. We've only just met."

"I've studied you. I'm not wrong. You've just lost your way, that's all. It happens. You're in a trough where you can't see yourself properly. Not long ago, I was trying to find a restaurant I'd been to only one time before, in a city I don't visit very often. I remembered its general location, but didn't know exactly how to get there. You know how I found it? I simply relaxed and let my instincts guide me."

Kit got the point but didn't want to admit it. "Why didn't you just look up the address in the phone book and get a map from the hotel?"

"There, see . . . natural intelligence, just like I said. So what do you think?"

"Well . . . maybe I'll give it a couple of days."

"Good for you. Call me tomorrow night and we'll see where we are."

After hanging up, Kit ate and took a long, hot bath, during which she remembered she hadn't asked Tabor what he knew about Tom Ward. Filled to the brim with Agrilabs, Inc., she decided to hold that discussion until they spoke tomorrow.

With her own needs met, she washed Lucky, who could always be found under the bed when there was water running in the tub. A few minutes before nine, he jumped up on the arm of the chair Kit was sitting in and stared at the phone. At nine, the call he was waiting for came in: Nolen wanting to know if she and Lucky were ready for their nightly walk with him and Mitzi. With that walk, Kit's first day as Kate Martin came to a close.

15

"Before we do anything this morning," Noell said as Broussard got in her car, "I want to say something about last night." She hesitated, looking through the windshield at a gardener collecting spent blooms from the Peabody's petunia bed. "I . . . may have given you the wrong impression. I admit I didn't have dinner with you just because we both like Louis L'Amour. It was more than that. And I think you felt it, too. But while it's true my husband and I don't have a perfect marriage by any means, I'm not ready to throw it away."

In one sense, Broussard was happy to hear this. Being unaccustomed to the feelings of sexual attraction, he found it disturbing, unsettling to the mind and the body. But as unwilling as he might be to enter into *any* impropriety, let alone with a married woman, Noell's declaration that nothing was going to happen was not entirely good news.

Finally, she looked at him. "I'm sorry if I led you to believe otherwise."

"I'm kinda slow to accept anything until there's adequate

proof on the table, so I was still in the speculation stage of that particular investigation."

Noell smiled at this, and despite what they'd both said, Broussard felt the issue was not settled.

The trip to the medical center was a short one, so after they'd been under way only a few minutes, Noell pointed to her left. "There's the UT physiology building."

Looking across the street, Broussard saw a venerable old structure adorned with lots of cut stone and Gothic tracery. The arch over the entrance matched the one in the picture Kit had found of Anthony Hunter.

Noell pulled into a McDonald's and ditched the car. Putting their lives at risk, they jaywalked across four lanes of traffic so dense that when they safely reached the sidewalk, Broussard muttered a small prayer of thanks.

Upon entering the target building, Broussard felt right at home, for it was as quiet as the morgue back in New Orleans and, in fact, had the same yellow tile on the walls. There was a directory to the left of the entrance, but there were so few letters on it, they spelled nothing.

"You get the feeling we came in the wrong door?" Noell asked.

"Obviously, we're in the restful wing."

Being that she was the detective and it was her city, Broussard let Noell lead the way. Ultimately, this took them into something called the Nash Annex, a tall, narrow, gloomy atrium with the exterior facade, including the windows, of the building they'd just left on one wall and four floors of exposed walkway and offices on the other. Even here, there was no one around.

"What are we suddenly . . . Adam and Eve?" Noell said in frustration. "Sorry, bad analogy."

The sound of a door opening echoed through the annex and a maintenance man appeared on the floor above, pushing a broom.

Noell put two fingers in her mouth and whistled like a sailor. When he looked down, she said, "Where can we find the Physiology Department's main office?"

He made a hitchhiking gesture with his thumb. "Fourth floor Nash." Then he pointed to his right. "Far end of the hall."

"How about that for detective work?" Noell said over her shoulder as she headed back the way they'd come.

"I don't think that kind of thing counts," Broussard replied, hurrying to keep up.

The only indication they'd found the right door was a departmental roster posted next to it, on which Anthony Hunter was still listed. Judging from the inattention to such things here, Broussard suspected his name would remain there for years.

Inside, they encountered a woman with two reams of copy paper clutched to her chest. She had skin the color of a gingersnap and only a bit more hair. She paused in her duties to offer assistance.

Noell made her standard introductions, then said, "And we'd like some information on Dr. Hunter."

The secretary's eyes rolled upward. "Dr. Hunter . . . We're all still in shock over that." Then the implication of Noell's affiliation sank in. "Homicide? You said Homicide. . . . You don't think . . . No . . ."

"That hasn't been established yet," Noell lied. "We're trying to determine exactly what *did* happen."

"And to do that, we need to learn more about Dr. Hunter," Broussard interjected. "For example, I'd like to know exactly what he's been doin' lately in his research."

"I don't know anything about those matters," the secretary said. "But you can find his published papers in the library."

"I've tried that. There's nothin' for the last two years. Did he submit any grant applications recently?"

"His competing renewal went to NIH for a March first deadline."

"Do you keep a copy in this office?"

The woman hesitated. "It's not a public document."

"This isn't idle curiosity," Noell said. "We're conducting an official inquiry. If necessary, we'll get a search warrant."

"No need to get pushy," the secretary said. "You can see it."

She led them into one of the rooms opening off the general area, put her load of paper on the desk there, and knelt at the bottom drawer of a long sideways file cabinet.

She thumbed through the folders inside and paused, then worked her way through those that remained. Obviously agitated, she began at the first folder in the drawer and methodically went through them all again.

"I'm sorry," she said, standing up. "Our copy doesn't seem to be here. But the dean of research has one and so does the Office of Research Affairs. I'll call one of them and have their copy sent over."

She picked up the phone, called the latter of the two offices she'd mentioned, and explained the situation. "They'll send it right over," she said, hanging up. "Mind if I go on with my work?"

"Feel free," Noell said.

"You can wait in here if you like."

Broussard fished in his pocket for a couple of lemon balls, which he offered to Noell. Seeing that they nestled in pocket lint like eggs in a nest, she waved them off. "Too early in the day for me."

It was the right time of day for Broussard and he popped one into his mouth, then dropped into a chair and folded his hands over his belly. In one of the other rooms, a phone rang.

Shortly thereafter, Ms. Gingersnap returned. "This is very odd," she said.

"Let me guess," Broussard said. "Neither of the offices you mentioned can find its copy."

"How did you know?"

"No other reason you'd have come in here lookin' so surprised."

"Dr. Hunter must have kept a copy," she suggested, entering now into the spirit of the search.

Broussard got out of his chair. "How about showin' us his office?"

"And finding us some rubber gloves," Noell added.

As they followed her into the Nash Annex a short while later, the secretary wondered aloud at the disappearance of the three copies of Hunter's grant. "It's almost as if—" she stopped walking and looked at Broussard with the glow of discovery on her face—"as if someone *took* them."

Too kind to point out that this was a conclusion she could have reached back in the office, Broussard simply smiled and nodded.

"Which also means we're not likely to find Dr. Hunter's copy, either," she said. "Ooooh, this is eerie."

Hunter's two file cabinets were unlocked. A thorough search of them turned up copies of his three previous grants, but not the latest. Nor did they find it in the file drawer of his desk.

"Who typed that grant?" Broussard asked.

"Dr. Hunter. Most of the doctors type their own work."

They all looked at Hunter's computer.

"Bet it's not there," Noell said. She pulled out the chair in front of the computer and sat down and turned the thing on.

"Can you operate it?" Broussard asked.

"Well enough to find the grant if it's in here and if we're not locked out of anything." The screen came on, displaying a bewildering number of icons. "This could take awhile," she said, double-clicking the mouse on an icon at the top.

Broussard turned to the secretary. "Hunter must have had technical help with his work. Are those people here today?"

"Unfortunately not. They both took some vacation time—

they're married. They left the day Dr. Hunter died, so they might not even know about it. They haven't called in, and I didn't see them yesterday at the funeral."

While Noell worked at the computer, Broussard went through Hunter's shelves, looking for data books. Finding none, he checked all the desk drawers, again without success.

"Would you like to see his lab?" the secretary volunteered.

"I would indeed." He turned to Noell. "Anything locked?"

"Not so far."

"I'm gonna look for data books in his lab."

She nodded and opened another file.

Hunter's lab was as neat as his office. The chemicals were alphabetically arranged, facing squarely forward, there was nothing lying on the benchtops, and all the drawers were labeled. Thinking of his own office and the piles of books and journals stacked all over it, Broussard wondered how a man got a decent thought in surroundings so sterile.

It did make it easy, though, to find Hunter's data books, which occupied the top three shelves of a metal cabinet in a small room off the main lab. As expected, they were arranged in chronological order, with the inclusive dates neatly written on their spines. The last book on the shelf contained data generated two years earlier. A search of the lab turned up nothing more current.

"Whoever's behind this sure isn't bothered by a locked door," the secretary observed, echoing a thought that had run through Broussard's mind a few minutes earlier.

"Who among Dr. Hunter's colleagues here might know what he was workin' on?" he asked.

She thought a moment. "That'd probably be Dr. Ivy."

"Is he in?"

"We can see. His office is at the end of this floor."

Taped to Ivy's door was a cartoon showing a guy in a lab coat looking through a microscope. Behind him, another scientist was about to put a few drops of a liquid from a bottle labeled "Sulfuric Acid" on the seated man's neck. The title of the cartoon was "Laboratory High Jinks." Arrows identified the seated man as Dr. Hunter, the one with the acid as Dr. Ivy. The labels weren't applied, but were actually part of the cartoon, indicating that someone with a lot of spare time had scanned the original into a computer and added the labels before printing it.

The secretary's knock was answered by a booming "Enter."

Dr. John Ivy rose from a littered desk to greet them. He was a big, lanky fellow with thin blond hair that hung to the nape of his neck like a sunscreen on a French Foreign Legion cap. He had the shoulders of an Olympic swimmer.

"Dr. Ivy, this is Dr. Broussard. He's here with a homicide detective investigating Dr. Hunter's death."

"Wasn't that ruled a heart attack?" Ivy said to Broussard.

"We're not so sure now," Broussard replied.

"All the copies of Dr. Hunter's grant have disappeared," the secretary said.

"Would you mind telling Sergeant Noell I'm gonna be a few more minutes?" Broussard said, wanting no more such interruptions.

"Of course."

Broussard accepted Ivy's offer to sit, then before Ivy could ask about the grants, he said, "I'm curious about what Hunter has been workin' on for the last year or two. The secretary said you two were friends, so I was hopin' you'd know."

Ivy rocked back in his chair and folded his big hands behind his head. "We were friends, true enough, but these days I'm afraid that doesn't extend to the lab."

"What does that mean?"

"Everybody's got a piece of some biotech firm or they're planning to patent something from their work. Free and open communication in science is a thing of the past. Everybody's looking over his shoulder, afraid a competitor is going to beat him to the pot of gold."

He rocked forward, dropped his palms to the desk, and slid forward until he was leaning on his forearms. "I'll tell you this—it's ruining science. Used to be, anybody would give you any reagent they'd developed. In fact, some of the big journals have that as a credo: If we publish your work, it's understood you'll make any probes you've developed available to your colleagues. Good luck. It just ain't happening like it used to. In the last six months, I've written three letters to a fellow at the Max Planck, asking for some antibodies he's developed. Still haven't heard from him . . . and I won't.

"I liked Tony . . . I really did. But I didn't agree with that attitude. Christ, I don't even work in the same area. What am I going to do, take his secrets and sell 'em to the highest bidder?"

"You think he had secrets?"

"Hell, he hadn't published for two years. I think it was because he was afraid to let people know what he was doing."

"And you have no idea what that was?"

"All I can say is, he must have thought it was pretty damn special to believe NIH was going to keep pushing money at him, with his publication record."

Broussard thanked Ivy for the information and went back to Hunter's office, where he found Noell, sans secretary. "How you doin'?"

"There's no grant in here," Noell said. "And no floppy disks around, either."

"As I understand it, if the grant *was* there and somebody simply deleted it, all they did was corrupt the file name so it can't be accessed. The rest of the file may still be on the hard disk. How about we take his cpu to your crime lab and see if they can find it."

"Sounds like a good idea. Didn't know you were so computer-literate."

"My deputy ME in New Orleans keeps me updated whether I want to hear it or not."

"Learn anything down the hall?"

"Just that Hunter's latest data books are also missin' and he didn't even talk with his best friend here about his work. His friend thinks it was because Hunter had stumbled onto somethin' he hoped would make a lot of money."

"Scientists motivated by greed? Say it ain't so. I guess you've realized by now you're not tracking one killer. You're up against a skilled organization."

"I was aware of that before I left New Orleans. I just didn't know if they were operatin' up here."

"You want to tell me about it?"

"I want to, but I can't."

"We've got some B and E charges here and probably theft. You're going to have to discuss it with somebody in the department."

"I know. Right now, though, I want to talk to Hunter's technicians."

He and Noell returned to the departmental office and got the address and phone number of the techs, Steve and Holly Keough, from the secretary who'd been helping them. A call to the Keoughs from a departmental phone went unanswered.

"They're probably just out of town," Noell said. "But I think we should take a drive over there."

For the secretary's benefit, she'd phrased her suggestion as though they just didn't have anything better to do, but Broussard knew what was in the back of her mind. Whoever had murdered Hunter was surely aware the Keoughs knew what he'd been working on.

With Hunter's cpu in the trunk, Broussard and Noell arrived at the Keough household twenty minutes later. The couple lived in the area generally known as midtown, in a brick bungalow shaded by fifty-year-old oaks and elms. Enough time had passed since the lawn had been mowed for dandelions to flower. There was no car in the drive, but Noell rang the bell anyway.

The house next door was a poorly maintained place with a big solar collector on the roof and a desert diorama out front made of Arkansas fieldstone and sand decorated with a few cacti, a dozen artificial snakes of various hues, and a ceramic parrot.

An old woman in a bathrobe came out onto its porch. "They ain't home."

"Do you know where they are?" Noell asked.

"Why do you want to know?"

Broussard and Noell left the Keoughs' house and walked over to her. Before they got there, she went inside and locked the storm door.

Noell's ID brought her back outside. They saw now that she was wearing slippers with fabric rabbit heads on them. Noell asked again about the Keoughs.

"They're on vacation—in Mexico. What's wrong?"

"We just want to talk to them about their work," Noell said. "When did they leave?"

"Last Wednesday . . . and today's Tuesday. So that's . . ."

She recited the days that had passed, keeping track on her fingers. "Six days. Would *you* go away that long and not call and check on your mother if she had arthritis so bad that some days she could barely get dressed?"

"You're Steve's mother?"

"Lord no . . . Holly's. She was a good girl, very affectionate to me, until Steve got hold of her. Since then, I get no consideration at all. You here because of somethin' he did? Always thought he'd come to a bad end."

"We're only seeking information," Noell said. "Do you have the phone number of their hotel?"

"It's inside somewhere."

"May we use your phone to call them? I'll charge it to the department."

"It's all right with me, but don't say you're here and don't try to get me on the line. They're not interested enough to call me, I don't want to talk to 'em." She opened the storm door and a big brown flop-eared rabbit hopped onto the threshold. "No you don't." She shooed him back inside with her foot. "Watch where you step. I ain't run the vacuum yet this mornin'."

Inside, Broussard saw three rabbits—the one the old woman had pushed back inside and two others under a rocking chair—a white one with black splotches on his back and another brown one with erect ears. The carpet was a minefield of fecal pellets.

Noell followed the woman to the phone while Broussard waited by the door, not wanting to soil his shoes.

Noell made the call and waited for someone at the hotel to answer.

In the interim, the black-and-white rabbit mounted the small brown one.

"Do you have a Mr. and Mrs. Keough registered?" Noell asked into the phone.

She waited for the clerk to check the guest list.

"I see," she said a moment later. "Thanks."

She hung up and looked at the old woman and then at Broussard. "They were expected last Wednesday but never arrived."

16

The new samples Kit and Jenny had prepared on Monday were run the following morning. Shortly before noon, the destaining had progressed to the point where the thin blue lines of protein were clearly evident.

Mudi was ecstatic. "In all of recorded history, there has never been a better gel than this," he gloated. "Kate, I am forever in your debt. May you come back as an eagle in your next life and find all your enemies furry and edible." He then disappeared down the hall with the gel to photograph it and begin his analysis.

Since it was too near lunch to begin anything else, Kit and Jenny walked down to Thrifty Fifties, where Jenny's shake of the head when Kit ordered the chili made her switch to a chef's salad.

"You certainly made a good impression on Mudi," Jenny said as the waitress carried their orders to the kitchen.

"Lucky, that's all."

"Don't be so modest. It wasn't luck. You've got a good head

for science. I'm not particularly bright, but I *am* careful. Have you done any graduate work?"

"A little."

"You should do more . . . get a Ph.D. and put some X chromosomes at the top of the peck order."

The conversation was getting very uncomfortable and Kit wished she were elsewhere. Lying to the others didn't bother her, but she regretted having to deceive Jenny. The girl was kind, considerate, and honest, and if anything illegal was happening at Agrilabs, she was certainly not part of it.

"What about Lewis?" Kit said. "She's pretty far up the ladder."

"Yeah, right. Like she *has* X chromosomes."

Shortly after they returned to work, Kit's duties took her past one of the windows that looked out on the bayou behind the institute. There, she saw Rose Lewis and a man, who, from what Jenny had said, must be the director. They were coming toward the building, each carrying a folding chair. Wanting to get a better look at the director, Kit remained at the window.

Suddenly, Lewis looked up—right at Kit. Startled, Kit darted to the side, out of sight. Then, remembering the windows were reflective, so you could see out but not in, her pulse slowed. Pulling back like that had been instinctive, but not the right move. Had that window been two-way, her actions would have appeared suspicious.

As she walked back to Mudi's lab, a small voice reminded her she was assuming the rear windows were one-way like the others. The same voice also pointed out that Lewis had been wearing sunglasses, which might have allowed her to see through any of the windows.

Late that afternoon, when Kit's scare at the window had largely been forgotten, Rose Lewis crept up and jabbed a finger in her back.

"Dr. Woodley, the institute director, wants to see you," she said with a mocking look. "He's waiting in his office."

Kit's first thought was that her true identity and purpose there had been discovered. The voice that had been whispering in her ear strongly advised her to run for it. A calmer influence reminded her there were many other reasons why Woodley might want to see her. Maybe he simply wanted to meet the new employee. After all, he *was* the boss. Besides, now she'd get a look at his inner sanctum.

At the door to Woodley's area, Lewis paused and spoke one word, "Access."

There was a faint hum and the door slid open.

Lewis pushed Kit through the doorway and went off down the hall. Inside was a long table filled with metal rods, glass cylinders, and plastic spaghetti tubing. From an open door at the far end of the room, she heard the squeak of a chair and the rustle of paper. On her right, something moved near the floor.

Turning, she saw a man in a blue lab coat kneeling in front of an electrical receptacle. A shock of straight black hair hung over his forehead. The rest was combed back in a single glossy sheet. His thin lips were drawn into a subtle sneer that made her feel as though she were being leered at through a keyhole.

For a moment, she stood rooted to the floor, hypnotized by the look of unmitigated evil in his glistening rodent eyes. Regaining her senses, she turned with a defiant tilt to her chin and moved toward the chair squeak, realizing she'd probably just met Tom Ward.

Through the open door, she saw the top of a balding head, its owner writing furiously in a notebook. The office looked as though it had been ransacked. The shelves lining the walls were filled with books that might have been thrown up there with a shovel. There were stacks of manila file folders and journals everywhere, even on the floor. The desktop was paper insanity. Amid the clutter, her eyes found the phone on a table behind the desk, just as Tabor had said. Encouraged by the absence of any evidence this was to be an interrogation, she knocked lightly on the door frame.

Woodley looked up. "Ms. Martin, so good of you to come."

Earlier, when she'd glimpsed him through the window, she'd thought him to be in his sixties. Up close, he looked older, his face more heavily lined than she'd realized. From this improved vantage point, she saw, too, that his lips were unnaturally red and he held them pursed, like a preacher who'd just caught the head deacon and the church organist in flagrante.

In an old management trick designed to make the bosses seem like just plain folks, Woodley came around to the front of his desk and cleaned the litter from two heavy wooden chairs. Sitting in one himself, he motioned Kit to the other. As she sat down, he smiled stiffly. "Dr. Mudi has been telling me some good things about you. It seems we made a wise choice in asking you to join us."

"Thank you. It's always nice to be appreciated."

"But mere appreciation isn't enough, is it? It can't clothe us or feed us."

Unsure where he was going with this, Kit said, "But I believe it *is* a fundamental human need."

"A perceptive comment to be sure, but not entirely appropriate for this conversation."

"Why's that?"

"Mostly because I say it isn't. That's the wonderful thing about being in charge. I get to have everything just the way I want it. And right now, I want you to have a fifty-dollar-a-month raise. And by my saying it, it's done."

"You're very kind."

A thunderhead rose in his eyes. "No. I'm *not* kind," he said sharply, pointing a finger at her. "Make no mistake. This is a reward for achievement, *not* a kindness."

As suddenly as the storm had blown up, it departed.

"I see from your résumé you've had some experience with gel chromatography."

He was referring to the process in which a protein mixture goes into the top of a glass cylinder containing sandlike spheres of a particular size and then separated proteins come out the bottom, biggest ones first. Quick and easy, if you knew what you were doing, and she did.

"I'm familiar with the technique, yes."

"From time to time, I may be needing some proteins purified. When I do, I'd like you to handle it. We've recently begun some new experiments and could use an extra hand."

"I'll be working in here, then?" she said, trying to conceal her excitement at being moved into a position where she could get at his phone.

"No. You'll set up your equipment in Dr. Mudi's lab. When we need something run, we'll deliver the samples and tell you what matrix to use. All you have to do is collect the fractions and give them, along with the strip chart, to Ms. Lewis. I know it doesn't seem like I'm expecting much from you, but let's start this way and see how things go."

Then, as though Kit's interest in it had set it off, the phone rang.

"I've got to take this call. . . . We'll talk again. The red button by the hall door will let you out."

Obviously dismissed, Kit got up and left his office. In the lab, Tom Ward stepped in her way.

"Anytime you want one of those fundamental needs filled, let me know," he said. "I'm good at filling things."

He leaned his face toward her neck. As she pushed him away and stepped back, she heard Woodley say, "Oh hell. Tom, come in here."

"Another time," Ward whispered.

A few seconds later, in the hall, as Kit was about to turn the corner, she saw Woodley and Ward leave the lab and head for the stairs. After waiting long enough to make sure they were gone, she went back to Woodley's lab, checked to make sure no one was watching, and stood in front of the door. "Access."

Nothing happened.

She tried again. "Access."

Still nothing.

Thinking this over, she went back to work.

"Brian . . . Andy Broussard. I've got more news. I just learned from Toxicology that the agent used to kill Hunter was batrachotoxin, a frog-derived dart poison five hundred times more powerful than curare. It depolarizes nerve and muscle cells, sendin' the heart into a lethal fibrillation. It also causes contraction of the rest of the body musculature, so the victim appears to be in premature rigor."

Broussard regretted he couldn't see the look of amazement on Tabor's face at how much he'd learned. "That's not all. Every copy of his latest research grant is missin' from the university here."

"So his death had something to do with his work," Tabor concluded.

"Not much doubt about that."

"Have you asked his colleagues what he was working on—or even better, his research techs? They should know."

"His colleagues don't know anything, and his two techs, a husband and wife, are missin'. They won a free Mexican vacation, but they never arrived at the hotel. The airline says they were on the flight, so they disappeared between the airport in Mexico City and the hotel. And guess what—the firm that awarded the free vacation doesn't exist."

"I'd sure like to know what he was working on."

"I thought we could get a copy of his newest grant from NIH, but they said they never received it. There was no grant on Hunter's computer, either, most likely because it was deleted by whoever stole the university copies. The crime lab here checked Hunter's hard disk to see if any of the grant was still there, but they found nothin'.

"On a different front, I *have* learned the curator of reptiles at the zoo here has a collection of poison-dart frogs. My detective liaison and I have an appointment with him tomorrow at four o'clock."

"That sounds promising."

"There's another thing—my liaison, Sergeant Noell, needs to talk to you." He gave Tabor the number of the Memphis Police Homicide Division. "I think she's in the office now."

"It's a woman?"

"And a very competent one."

"I'll give her a call."

"I'm sure she'd appreciate it. What's happenin' with Kit?"

"At this moment, I expect she's at work in Thibodaux."

"You let her go back?"

"She wasn't influenced by Hunter's death. Said she thought he was murdered from the start."

"But *you* didn't know it."

"We've always assumed the people involved would be capable of murder. If you recall, the governor pointed that out in your office. That's why we made sure she could protect herself. Andy, she's a grown woman. She was given all the facts and she decided to continue."

"I'm just worried about her."

"I am, too. But the fact you've uncovered one definite murder and two probables makes it even more important these criminals be stopped. I'm a good judge of people. If it makes you feel any better, Kit is uncommonly suited to this job. She could use a little more confidence, but other than that, she's solid. And she's always known she should get out of there at the slightest sign of trouble. Did you leave a message for her about the two techs disappearing?"

"No."

"When I talk to her tonight, I'll tell her."

"Despite what you've said, I'm still gonna worry about her. There was something else I wanted to . . . Oh yeah—the business card you gave me had a name and phone number handwritten on the back. Thought you might need it."

He recited what was on the back of the card and hung up, wishing he'd never sent Kit to Angola.

"I met the Agilabs director today," Kit said into the phone. "He wants me to do some work for him."

"So the fly blundered into the web," Tabor replied. "I told you something would develop. Does this mean you've moved into his personal lab?"

"No. I was in there today, but any work he gives me is to be done elsewhere. It's too bad we don't already have the tap in place. While I was talking to him, he got a call that seemed to shake him up; then he and Tom Ward went somewhere in a hurry."

"Who's Tom Ward?"

Kit described Ward.

"That's not someone I know about. But he sounds like their enforcer. If you decide to continue, he's the one to watch out for."

"*If* I decide to continue?"

"I heard from Andy. Hunter's techs have disappeared. We have to assume they're dead, too. That raises the ante to where, once again, you can drop out gracefully if you wish."

"Drop out . . . I don't think so. Not when I've just figured out how to get to Woodley's phone."

17

Finally . . .

After spending most of the morning on supposed trips to the bathroom in response to a feigned intestinal disturbance, Kit caught Rose Lewis pushing a cart of clean glassware toward Woodley's lab. Counting on the fact that Lewis never acknowledged the presence of an underling when she passed one in the hall, Kit timed her own approach to coincide with Lewis's arrival at the lab door just as Lewis said, "Access."

It wasn't likely Lewis could have heard it over the sound of jiggling glassware, but Kit still waited until the lab door had closed before she pushed the stop button on the tape recorder in the pocket of her lab coat.

Her luck held awhile longer when she ducked into the restroom and found it empty. She took out the recorder, ran it on rewind for a few seconds, then pressed the play button.

A few bars of "Stayin' Alive" echoed off the tile walls; then there was only the faint sound of jiggling glass, which gradually grew louder before that, too, played out. A scant second later, Rose Lewis said, "Access." Kit stopped the tape and rewound it to the beginning.

The plan was to get away from Jenny at lunch and rig Woodley's phone while he and Lewis sat out back and ate—that is, if the recorder hadn't distorted Lewis's voice in some minor way so the door control wouldn't recognize it. It certainly sounded just like her, but there was no way of knowing how sensitive the control was. The wild card was Tom Ward. She knew nothing about his schedule, but did know his car, and so far today, it wasn't in the parking lot.

It wasn't a perfect plan. Her chances of being seen as she invaded Woodley's lab would be far fewer if she made the attempt at night, but the previous afternoon, on a real trip to the bathroom near quitting time, she'd seen Rose Lewis enter a series of numbers into a keypad mounted on the wall next to Woodley's door. Lewis had then tested the voice sensor, which had failed to respond. Apparently satisfied with what she'd done, Lewis had then walked away.

The keypad was obviously used to switch off voice control of the door. Kit had described all this to Tabor, hoping he'd be able to reactivate the control so they could go in together at night. But he'd said he couldn't.

To get the activation number, Kit would have needed to watch over Lewis's shoulder while she punched it in. That left only one alternative: to go in during the day—alone.

In addition to the risk of being seen, it was possible the voice control was also switched off during lunch—more of that slippage Tabor was always mentioning. The only way to know was to try it.

Heart in her throat at the knowledge of what she was going to do, Kit left the restroom and put the recorder with the other one in her locker.

For the next hour and a half, she was practically a zombie, mentally rehearsing and refining what she was going to say to Jenny come lunchtime, and planning each movement of her assault on Woodley's phone.

All too quickly, it was noon. As expected, Jenny assumed they'd go to lunch together.

"I wish I could," Kit said with as much sincerity as she could muster. "But I've got to meet the plumber at my place."

"What's wrong?"

What's wrong? . . . What's wrong? The question rattled around in Kit's skull. "The kitchen sink won't drain."

"Which one did you call? Some of the plumbers in this town are real crooks."

Good God. Who'd have thought she'd ask *that?* "I don't know. Somebody out of the phone book. I forget the name."

"I hope they don't take you for a ride."

"Me, too."

"And I hope they show up."

"I expect they will. I better get going, so I don't miss them."

Kit went to her car, left the parking lot, and drove around town, returning at 12:35. She took a quick tour around the lot to make sure Ward's car wasn't there, then went inside through the side door to avoid the receptionist, who usually ate at her desk.

Feeling like her rib cage was full of helium, she went up the back stairs and headed for the window through which she'd seen Woodley and Lewis the day before. And yes . . . there they were!

Returning to the first floor, she walked quickly past the lunchroom without looking inside, then went to the locker room.

Thankfully, it was empty.

She donned her lab coat and slid the recorder with Lewis's voice on it into the right pocket. The other recorder went in the left pocket, along with the duplex plug and the connector cord. She then went up the back stairs to the ladies' restroom to prepare the tape, forcing herself to appear casual and take her time.

When she stepped into the restroom thirty seconds later, her heart sank, for she saw feet in the first stall.

Afraid it would appear suspicious if she left, she entered
the other stall, took off her lab coat, and hung it on the back
of the stall door. She lowered her slacks and her panties and
sat down to wait the other party out, making sure the Ladysmith didn't show.

Seconds ticked into minutes and nothing was happening
next door. Feeling that she ought to be making some appropriate sounds herself, she tried, but was too keyed up to succeed. Another quiet minute passed in silence. Jesus, was that
person in the next stall even real?

Kit checked the reserve watch she'd pressed into service
after Snake Bayou had ruined her good one.

Twelve-forty.

Damn it. . . . Woodley and Lewis would be gone until 1:30.
Another twenty minutes and most everybody else would be
back from lunch; then the chance of getting in unseen would
be greatly diminished. And Jenny would start wondering
where she was—might even call her where she was supposed to be living.

Suddenly, the toilet next door flushed, carrying away all
those fears.

Kit waited until she heard the hall door shut, then waited
a few seconds more to be sure no one else had come in. Detecting no further sounds, she adjusted her clothing and got
out the recorder with Lewis's voice on it.

She fast-forwarded the tape, stopped it, and hit the play
button.

The restroom became a disco.

Two more cycles of that brought her to the sound of jiggling glass. She let it play until Lewis spoke, then rewound
slightly and let it play again, stopping at a distinctive glass
noise she'd noted just before the all-important word.

Satisfied, she slipped the recorder back into her lab coat,
left the stall, and donned the coat.

Twelve-forty-five.

Fifteen minutes to go. No need to panic—plenty of time. Once she got into the lab, it'd be easy to finish. She went into the hall, walked down to where it intersected the one leading to Woodley's lab, and froze at the corner.

Voices ... male ... by Woodley's door.

She remained around the corner, unseen by the two men, silently urging them to wrap it up and go away. She recognized one of the voices as Mudi's. He was telling a story that sounded as though it could go on forever.

"I put the cobra in a bag and tied it to the back of my bicycle, thinking it was dead. . . ."

Till that moment, she'd found his accent charming. Now, it was like a jackhammer in her ear.

"When I got home, I put the bag in my room, intending to take it to the university after lunch. . . ".

Twelve-forty-seven. Thirteen minutes left. Her safety margin was slipping away. The coiled spring on which her heart was balanced threatened to launch it through her chest. In her desperation, she wanted to pull the Ladysmith and tell them to move their asses.

Then the other man was laughing. Mudi's story was over.

She prayed the other guy wouldn't counter with a tale of his own. Miraculously, he didn't. They broke off the conversation and Mudi moved off down the hall. The other guy walked a short way in the same direction and went into his lab.

When Mudi was out of sight, Kit walked quickly to Woodley's door, stood in front of it, and got out the tape recorder. Until this moment, she'd thought the chances were even that the door's sound sensor was still on. But as she pressed the play button on the recorder, she was engulfed by pessimism.

"Access."

And ... by God, the door opened.

She darted inside and it closed behind her.

Even though she knew Woodley and Lewis were behind the building eating lunch, a part of her expected them to leap out of hiding. But they didn't. She was in, and she was alone.

She moved quickly to Woodley's office and went to the table that held the phone. She knelt to start work and her eyes fell on an appointment book open beside it. In the blank for 8:00 P.M. was an address in La Place.

Turning to the job before her, she dumped the contents of her left coat pocket on the carpet and pulled Woodley's phone cord free from the jack. As she plugged the duplex into the old jack, the hairs on the back of her neck prickled.

The hall door had opened.

Suddenly so short of breath that she felt dizzy, her hand went to the cuff of her slacks and raised the fabric so she could ease the Ladysmith from its holster. With the gun resting solidly in her hand, she got to her feet and slowly crept to the office door, where she posted herself on the right, a few feet away from the opening, and waited to see who had come in.

But no one came, nor did she hear any more noise. Of course it was hard to hear anything over her own labored breathing. Were they waiting for her just outside the office door?

"Who's there?" she said, her voice cracking.

No answer.

She thought about saying she was armed, but why warn them? God but it was hot in here.

Unable to take the tension any longer, she burst through the door at an angle that would take her away from anyone waiting just outside. Reaching the long table that stretched from one side of the lab to the other, she spun quickly to her left, brought the gun up, and supported it with her free hand.

Had she fired, she'd have shot up a wall chart showing all the sugar-specific enzymes available from Boehringer Mannheim Biochemicals—and that's all she'd have hit, for there was no one else in the room.

Elated at not having to shoot her way free, yet despairing

at the amount of time she'd lost, she holstered the gun and went back to work, her hands shaking.

In less than two minutes, she was finished and standing at the door to the hall. One last hurdle—one that no preparation could minimize. Would anyone see her leave? The door was windowless, so she had no way of knowing if anyone was passing in the hall. If they were, she'd be seen leaving and word could get back to the wrong people. It was a problem without a good solution.

With no means to choose one moment over another, she pressed the red button that would let her out. As the door slid into the wall, the apprehension cramps in her belly stopped. The hallway was empty. After a quick look in both directions, she stepped out of Woodley's lab, immensely relieved, the only tarnish on the moment the knowledge that at some point she'd have to go back in and retrieve the recorder she'd left.

18

"I'm sorry, but something's come up here at the office, so I won't be able to drive you to the zoo," Noell said. "How about catching a cab and I'll meet you there?"

"I can do that," Broussard said into the phone. "What about the Tate County sheriff? Is he comin'?"

"He's got another commitment. Said for us to get the lay of things and he'll follow up if we find gold."

"Should I wait until you arrive before startin' any discussion?"

"You begin, and when I get there, you can fill me in."

Fifteen minutes later, Broussard's cab dropped him at the zoo entrance, which was impressively done like an Egyptian temple colorfully decorated with rows of hieroglyphs and stylized human figures. In front of the temple, two screaming kids up on a ribbon-thin statue of a hippo were defending their position against three noisy pretenders on the ground by flailing at them with rubber snakes. It was almost enough to make Broussard sorry he was childless.

Yesterday, it had been spring. Today, the late-afternoon sun had run the temperature up to ninety, baking the pavement leading to the entrance until it radiated heat like a sauna. The humidity, too, had crept up to New Orleans standards.

Dodging an oncoming twin baby carriage being pushed by a woman so busy talking to her friend that she almost ran him down, Broussard headed for the members' entrance, where he explained his business and was directed to the administration building.

The Egyptian theme continued inside the gates, with a columned temple gift shop on his right and a temple ad building on his left.

Suddenly, he got the connection: Memphis, there was one in Egypt, too. Give the man a round of applause.

He walked to the ad building entrance and went inside, finding the rush of cold air that met him a welcome treat. He stated his business to the receptionist on duty and she paged the reptile curator.

While waiting, Broussard walked around the reception area, looking at framed color photos of zoo scenes hanging on the wall. When he'd done them all, he stood at the glass door through which he'd come and watched a parade of zoo employees outside, trucking the props for an educational program back to wherever they were stored.

"Dr. Broussard?"

He turned, to see a lanky, long-faced fellow in khaki zoo clothes coming his way, hand outstretched.

"I'm Icky Carr, the reptile curator," he said, echoing the words written on his name tag. "I also do amphibians, but we don't have many of those—at least not on display." His handshake started out lax, then tightened, like a boa choking its prey. "Are you alone? I thought you were coming with a detective."

"She was detained."

"They've got women detectives now? I mean, I've seen *Cagney & Lacey*, but this is Memphis."

"They've got at least one."

"You think a woman could make a guy talk if he didn't want to?" Carr glanced at the receptionist, who was giving him the fish eye, or, in this case, the snake eye. "Meena, don't look at me that way. I got nothing against women, you know that. I just think there are some jobs men can do better." He looked back at Broussard. "I'll bet when she wants to sweat a guy, she asks for male help."

Not wanting to be a party to any criticism of Noell, Broussard tried to put an end to this line of conversation. "Let's hope neither of us ever has reason to find out."

Carr's brow furrowed as he sought the meaning of that. Obviously still puzzled, he turned and motioned for Broussard to follow. "Come on back where we can talk in private."

Broussard glanced at the receptionist and she gave him a thumbs-up.

Carr, too, unexpectedly turned her way. "Meena, I saw that. Where's your loyalty? When the illustrious female detective arrives, send her back."

In Carr's office, the chair behind his desk and the one in front of it were the only concessions to people. The rest was a shrine to frogs. On the table behind the desk, there was a large terrarium in which Broussard saw tiny flashes of orange and black hop across its simulated forest floor. To the left of the terrarium, the remaining tabletop was filled with jars whose sides were covered with tiny flies—a mutant drosophila with vestigial wings, Broussard guessed, easy prey for the frogs.

There was another, slightly smaller terrarium on a table against the right wall. This, too, contained little living, hopping jewels. Carr's desk was paved with shallow water-filled porcelain containers, each housing a single tadpole. To the left of the door, another table held two rows of plastic shoebox terraria that housed more tiny frogs. On the left wall, a chart depicted an incredible array of the most beautiful frogs one could imagine, each a little work of art. In testimony to Carr's amphibian husbandry skills, the office was filled with froggy trills and peeps of satisfaction.

And why not? Even the temperature in the place had been adjusted to frog comfort. Unsure of how long he'd be able to take the heat, Broussard accepted the chair Carr offered.

Carr sat, too. "What did you mean back there when you said you hoped neither of us would ever have reason to learn whether your detective friend is good at sweating out the truth?"

Broussard didn't want to get into the substantive part of his inquiry until Noell arrived. He therefore parried Carr's question.

"We'll certainly discuss that. But for now, I'd like to explore what you know about poison-dart frogs."

"Dart-poison frogs," Carr said.

"What?"

"You said, 'poison-dart frogs.' That's not what they're called. That makes it sound like they shoot poisonous projectiles at people. The real name is dart-poison frogs."

"Of course. It's always best to begin with the correct terminology."

Carr turned to face the wall, rocked back in his chair, and folded his arms over his chest. "There are about fifty-five species of poisonous frogs, all belonging to the family Dendrobatidae. They're all quite small and all lay their eggs on the forest floor, where, in some species, one of the parents keeps them moist by periodically urinating on them. When they hatch, the young climb onto one of the parents and are carried to water—often, small pools that collect between the leaves and stems of certain plants."

This was not the kind of information Broussard was after. "That's very interesting, but—"

Acting as though he hadn't heard Broussard speak, Carr rolled on.

"In some species, only one tadpole is left in each of these little pools, which are often practically devoid of nutrients. To compensate for this, the female lays a single unfertilized egg in each pool to serve as a food source."

The floor began to vibrate and the sound of running feet could be heard in the hall. Carr rocked forward and grabbed a two-way radio from between the terrarium behind his desk and the bottles of flies. He raised it to his lips, obviously concerned. "This is Carr. What's happening? Come in. This is Carr. Do you need me?"

"Negative on that," the radio belched. "Everything's under control."

Carr put the radio back on the table and turned to Broussard. "From time to time, people fall into the tiger pool and I have to help get them out. Where was I?"

Not wanting to hear any more little frog natural history, Broussard said, "How is the poison obtained and coated on darts?"

"Apparently, there are two ways. The northern Choco Indians impale the frog on a stick they run into his mouth and out one hind leg. The stress causes the frog to secrete the poison, which comes from glands in the skin. Sometimes the Indians hold the frog over a flame, which increases the yield. I must say, I don't care for that method at all."

"I'm sure the frogs don't, either."

"Apart from the cruelty involved, that approach negatively impacts the frog population. I much prefer the way the southern Chocos do it. They keep the frogs like pets and simply wipe their darts across the frog's back without stressing it beyond what handling induces."

"How long does the poison remain active when it's dried onto a dart?"

Carr's answer was delayed by a knock on the door. At Carr's invitation, Sergeant Noell joined them, with apologies for being late. Both men rose and she and Carr shook hands.

"Here, take my chair," Broussard said.

"It's all right. I can stand."

Reluctantly, Broussard returned to his seat. "Mr. Carr was about to say how long frog poison remains active after it's coated onto darts."

"Anywhere from six months to a year," Carr said, also sitting.

Noell took a small notebook from her linen blazer and wrote that down. When she looked up, Broussard said, "Do you want to take over?"

"Sure, thanks." She gestured to the terrarium and the tadpoles on Carr's desk. "Are all these poison frogs?"

"If you mean are they all species generally classified as poisonous in nature, yes."

"Where'd you get them?"

"The tadpoles are from eggs laid by the ones in this terrarium." He gestured to the frogs behind him.

"What about the adults?"

"I bought them."

"From where?"

"Various zoos around the country—from their surplus animal lists."

"Is this the only place here at the zoo where poison frogs are kept?"

"I've got some at the education center, some at the reptile house, and some at the aquarium."

"So a lot of other people have access to your frogs?"

"Quite a few."

"Would you know if any are missing?"

"I know how many I have, but as you can see, it's hard to inventory a terrarium. Would you mind telling me what's going on?"

"Do you know a man named Anthony Hunter . . . a professor at UT?"

"I've talked to him a couple of times—at zoo functions—but we're not friends or anything. Didn't I hear he died?"

"He's dead, yes. Poisoned, we think, by"—she checked her notebook—"by batrachotoxin, a poison from frogs like these."

"And you think that toxin was from my frogs?"

"We don't know, but it certainly seems possible."

"No, it isn't."

"How can you be so sure?"

"Two reasons. One is, the toxins in poison frogs are not manufactured by the frogs; they're acquired from the insects they eat, which, in turn, get them from the tropical plants *they* feed on. Since captive frogs don't get the same diet they do in the wild, they aren't really toxic."

"You're saying all your frogs are captive-bred . . . no wild-caught specimens among them?"

"None. And they're the wrong frogs."

"In what sense?"

He pulled open one of the drawers in his desk and leaned over. After a lapse of a few seconds, he straightened up, holding a stapled sheaf of papers in his hand. He riffled through them, folded some of the pages back, and handed the sheaf to Noell. "That's a copy of an article from *Scientific American*. The five frogs shown there, comprising all the known species of the genus *Phyllobates,* are the only ones that secrete batrachotoxin. It's true. . . . Turn a couple of pages. I've circled the part about batrachotoxin being limited to those frogs. And I don't own any of the five."

Noell flipped some pages and stopped to read. When she finished, she handed the article to Broussard.

"As I said, even if I did have one, unless it was recently wild-caught, it'd be harmless."

Broussard looked at the picture on the page Carr had first found for Noell. It showed that two of the frogs were from

Central America and three were from South America. Beside the picture of *Phyllobates terribilis,* Carr had added a note indicating it was the most toxic of the five. Finding that note of more than passing interest, Broussard turned to the passage about batrachotoxin's limited amphibian distribution, verifying what Carr had said.

"If what you say is true, you wouldn't mind if we inventory your frogs," Noell said.

"Actually, I would. To do a careful job, you'd have to dismantle the terraria they're in, so unless you get a search warrant, I'm going to be a bastard and refuse to cooperate."

Noell studied him for a few seconds, her jaw set. Finally, she said, "Where could someone buy a wild-caught frog like those in the article?"

"I have no idea. It may not be legal in their countries of origin to export them."

"Still, I'm sure it happens."

"I wouldn't know."

"What about batrachotoxin—where could someone buy that?"

"Now you've really exceeded my knowledge. If you like, I'll give you the Internet address of the poison-frog home page. Maybe some link on it will help you."

"There's a home page for poison frogs?"

Carr shrugged. "If the Joe Nobody family in Kokomo can have one, why not poison frogs?"

"If you've got the address handy, I'll take it."

Carr thumbed through his Rolodex, stopped, and recited a string of letters and symbols that Noell jotted in her notebook.

"Now, if that's all you wanted, there's a shipment from the St. Louis Zoo waiting for my attention."

Noell flipped her notebook shut. "Yeah, that's all. Thanks for the information."

"Aren't you going to tell me not to leave town?"

"Don't leave town."

As Noell reached for the doorknob, Carr said, "Detective . . ."

"Yes?"

"When you see Sergeant Cagney and Sergeant Lacey at your next gender neutral meeting, tell them I love their work."

"I'll do that."

When Noell and Broussard were outside the building, Broussard said, "Why'd you tell him not to leave town. You really think he's a suspect?"

"No. I was considering shooting him, but there'd be all that paperwork. . . . Better I just curtail his travel."

"I admire your restraint."

"I might have stayed awhile and traded insults, but I was anxious to leave."

"Why?"

"I was late because there's been a break in the case."

"What's happened?"

"The state police in the next county have tracked two guys who burgled a jewelry store to a cabin in the woods, where they found Anthony Hunter's notebooks and a bunch of floppy disks that are probably his, too."

"How'd they connect all that to the Hunter murder?"

"The notebooks had UT Memphis and Hunter's name on each one. They were so obviously stolen, one of the cops called UT and learned Hunter was dead. Then they called us."

"Sharp police work."

"We're not the hicks some people think we are."

"You don't mean me?"

"No. You still want to see those notebooks?"

"Absolutely. Where are they?"

"At the cabin. Most of the take from the jewelry store is still missing, so everybody's there looking for it. If we want those notebooks anytime soon, we'll have to go get them."

"Let's do it."

19

While Broussard and Noell fought the flow of late-afternoon traffic out of Memphis on their way to the cabin in Fayette County, Kit sat at an EdgeGARD tissue culture hood in Thibodaux changing the growth medium on Mudi's cell cultures. It had been hours since she'd invaded Woodley's lab, but her nerves were still sizzling, so the pipette she was using to dispense medium danced over the culture dish. When no one was looking, she'd resorted to holding the pipette control in both hands, similar to the way she'd been trained to steady a pistol. It was, therefore, with great relief that she finished the last dish and carried the stack of ten she'd been working on back to the incubator.

She carefully distributed the dishes around the lower shelf in the incubator, then returned to the hood to wipe the stainless-steel work surface with alcohol prior to shutting off the lights and the blower that kept bacteria in the room from entering the work area.

Five o'clock . . . quitting time . . . glorious words. She reached for the hood's power switches.

"Leave it on."

Turning, she saw Rose Lewis, who was carrying a cardboard box.

"I need this calf serum aliquoted into fifteen-milliliter tubes," she said, putting the box on the nearby benchtop.

Kit walked over and looked in the box, where she saw twenty-five small bottles of *frozen* serum. "Can't this wait until morning? It'll take twenty minutes to thaw them and another half hour or more to aliquot."

"If it could wait, I wouldn't have brought 'em in here," Lewis said. "So, do you follow orders or do you hit the road for good?"

"I'll give you a hand," Jenny said from the doorway to the next room.

"Did I ask you to help her?" Lewis said sharply.

"I just thought—"

"It's time you went home," Lewis said.

Confused, Jenny remained in the doorway. "I was only—"

Lewis pointed a finger at Jenny. "One more word and you're fired."

"Jenny, it's all right," Kit said. "I can do it."

Lewis turned on Kit, her face contorted with rage. "You're not in charge here. *I* am. She'll be leaving because *I* say so, not because *you* allow it."

In her vehemence, Lewis sprayed Kit's lab coat with spittle.

Kit was about to make an exaggerated gesture of wiping it off and say something devastatingly appropriate, but the thought that if she got fired there'd be no one to reclaim the tape in Woodley's office made her say and do nothing.

Lewis stood in the doorway and watched until Jenny was out of the lab. She then turned to Kit. "I want each individual tube labeled. When you're finished, put the tubes on Dr. Woodley's shelf in the walk-in freezer. You know where it is?"

"I've seen it."

"And between now and tomorrow, I want you to learn to keep that expression off your face."

"What expression?"

"The one that shows how much you despise me. I can't stop you from thinking it, but I don't want to see it every time I look at you."

Lewis turned and walked away, leaving Kit with the best example yet of the expression they'd been talking about.

Kit put the bottles of frozen serum in the 37°F water bath that was always kept switched on, then lined up in the hood enough test tube racks to hold the 167 tubes she'd need.

By the time she'd labeled all the tubes and put them in the racks, the serum had thawed. The anger she felt toward Lewis was not an entirely unproductive emotion, as it washed away the nervous hand tremors she'd been experiencing all afternoon, allowing her to work quickly and smoothly.

When all the tubes were filled, she put the empty serum bottles in a dish of soapy warm water in the sink and packed the tubes in groups into the compartmentalized box in which the bottles had arrived. She then bedded the hood down for the night. On the way out of the lab with the box of tubes, she shut off the lab lights and locked the door.

By now, everyone else in the building had gone home, so through the narrow vertical rectangles of glass in the door to each of the other labs, she saw only darkened rooms. This reminder that she had been singled out to stay late for a task that could just as easily have been done in the morning fanned her resentment of Rose Lewis.

Her thin lab coat was little protection against the frigid air the two fans at the rear of the walk-in freezer blew against her when she opened the door. Stepping inside, she shut the door gently without engaging the latch.

Lewis had said to put the serum on Woodley's shelf, but that one and the shelf below it were full. While she was deciding if it would be worthwhile to rearrange Woodley's things to make room, the door behind her clicked shut.

With an icicle through her heart, she rushed the door and rammed the cardboard box in her arms against the metal piston that prevented lock-ins.

The piston slid into its sleeve, but the door wouldn't open.

She chucked the box of serum onto the floor and threw her shoulder against the cold metal door, which moved a fraction of an inch before colliding with something on the outside.

Amid the crystals of fear spreading through her, she remembered the sound she'd heard while tapping Woodley's phone. It hadn't been someone *entering*, as she'd thought, but someone *leaving*, someone who'd been in one of the small adjoining rooms she'd neglected to check. Lewis had set her up and she'd fallen for it.

Stupid . . . stupid . . . stupid . . . She slammed her shoulder into the door twice more, the exertion sucking frigid air into her lungs. No good—this was not helping.

Fingers already so cold that they hurt, she thrust her fists into her chilled pockets. With the fans at the rear blowing numbing air over her, it was like standing on an Arctic tundra. She tried to think, but the clattering fans and the ache that had begun in her ears made that difficult. In such cold, she wouldn't last thirty minutes.

Her eyes strayed to the opposite wall, to the sixty-watt bulb covered by heavy glass that at least gave her some light. Crossing the freezer, she reached for the glass with shaking hands, hoping the bulb might provide a little heat. But she could feel nothing.

More than ever before in her life, she needed clarity of thought, but ice buildup left her mind earthbound.

As the minutes passed, hopelessness became a thriving malignancy that threatened to drive her screaming to the freezer door, where she would claw at it until her fingernails shattered and her blood turned to icy sludge. She put her hands to her ears, but it was like trying to warm them with blocks of ice. She was shivering madly now, her teeth clacking nearly as loudly as the fans. Her feet were numb and heavy. If she didn't do something fast, she was going to die. . . . But there was nothing to work with.

Wait . . . the Ladysmith . . . She was actually reaching for it before she realized it couldn't help.

Think . . . think. But all that came was a barren wind.

Eventually, she opened to the finality of her plight. She slumped against the metal shelving and closed her eyes. If she couldn't escape physically, could she at least imagine herself free? And this, she found her mind could do.

She was home, not the dump she now lived in, but the first home she'd ever owned, in bed, wrapped in Teddy's arms, Lucky waiting patiently on the other side of the bedroom door for them to let him in.

Lucky . . . Nolen would take him. . . . He'd like living with Mitzi.

Then, deep in Kit's mind, icy plates overrode one another, dislodging a small snowdrift that fell into a larger drift. A buzzer . . . There was something about a . . .

She struggled to think, tried to blot out the narcotizing images carrying her to her grave. *If the temperature goes up even a few degrees, a buzzer will sound.* That's what Jenny had said—*a buzzer will sound.*

A buzzer will . . .

There must be a heat-sensing device somewhere inside the freezer.

Her eyes scanned the metal walls but saw nothing that looked likely. Shivering violently, she turned and saw a copper tube that went into the front wall near the low ceiling. On the end of it, slightly above her head, was a cylinder of the same color.

Dropping stiffly to one knee, her hands wooden, she pulled a stout cardboard box from a low shelf onto the floor. With her foot, she slid the box across the floor and stepped onto it. Cupping her hands on either side of the metal cylinder, she leaned forward and exhaled her warm breath against it through teeth that sounded like rattling bones. Her shaking hands threatened to knock the cylinder loose.

Inhale . . . exhale. Inhale . . . exhale.

The frigid air stabbed at her lungs, but she kept going. Inhale . . . exhale . . . again and again.

Hyperventilating, she began to feel light-headed. Inhale . . . exhale. Her temples throbbed and the sound of her breathing thundered in her ears. Inhale . . . exhale. Everything grew fuzzy.

Ring, damn it. . . . Ring.

The dull roar in her ears grew louder and its pitch went up to a shriek. And then there was no more noise, only black velvet.

20

"This is Matt Easter at the Agrilabs building. I got a woman here suffering from hypothermia. . . . I don't know how to answer that."

Kit's eyes fluttered open. "No . . . I'm fine." As she struggled to a sitting position from where she lay on the floor, Easter turned from the wall phone and looked down at her. "Oh man, am I glad you woke up. But we can't be sure you're okay. You may have frostbite or something."

Kit's hands and feet were so terribly cold, she couldn't say he was wrong. Though her mind was working poorly, she was also aware that whoever had trapped her in the freezer might still be in the building and that Easter's presence alone might not prevent them from a more direct attack. By all means, get more people in here. "You're right. Ask them to come."

Easter recited the institute's address into the phone and hung up. He came to Kit's side and squatted on his haunches. "I got some instant coffee in my lab. It tastes like shit, but I can make it, well, instantly."

Matt Easter . . . Kit vaguely remembered meeting him on her first day when Jenny had shown her around. "What kept the freezer door from opening?"

Easter gestured to a point behind her with his chin. "That cart full of crap. Someone must have moved it and accidentally wedged it against the door while you were in there."

There was no point explaining things to him, so she didn't respond to this.

"How'd you make the alarm go off?"

"I breathed on it. I think that's why I passed out—from hyperventilating."

"Lucky for you I was here and had things in the freezer I couldn't afford to lose if the thing failed."

"Yeah, everything's going my way. Thanks for the help."

"You never answered me about the coffee."

Kit didn't want to stay in the building a second longer. "I'd rather just go out front and wait for the ambulance."

Easter assisted her to the front entrance and out onto the steps. By now her circulation had improved to the point where she was convinced she didn't need medical assistance. Nor did she want any well-meaning paramedic discovering the Ladysmith. "Actually, you know . . . I'm feeling much better. I don't think I need that ambulance after all." She began backing away. "I'm just going home. I appreciate what you did . . . really. Thanks a lot."

As she turned and hurried to her car, she saw only one other vehicle, which she presumed belonged to Easter. That was good, because it meant she wouldn't be followed.

It was only when she reached her car that she realized she didn't have the keys. Damn. After putting the serum in the freezer, she'd planned to dump her lab coat in her locker and get her bag. Damn.

Fortunately, Easter had been so puzzled at her rapid departure, he was still on the front steps when she returned.

"Change your mind about getting checked out?"

"My handbag is in my locker, but I don't want to go back in there. Will you get it for me?"

"Which locker?"

She told him the number and the combination of the lock and he went back inside. But now she was left alone *outside* the place. Surely no one would try anything out in the open like this where a passing motorist might see it. Of course, this late, there wasn't all *that* much traffic going by. If they waited until just the right moment . . .

Suddenly feeling far too vulnerable, she thought about going back inside and waiting in the reception area. But then that seemed worse. In the distance, she heard the wail of a siren.

Come on, Matt, get me out of here.

Finally, Easter came out with her bag. Leaving him with a hurried thanks, she ran to the car and piled in. She pulled onto the street just as the ambulance arrived.

"How far back in here is this cabin?" Broussard asked.

Noell inched the car to the left to avoid a large branch from a tree that had fallen beside the two dirt tracks they'd been following for the last twenty minutes. "We're almost there."

The tracks made an abrupt right turn around a rotted stump and then dropped into a moist hollow filled with ferns. Fifty yards farther on, they followed a gentle rise into an old-growth forest of great oaks. A few minutes later, when the canopy overhead thinned and the dirt tracks curved both right and left around a poplar that had probably been a sapling long before Broussard was born, Noell eased the car off the tracks into a patch of scrubby weeds.

"Is this it?" Broussard asked, seeing no cabin.

"That's got to be the tree they described." She looked to her left, where the land sloped sharply. "And there's the footpath to the cabin. But where is everybody?"

"Could be they finished and left."

"Damn . . . of all the times to be without a radio."

She was referring to the already-discussed fact that they had come in her personal car because the official car she'd been driving had developed a mechanical problem earlier in the day and the department had not been able to come up with a replacement. "I wonder if some of them are still down at the cabin?"

Not one to speculate on an issue when direct data could be easily obtained, Broussard reached for the door. "Only one way to find out."

Noell followed his example.

Enjoying his role as a man of action, Broussard quickly headed for the path.

"Andy . . ."

He noted the odd tone in Noell's voice even as he turned. This did not, however, prepare him for the shock of seeing a 9-mm Beretta leveled at his heart.

21

No way was Kit going to her phony Thibodaux address to change cars. With the heater on the governor's loaner turned all the way up and the gas pedal flirting with the floorboard carpet, her trip home was hot and fast. Thankfully, no one behind her seemed to have the slightest interest in following her.

When Lucky came running as she entered the courtyard behind the gallery, she swept him into her arms and hugged him until he yelped. She put him down only when a few minutes later, in her apartment, she needed both hands to make coffee. To get it as quickly as possible, she put a mug instead of the pot on the Mr. Coffee hot plate. While waiting for the water to percolate through, she stripped off her lab coat, balled it up, and stuffed it in the kitchen wastebasket.

She couldn't wait for her mug to fill, so she snatched it off the coffeemaker as soon as it contained something, replacing it with the pot so inexpertly, a small cascade of the dark brew hit the hot plate.

Sipping the coffee and warming her hands on the bottom of the mug, she roamed her apartment, which now didn't seem as bad as she'd remembered, mostly because anyplace was better than the inside of that freezer. She even found a certain bizarre comfort in the two-by-four brace holding up the ceiling.

She drank two more full cups of coffee before turning to a job she faced with mixed feelings—talking to Tabor.

He called back promptly after her page.

"I screwed up. . . . I got the recorder placed, but someone saw me do it. They set me up so I had to work late and put something in the walk-in freezer. While I was in there, they wedged the door shut. I nearly froze to death."

"You sound okay now. Are you hurt?"

"No. But you can forget the phone tap. Oh hell . . ."

"What?"

"When I left, I forgot to get the recorder that was in my locker. So I've lost both of them."

"That doesn't matter. The important thing is you got away safely. How'd you get out of the freezer?"

"I breathed on the temperature sensor until the alarm went off. Someone working late let me out."

"That was good work."

"I'm pleased with it. Sorry I let you down."

"You did your best."

"What does *that* mean?"

"I don't blame you for what happened. It was just . . ."

"Slippage?"

"Exactly."

At this point, Kit remembered something else she'd intended to pass along. "I don't know if it means anything, but when I was tapping Woodley's phone this afternoon, I saw in his appointment book he's meeting someone at eight tonight in La Place."

"Where in La Place?"

She gave him the address. "What will you do now?"

"From this point on, it's my problem. You're a civilian again. Is it possible anyone followed you home?"

"I checked, but I'm sure not."

"I'm confident we took sufficient precautions to hide your identity, but just to be ultrasafe, you should continue to carry the Ladysmith. And if you go out at night, avoid deserted, poorly lit streets."

"Am I going to have to join a witness protection program?"

"Like I said, they don't even know who you are. And if they did, there's no reason for them to believe you've witnessed *anything*."

"But I should wear the gun and be careful where I walk."

"Probably good advice even if none of this had happened. And of course, you won't want to discuss this even with friends."

"Loose lips sink ships."

"Something like that. Don't worry, we'll get this unraveled and have those thugs under indictment before you know it."

"Now I've alerted them, they'll be more cautious."

"That won't save them. I'll tell the governor you're out of the picture. I'm sure he'll want to thank you personally."

"For lousing things up?"

"For being a good citizen. We'll talk again soon."

Then he hung up.

This conversation left Kit troubled. The part where Tabor released her was what she thought she wanted. But his suggestion she watch her step for a while put that in a different light. He'd said she was likely not in any further danger, but suppose that opinion, too, turned out to be slippage. The risk she'd assumed when she'd agreed to help was acceptable because the actions that would lead to risk could ultimately put an end to any long-term threat. Now she was facing a long-term risk and personally doing nothing about it.

How long would she have to wear the gun—a week . . . two

weeks? Would she be jumping at shadows for a month . . . two months?"

She looked at her watch. Jesus, Woodley's meeting in La Place would be getting under way in twenty minutes. And La Place was about eighty miles from Baton Rouge. There was no way Tabor could get there in time.

But she could.

The voice of reason kicked in, telling her it was nothing but a dinner party at a friend's home, that even if it *was* a clandestine meeting where incriminating things would be said, there'd be no way *she* could hear it. This calmed her and she dropped into a chair to reflect.

Her thoughts quickly turned to the freezer and what a close call that had been. She had Rose Lewis to thank . . . and maybe Tom Ward. And who knows how many others. Woodley, to be sure . . . the warden at Angola and his brother at the funeral home . . . She relived her escape from her sinking car in Snake Bayou, feeling again the seat belt around her ankle as she fought to reach the surface. And Sheriff Hubly . . . so helpful . . . Bastards, one and all.

In the end, the accumulated sins of this villainous cadre pushed her over the line.

22

Broussard's shirt was stuck to his back and rivulets of sweat spilled from his eyebrows and ran down his glasses. His bow tie was long gone—thrown aside and covered with dirt. As his shovel once again plunged into the sandy loam, he recalled the old forensic axiom: Bodies will putrefy at a set rate in which one week in air equals two weeks in soil and eight weeks in water. If he didn't come up with an idea quickly, he'd soon be fulfilling the second part of that axiom instead of thinking about it.

The grave Noell was making him dig was now about two feet deep. When killers bury their victims, they rarely go deeper than three. Allowing for his extra bulk, he maybe had two more feet to live.

He was working at the end of the hole opposite the edge where Noell stood looking down at him, her gun ready to drop him if he should try throwing a shovelful of dirt in her face. He still couldn't believe or understand what was happening. And so far, she hadn't responded to anything he'd said.

During dinner at the Peabody, they'd definitely connected. He hadn't imagined that. So how could she do this, and *why?* Surely she wasn't involved in Hunter's death, and if she was, he hadn't found anything to point to her. This made no sense. But they *were* here, and he had no doubts she was planning to finish what she'd started.

He stood the shovel in the ground, removed his glasses, and wiped the sweat from his eyes with his arm.

Noell swatted at a mosquito with her free hand. "Keep working. I don't want to be here any longer than I have to."

Broussard looked up at her. "Why do you have to be here at all?"

"Shut up and dig."

"I don't think you want to do this."

"Look, I could just as easily leave you in the open for the animals to eat like a sack of garbage. But you deserve better. I swear, though, I will if you don't get back to work."

Buried or left in the open—Broussard figured the dead didn't care either way. He returned to his labors only because it bought him a few more minutes to devise a way out of this difficulty.

Whenever he moved to Noell's end of the grave, she retreated a safe distance, out of his reach. When he was digging at the far end, she would return to the grave's edge. That, he concluded, would be her undoing.

To set the first part of his plan in motion, he slowly worked his way toward her. As expected, she backed up a few steps. Upon reaching the edge of the hole, he set to work, deepening it. But with each bite the shovel took of the bottom, he also removed some of the side wall.

In a few minutes, he had undercut the wall as far as he could without arousing her suspicions. But was it enough? If not, Charlie Franks, the deputy ME in New Orleans, would soon be getting a promotion.

To coax Noell onto the weakened ground, he worked his

way to the opposite end of the hole. She returned to stand at its edge.

And stand there . . .

And stand there . . .

It wasn't enough. The blasted thing was *not* going to give. The hole was probably now deep enough to contain his body. Any moment, she would halt the digging. Before making a wild last-second move that would likely succeed only in getting him shot, he tried fitting the pieces of his predicament together in new ways, but all that emerged was dross. He thought about the fairy tale where the girl has to spin flax into gold. At least she had flax.

"All right. That's"—Noell's voice rose two octaves and she practically shouted the last word—"enough," as the undercut edge crumbled and she slid into the hole.

She didn't drop her gun, but the hand holding it flew upward as she fell, pointing it at the darkening sky. Broussard crossed the hole in two steps, the shovel cocked behind him. He brought it around hard and the blade clanged against the gun, knocking it from her hand, over the pile of dirt at the hole's edge.

She lay propped against the canted side of the hole, anger and surprise distorting her features.

"Now you've got some explainin' to do," Broussard said.

She was on her feet instantly, charging toward him. The crown of her head hit him in the chest, backing him into a dirt ridge that caught his heels and sent him toppling with her on top of him. His shoulders hit the other edge of the hole and she rode him down into a sitting position.

Feeling her trying to get up, he wrapped her in a bear hug, pulling her breasts into his face. She punched him hard in the left ear. Shocked at the force of the blow, his hold on her loosened. Realizing she'd gained an advantage, she slithered upward, knees pummeling his belly until she got a foothold in his groin. He renewed the bear hug and her legs folded, both knees striking him in the face.

She began clawing at the soil he'd piled at the hole's edge, sending an avalanche onto his head. Then she was ramming handfuls of it around her knees into his face, up his nose. His grip loosened enough that she could rock her right knee back a couple of inches. With this maneuverability, she drove her knee twice into his nose, bringing forth a cascade of blood that washed the dirt from his nostrils.

Holding on as tightly as he could with his left arm, his right hand roamed over her buttocks until his fingers got hold of her belt. While this grip kept her from climbing him, his left hand slid up onto her stomach. Pushing with his left hand and pulling on her belt with his right, he rocked forward as forcefully as he could, standing her up, then driving her backward, off her feet.

She managed to get up a scant second before he could, so as his head lifted, she drove her knuckles into his left temple with a roundhouse punch. Dazed, he still managed to get fully to his feet. Through the light show playing behind his eyes and the dirt sticking to the sweat on his glasses, he indistinctly saw her in a crouch, fists raised.

This woman was whipping his butt, partly because she was a skilled street fighter, partly because he believed there was never an excuse for hitting a woman. But with bloody dirt matting his beard and mustache, his temple throbbing, and a knot rising on his cheek, he thought it might be time to reassess that position.

Noell charged and threw a fist at his face. Dodging to the side, he sloughed the punch. As her momentum carried him past, he fired his own right fist into her stomach.

Her eyes rolled up, her mouth hinged open, and she dropped to her knees. She balanced there for no more than a second, then fell over in the dirt in a fetal position, gasping for air.

Not completely pleased at what he'd done, Broussard considered stretching her out and helping her catch a breath. Then, imagining what she might do to him given the least advantage, he rolled her over, loosened her belt, and pulled it from the loops. He used the belt to tie her hands behind her, ignoring the horrid rasping sounds she was making.

He was certain it would be a huge mistake to leave her feet free, but he didn't want to sacrifice his own belt. Flax . . . Here he was again without flax. While grappling with the problem, he pulled his shirttail free and wiped the dirt from his glasses.

Able now to see more clearly, he also remembered the long willowy tree roots he'd removed from the hole. This sent him looking for a suitable specimen.

He returned with one just as Noell was starting to breathe normally. The couple of minutes she'd spent without air had drained her strength to the point where she exhibited little resistance as he trussed her feet with the root.

Believing she was now capable of talking, Broussard tried again for an explanation. "Now will you tell me what this was about?"

"I've got nothing to say."

"Then maybe I'll just leave you here for the night."

"Is that supposed to worry me?"

She was right. It was a lame threat. But not being in the business of forcing information out of people, it was all he could think of. That left only one alternative.

He frisked her for the car keys and transferred them to his own pocket. Then he picked her up and put her on the ground at the hole's edge. After climbing out, he threw her over his shoulder and carried her to the car, where he dumped her on the backseat.

The sun was now nearly gone and a deep gloom had settled on the woods. Dispelling the darkness with the car's headlights, he circled the big poplar and headed back the

way they'd come—through the oak forest, down into the fern
hollow, past the rotted stump. And . . . He brought the car to
a stop and stared out the windshield.

The two dirt tracks he'd been following diverged into two
identical sets. Coming in, he'd been glancing at Noell so
often, he hadn't paid a lot of attention to the route they were
following. Left or right?

Right, he thought. But maybe . . .

He looked over his shoulder at Noell. "Which way?"

"You figure it out."

Her response was about what he'd expected, but it had
been worth a try. He chose the track on the right.

Had this been a situation like the one Tabor had discussed
with Kit, such that Broussard was trying to find a route he'd
driven before, the odds would have favored his choice. But he
hadn't ever driven the route, so when he navigated the car
around a sharp right turn that blocked his view of the tracks
ahead, the car plunged into a mud hole they hadn't encountered coming in. Lacking the momentum it had before it took
the curve, the car became trapped in the thick muck.

Rocking it forward and backward by quick shifts of the
transmission did nothing to improve matters.

He got out to inspect the situation and found the tires in
so deeply, only the upper half of the wheel covers were showing. Now he really *could* use some flax.

In the ever-deepening dusk, amid hordes of mosquitoes
with no compunction about biting a man when he was down,
he scouted the adjacent brush and woods until he found an
old fallen tree. By the time he got back to the car with an
armful of branches, there was barely enough daylight to per-
mit their proper deployment in front of the rear tires.

Feeling like the featured item at a mosquito buffet, he returned to the driver's seat and started the car. Forward and
back . . . forward and back . . . Over the sound of the engine,
he heard the crackle of snapping branches. His hopes rose.

Forward . . . backward . . .

The tires were eating into the branches, gripping.

But in the end, they were merely ground into muddy pulp and the car remained stuck.

He looked into the backseat. "I'm afraid we're gonna have to spend the night here."

"Here . . . back in that hole . . . what does it matter?"

Giving up on a problem was not a decision that rested lightly on Broussard's mind. But his face hurt, he itched all over, and he was dead tired. Waiting until morning wasn't exactly giving up. It was more like taking an extended break.

He closed his eyes to rest, but his mind picked up a thread of self-criticism. Noell had made up the whole thing—the jewelry store burglary, the found notebooks. There wasn't even a cabin. And he'd swallowed it like a big bream sucking in a fat cricket. She'd driven her own car here because she didn't want to be in radio contact with Homicide. He should have found it odd that the department didn't have another car for her to take on official business.

She'd also neglected to bring a Handie-Talkie. *That* was another clue. He didn't even catch on when there were no police cars at the supposed cabin site. That was a *big* clue.

He'd been a fool all right. Had even thought about the two of them . . .

This line of inquiry was far too painful to pursue. Better the mind rest along with the body.

During the next few minutes, while he believed the attic lights were out, a small bulb continued to glow. In that pale light, the boxed stack of events leading him to this mud hole shifted, tilting the stack to one side.

Eyes shut, on the verge of sleep, he scratched an itch.

In the attic, the boxes tilted another five degrees.

Eyes still shut, his chin fell onto his chest.

In the attic, the boxes tilted a bit more.

He brushed at a mosquito buzzing in his ear and the boxes collapsed, spilling and mixing their contents.

His small eyes popped open.

"Oh my God."

23

Before running out the door, Kit paused to think. In the past, whenever her investigations had led her into potentially dangerous situations, she took Bubba along for protection, which he provided by bringing his revolver. But with the Ladysmith, she could now protect *herself.*

Still, it didn't seem wise to do this without letting someone know where she'd gone. But to tell a friend like Nolen would just drag him into the whole mess. That eliminated Teddy as well. The logical choice was Tabor, who would, of course, order her to desist.

Unless . . .

She went to the phone and punched in Nolen's number. Please be home . . . please. "Hi, Nolen, this is Kit. Would you do me a couple of favors?"

"Depends," Nolen said. "If it'll cost me money, probably not."

"There's no money involved. I have to go out, and I probably won't be back in time to walk Lucky. Will you take him when you walk Mitzi?"

"Sure, what's the other favor?"

"I want to give a friend of mine a message, but I only have his pager number, and I can't wait for him to call back. Could I leave your number for him and have you relay the message? He usually returns calls within fifteen minutes."

"What message?"

"Tell him I decided to go to that meeting, too. He'll understand."

"No problem. Just drop Lucky by as you leave."

She thanked him and broke the connection with her finger. She started to enter Tabor's number, then paused. He was likely already on his way to La Place, so he'd probably return her call on his cell phone, which meant he might be on the line exactly when she reached Nolen's apartment. Not wanting that to happen, she grabbed her bag, whisked Lucky up in her arms, and headed downstairs, where she made the call to Tabor on Nolen's phone.

It was a good plan. By not giving Nolen the address where she was headed, he was not being sucked into anything. Of course, Tabor would be angry when he heard where she'd gone, but he'd have to agree that under the circumstances, with him so far away and her so close, she'd made the right decision.

Traffic was light all the way out of town and she made good time. Having never been to La Place, when she hit its city limits, she stopped at an Exxon station for directions. The clerk there was apparently still so much in shock over the Exxon *Valdez* incident, he couldn't yet handle anything that complex.

She tried again at a Shell station, with good results. At least it seemed that way at the time. After following those instructions to a desolate road with another of those damn duckweed-carpeted bayous constantly nudging its right shoulder and the only sign of civilization on the left an occasional run-down bait shop, she began to wonder. But then the dry side of the road produced a prosperous-looking Our Lady of Prompt Succor church. Beyond that was something behind a fancy brick wall too tall to see over. Hoping it wasn't the parsonage, Kit drove on, following the wall for about 150 yards to an iron-gated entrance with a guardhouse just inside. On an illuminated plaque beside the gates was the address she sought.

She tried to get a look down the driveway, but a uniformed ape came out of the guardhouse and scowled at her. Giving the car some gas, she followed the wall for another fifty yards, to its end. Beyond that, the land reverted to inhospitable scrub and stands of willow.

She drove on until the shoulder allowed a U-turn, then headed back the way she'd come, maintaining a businesslike speed and making sure she kept her eyes straight ahead when she passed the gates. The frontage between the wall and the road contained a row of Bradford pear trees, so when she turned into the church driveway, she was confident the guard at the gate didn't see it happen.

In front of the church, a parking lot ran right up to the wall of the adjacent property. Visible as it would be from the road, it was no place for Kit's car. She therefore followed the drive around to the back of the church, where there was another paved area.

The sun had fully set, but the rear of the church was illuminated by an arc light mounted high over the back door. In its harsh illumination, she saw a volleyball net suspended between two metal poles anchored in cement-filled tires. The surrounding asphalt had yellow boundary lines painted on it—not the greatest place to go to your knees after a ball. This paving stopped several feet short of the wall next door, with a grassy strip intervening.

Kit maneuvered past the volleyball net to the grassy strip, where she eased the car forward until the front bumper was an inch from the wall. A glance to her right verified that the bed of crepe myrtles and shrubs between the church and the brick wall effectively concealed her car from anyone passing out front.

She switched off the lights and the engine, then took the car key off the ring holding her other keys and put the key ring in her handbag. She tucked the bag under the passenger seat, got out, and eased the door shut until it latched. She locked the door and pocketed the key.

She walked to the front of the car and gingerly tested the bumper to see if it'd support her. Convinced it would, she used it as a step to help her onto the fender. The added height allowed a good view of the grounds on the other side of the wall, where to her left, about a hundred yards away, her attention was drawn to a huge Greek Revival mansion with welcoming warm light spilling from all the windows. Almost as soon as she looked that way, she ducked.

There were people on the front porch.

Heart racing, she dropped to one knee. Had they seen her? With the church arc light behind her, it probably wouldn't have been hard to do. Hell, her head must have been at least a foot above the wall.

She climbed down and dug in her pocket for the car key, feeling as though she should run for it. But there were no whistles, no shouts coming from inside. Maybe they hadn't seen her—or maybe, right this minute, the guard was running along the outside of the front wall, coming her way.

On the verge of panic, she unlocked the car, got in, and started the engine. Without turning on the lights, she yanked it into reverse and backed up fast, nearly taking out one of the volleyball poles. She cut a sharp turn, shoved it into drive, and headed for the road.

As she cleared the church, she looked for the guard.

Nothing.

Nor was he in sight when she reached a position where she

could see along the front wall. No cars coming her way, either.

She sat there for about thirty seconds, waiting for them to come for her, but they didn't. Believing now that she hadn't been seen, she turned around in the front parking lot and went back to the wall.

Afraid to look inside again with that light behind her, she searched the area for a better spot. About ten yards behind the paved area, out of the glare of the light, she saw a small grove of trees. There, she found one whose branches permitted a manageable ascent to where she could once more see over the wall. Hidden now from view of the gathering on the porch, she took her time and looked the place over.

The mansion was ringed with columns supporting a second-floor balcony that also circled the house. Two lines of giant trees, most likely live oaks, with lights in their boughs, formed a canopied walkway leading from the front door to the front wall. The guard she'd seen was posted on the opposite side of the treed walkway, a position that gave him an obstructed view of the grounds. Between the walkway and the wall in front of her, the estate was too dark to make out any detail beyond a few scattered trees whose leafy branches were mere suggestions against the night sky. As her eyes turned back to the gathering on the porch, the group adjourned to the house.

If she was ever going in, now was the time. But was it the place? Neither the trees she was in nor any of the others nearby was close enough to the wall to assist her over it. And she couldn't go schlepping around the dark perimeter looking for one she *could* use. She'd have to go in here or forget it.

She climbed down from the tree and went back to her car, telling herself that even though she'd be backlit by the church light, no one would see her. And even if they did, she *was* armed.

My God but it was hot. Her blouse was already sticking to her skin and her moist panties were eight miles up the Amazon.

Before climbing onto her car again, she realized if she got in, she'd need some help getting out.

For once, an answer came as a gift.

She went to the volleyball net and untied it from its supports. She dragged the net to the bed of crepe myrtles and tied one end to the tree nearest the wall. After twisting the net into a rope, she threw the free end over the wall.

By now, she'd perspired so much into her hair, it felt like a wet rag against her skull. And her bra was soaked.

Returning to her car, she climbed up on the left fender and carefully looked over the wall to make sure the situation hadn't changed. Satisfied that nothing had been added to the equation, she hoisted herself onto the wall and dropped into a crouch.

Get up there and jump down—that was the plan, but the height made her hesitate. What if she should sprain an ankle?

She slapped a mosquito on her cheek and brushed it from her skin.

Get off the wall.

But it was so high.

GET OFF.

The net . . . She could . . .

She crouch-walked as quickly as she could to the volleyball net and eased herself down onto the deep grass inside.

No alarms went off; no shouts rang out. So at least they didn't have pressure sensors on the lawn.

Needing to stay out of the lights, she made her way along the wall, back to the point where she'd first climbed up. As she continued in that direction, a line of dim shapes far across the lawn momentarily blocked her view of the mansion. Then, as her angle changed, it reappeared.

Soon she was directly opposite the mansion. Using the scattered trees for cover, she zigzagged across the grounds until she reached a grape arbor about thirty feet from it. There, she paused to reconnoiter and catch her breath, which the humid air reluctantly provided.

The first-story porch also circled the house. It was ringed by a wide bed of flowers that in the light spilling from the windows appeared to be begonias. The porch was only about a foot above grade and there were no obstructing balustrades to navigate. Nor did she hear evidence of anyone lingering outside.

Apart from her own fear, which had given her a few bad moments, everything had actually gone very well up to this point . . . almost *too* well. Maybe this *was* nothing but an innocent dinner party. Either way, hiding in a grape arbor wasn't the way to find out.

She took a deep breath and darted to the house, where she stepped over the begonias and onto the porch, then tried to blend with the paint on the mansion's outside wall, bracing herself for the sound of sirens.

Still nothing happened.

She turned to the wall and edged her face out so one eye could see through the window. A moment later, she pulled back.

Innocent dinner party?

Dinner, maybe.

Innocent, no way.

Inside, facing her over a long table in the room across the hall, she'd seen Warden Guillory and his brother. Woodley was at the head of the table and Tom Ward was seated against the wall to his left. Another man at the table had his back to her.

This seemed like a major discovery, but then she remembered what Tabor had said when they'd first met—that he had evidence of a connection between Agrilabs and the funeral home in Courville. So, by itself, this was nothing new. She needed to hear what was being said. And she wanted a look at the other guy.

Hoping their conversation would carry through glass, she left her post and circled around to the back, intending to creep up to a window on the other side. Reaching the corner of the house, she encountered two obstacles to that plan. First, there was a clear visual trajectory from this side of the house to the front gates and the guard out there. Second, even if there was no risk of being seen, there were three central air-conditioning units behind her making such a racket, she'd never be able to hear anything from inside.

Now what?

Go home and butt out? Let Tabor handle it?

But she was so *close*. What *were* they talking about?

Unwilling to cave just yet, she returned to her first position and gave the matter some thought.

She soon noticed that the windows on the ground floor were all actually French doors. This explained why, when she'd seen the conspirators go inside from the porch, they hadn't appeared to use the home's main entrance. Staying well to the side, she looked again through the window, directing her attention to the door they *had* used.

There were actually two sets of French doors on the front wall, one on each side of a chest that sat under a painting depicting a fox hunt. She was sure Woodley and his cronies had gone through the pair on the left. She figured the odds on those doors still being unlocked were at least even.

Jesus, what was she thinking? Walk right in?

Even as she dismissed the thought as lunacy, she stared at a tall Chinese screen that formed a hypotenuse with the room's far-front corner. It was mesmerizing, that screen.

Under its spell, she retreated to the grape arbor and fell back to the protection of a tree beyond the house lights. Even here, the screen spoke to her.

Responding, she ran to another tree that stood opposite the second oak in the row that formed the canopied walkway. Faced with leaving the night's dark embrace, she nearly fled deeper into it. But the weight of all she'd suffered at the hands of those inside pushed her from its safety into a mad dash toward the big oak.

She reached it breathing hard and sank against its rough bark. A minute later, with her wet panties soaking into her slacks, she ran for the first tree in the row. Well short of it, a root caught her foot and she stumbled the rest of the way, nearly ramming the tree with her head.

The point of this exercise was to reach the front porch without being seen through either of the two sets of French doors on the side of the house where she'd looked inside. She completed the final leg of that journey by darting from the last oak to the mansion's nearest column.

The porch contained several white wicker sofas and a couple of fan-back wicker chairs. Dropping to her knees, she crept behind a nearby chair and crossed a small open space to a settee by the pair of French doors she thought might be unlocked. With the decisive moment at hand, she saw with greater clarity what a chance she was taking. It seemed very unlikely that opening those doors would set off an alarm. But a squeaky hinge, a loose floorboard, Tom Ward wandering around to stretch his legs—any of those things would do her in.

A sensible voice urged her to leave the job unfinished and go home. Indignant, its stubborn sister demanded that she stay. They compromised. If the doors were locked, she'd leave. If a hinge squealed, she'd leave fast. If a floorboard squeaked, she'd run like hell. If Tom Ward got up to wander and discovered her, well, she'd deal with that when she had to.

The first test would be the French doors. Were they locked?

When she could breathe without sounding like a dying

buffalo, she reached up, took hold of the doorknob on the right member of the pair, and slowly turned it.

So silently that it might have been in league with her, the door opened.

24

A man was speaking.

Even here on the porch, she could tell it was Woodley. For a scant moment, she thought she might be able to hear everything without going any farther. She paused, listening hard. but a few words here and there were all she could decipher. She'd have to go in.

This was even worse than her invasion of Woodley's lab. There, the place had been empty—at least she thought it had been. Here . . .

Contemplation of what she was about to do sent waves of gooseflesh down her back and onto her arms. Sensible Kit made a final plea for an end to this reckless behavior. Ignoring her, Kit got up and slipped inside.

The room's cooled air against her hot skin put gooseflesh on her gooseflesh. Fearing everyone in the next room could hear her heart beating, she almost broke and ran, but was restrained by stubborn Kit. Before a dissenting opinion could be filed, she crept into the hidden pocket behind the Chinese screen, where she leaned her back against the wall, folded her arms, and tried to concentrate on what was being said next door.

"I can't give you a definite timetable," Woodley said.

"Suppose there's no way to separate the side effect from the beneficial effect?" a voice that sounded like Warden Guillory's said.

"I think that's highly unlikely. It's a big molecule. The odds that the two effects reside in the same amino acid sequence are remote."

"Considering what's happened, we may not have much more time," Warden Guillory said.

"That's all being taken care of," Woodley replied. "Which brings me to the main purpose of this meeting."

Eager to hear what was coming, Kit concentrated harder. Then, as Woodley began to explain, she felt something brush her leg. Alarm bells clanging in her head, she looked down, to see a small white dog sniffing her. *Jesus, if it should bark . . .*

She knelt and saw from his collar that his name was Bobby. Desperately afraid he'd give her away, she scratched him under the chin. With this attention, he looked up at her, mouth open, panting happily. It was a Westie. Continuing to scratch him, she also listened.

"Because of that increased risk, our remaining partner feels he's entitled to a larger share."

This brought angry murmurs from the others.

"Nevertheless, that's what he's demanding. In fact, he now wants half."

"There's no way I'm agreeing to that," Warden Guillory said. "We're *all* taking a risk. He agreed to the existing terms. Let him abide by them."

The Westie began to wag his tail, hitting it against the Chinese screen. Afraid the sound might bring someone to investigate, Kit lifted his hind legs off the floor and replanted him so his tail merely fanned the air.

"What if we refuse?" Trip Guillory said.

"He made reference to how interested a grand jury would be in our activities and how easily he could distance himself from us."

"I don't believe he's thought this over very carefully," an unfamiliar voice said.

"What do you mean?"

"He's treating us as though we don't have options."

"What options?" Trip Guillory asked.

"Perhaps Tom could help us there."

"If you mean can I make this problem go away, it wouldn't be the easiest job I ever had, but it's possible."

"How?" Trip Guillory said. "He's too well protected."

"Any man can be reached. Give me three days and we'll be a smaller family."

"Damn it," Trip Guillory said. "If there just wasn't so much at stake."

"I sense we've reached a decision here," Woodley said. "Is there any other discussion? No?"

With a start, Kit realized the meeting was about to end. Any second, they all might be heading for this room and the door she'd come through. She had to get out—now.

She shot to her feet and stepped over the dog. Startled by her sudden movement, he shied against the screen, tipping it off its legs and sending it slamming to the floor. Frightened by the sound, the Westie did a wheelie on the bare floor, clattered across the fallen screen onto the Bessarabian kilim carpet, and bolted from the room.

Before anyone at the meeting could clear their chairs, Kit was past the porch and into the darkness.

His automatic already in hand, Ward pushed Woodley out of the way and ran after her, trampling over the Chinese screen in his haste. He darted through the French doors and out onto the porch, where he stopped, gun raised to his ear to scan the grounds. Behind him, the others crowded through the doors.

"Goddamn it," the owner of the estate said. "I've got a fifty-thousand-dollar security system here. So where is it? There are infrared motion detectors in all the trees. The entire place should now be bright as day."

"Well, as you can see, it ain't," Ward said. "I got no idea where to look."

"Never mind. There's a backup. But you've all got to get inside."

"What kind of backup?" Ward said.

"One that can locate its target even in the dark. But it'll find you, too, if you don't get inside."

As Kit ran, she wondered if she'd hear the bullet fired before it hit her, or would the two happen so close together that she'd have no warning? She was really burning up yardage now as she angled for the point where she thought she had come over the wall. But where was the glow of the church light? It should have been visible. She looked to her right. Not there, either.

She strained to see into the darkness, trying to keep from colliding with a tree. Detecting a subtle form in the void, she veered right, skirting a tall yew hedge.

In a small building behind the mansion, the security backup lay curled in sleep. But with the first sound of the metal door sliding open, he was up, ears erect, eyes bulging. Then he was free. A killing machine of bone and sinew, a minion from hell anointed by Lucifer, a creature born to his name, and he was called Death.

He smelled the men who'd been on the porch and the gate guard who'd just been warned to stay in the guardhouse. Their odors were faint—prey that might already be out of reach. But there were two other smells, bright and strong.

His choice was instinctive, made a thousand years before his ancestors knew the hand of man. Stringy saliva trailing from his muzzle, snot bubbling from his nose, he gave chase, following fear.

Muscles rippling under his sleek coat, he consumed the distance to his prey in great powerful strides. At the yew hedge Kit had passed seconds earlier, he slowed to stalking speed.

Fifteen yards away, Kit had just realized to her horror that a second hedge intersected the one on her left. With a sinking feeling, she ran along this new obstruction, searching for an opening. When she found a third hedge intersecting the second, fear made room for anger. How could she be so dumb?

The hedges were what had blocked her view of the church light and were what had kept her from seeing the house when she'd first come over the wall.

Jesus.

The third hedge ran back toward the house. Unwilling to give ground in that direction, she tried to push her way through, but couldn't penetrate the wall of thick branches. Aware of the time flying by, she moved along the hedge, praying for an opening. Her right knee banged against something. More by osmosis than sight, she determined that it was a sort of overgrown baby carriage with wheelbarrow handles.

She couldn't see him, but Death saw her. His ears flattened and his lips curled back in an ugly sneer. Slowly, he closed the distance between them.

Kit moved out to go around the lawn cart and heard a throaty growl that could not have come from a little Westie. Fear clogging her own throat, she reached down and released the Ladysmith. She came up with it in her hand and assumed a textbook stance.

Unable to pinpoint the source of the sound she'd heard, she

swept the air in front of her, keeping the gun moving. Another malevolent rattle that quickly grew louder and more malignant came out of the darkness. Zeroing in on its apparent origin, she narrowed the focus of her attention.

Death's eyes were now bulging out so far, the whites were showing, ringing the black centers, giving them the look of taxidermist's accessories. Still unable to see him, Kit continued her focused sweep.

The tension was unbearable. If she moved, the animal would certainly attack and she'd be caught out of position, off balance. At least here, she was as prepared as she could be. But she needed to be gone. She couldn't stay here, couldn't allow herself to be held until the men inside came for her.

Her finger tightened on the trigger. Empty the gun into the night and hope for the best—that could work. But it might not.

Do something.

Then Death took the decision from her. With a sound first heard before there was written history, he launched himself at her throat.

As he came hurtling out of the darkness, she finally saw him against the sky. She swung the gun that way. But she was too slow. He hit her and she went over backward into the lawn cart without getting off a shot.

When the world stopped spinning, she found the cart upside down on top of her, the rim of the bucket resting against the backs of her knees. She turned on her side, pulled her legs up to her stomach, and lay there inside the bucket, under a carpet of sour grass clippings, her heart threatening to explode, all too aware that she'd lost the gun.

Death was in a crazed frenzy, circling the cart, trying to thrust his muzzle under it. Hearing him slobbering behind her, she rolled in the opposite direction as much as she could. A second later, the tip of his snout was practically in her face, so close, she could smell the mole he'd eaten that morning. She rolled away from him onto her back and felt a hard object beneath her. Confined to such a small space, her body heat and sweat had nowhere to go, so she felt as though she were being steamed alive.

Death began to dig.

Trouble . . . this was big trouble. The estate's heavy turf would slow him briefly, but when he got through that, he would quickly open up a hole large enough to get his head through, and then he could either grab her or flip the cart over.

With her left hand, she managed to get hold of the object punishing the small of her back. In the dark, it was impossible to see it, but she knew from its shape it was an aerosol can, or, more correctly, her possible salvation.

But it was so lightweight. Could it have been tossed in with the grass clippings because it was empty?

No. Let it not be empty.

She shook it against her ear but could hear nothing. Her fingers found a dimple on one side of the nozzle and she turned the can, facing the dimple away from her.

So many things to go haywire.

If she guessed wrong about the direction of the nozzle, she'd spray *herself*. And she couldn't afford to waste what little might be left on a test spray into her hand.

Death had cleared away all the grass from his hole and the air behind him was filled with dirt as his front legs churned the ground. Soon the hole was big enough. He thrust his entire head under the cart, jaws snapping. In the dark, his hot saliva splattered onto Kit's face.

To protect her own eyes in case she had the nozzle pointed the wrong way, she shut them and depressed the button on top of the can. There was a hissing noise followed by a yowl of agony as the dog yanked his head out of the hole. Blinded and howling in pain from the wasp spray in his eyes, he began turning in circles, snapping at phantoms.

Hearing his reaction, Kit kicked the cart off herself.

How long would the spray keep him occupied?

No way to know.

Fighting the desire to get away, Kit swept the ground with her hand, looking for . . .

There . . . the gun.

Snatching it up, she ran for the open end of the hedges without looking back.

25

For the second time this month, she'd lost the combs that held her hair out of her face, but she was running so fast, the resulting wind kept it from her eyes. As she rounded the end of the hedge, she glanced toward the house, expecting to see a covey of flashlights bobbing toward her, but there was nothing there. Fearing that any moment the dog would recover, she sprinted hard for the church light, which appeared ahead as a welcoming beacon.

She reached the volleyball net with a three-alarm blaze in her chest and a stabbing pain in her side. She'd heard no evidence the dog was close behind, but believed that meant nothing. Still, needing both hands to climb the net, she paused to holster the Ladysmith and secure it with the Velcro strap.

Sweating like a stevedore, she grabbed hold of the net and started climbing. It wasn't pretty and, with her wet hair now dangling in her face, it wasn't easy, but she managed to get onto the wall, where, realizing what a great target she made, she jumped.

The ground came up fast and she hit with a jolt. Her ankles hurt but held. Her car sat where she'd left it, apparently undisturbed. Afraid they might be waiting for her in the shadows, she reached for the Ladysmith.

Warily, she moved toward the car, trying to see in all directions at once. There were a lot of crickets chirping. Would they be doing that if anyone was around? Dumb question... *She* was around.

If it was a trap, when would they spring it? Probably when she was unlocking the car.

Unlocking ... The key ...

She switched the gun into her left hand and dug for the car key, tormented by visions of it lying back there with her combs, under the grass clippings. But by all that's good and right in the world, it was in her pocket.

She reached the car safely and put the key in the lock, craning her neck for any signs of an ambush. There was no place anyone could hide within thirty yards, so she'd clearly have time to get in and lock it before anyone could reach her.

But what if this very second she was in the crosshairs of a rifle? She ducked and yanked the door open. Sweating and frightened and sorry she'd ever become involved in this, she threw herself inside and locked the door. Expecting at any moment to hear the sound of shattering glass as a bullet came out of the darkness, she tattooed the ignition switch with the key, her hand shaking so badly, she couldn't hit the hole.

Finally, she did. A touch of the starter filled her ears with the sweet sound of the engine. Once again, the closest volleyball support survived her departure. And she was soon on the road, every second that passed taking her farther out of harm's way—*if* no one was following.

She couldn't shake that last thought, so every car approaching from behind on the way back to New Orleans fell under suspicion. Then they'd take a side road or pass her and she'd relax until another appeared. When she finally turned onto North Rampart, a tailing car she'd picked up three blocks earlier followed. From the lights behind it, she could see only one occupant.

Normally, she would have turned down Toulouse, then taken Dauphine to Nolen's garage. Tonight, on a stage-two alert, she kept going on Rampart for another nine blocks. The car behind did the same.

Reaching Esplanade, she turned right. In the mirror, she saw the suspect car follow, sending her alert status to stage three.

She passed Burgundy and turned onto Dauphine, keeping her eyes more on the rearview mirror than on the street ahead. The car that was giving her so much concern came, too. Skin prickling, all internal alarms flashing, she decided to look for a patrol car she could flag down. But then the suspect car turned onto Barracks and was gone.

There was, however, another car behind him that didn't turn. Considering there might be two cars following her, she turned right on Ursulines, so she was headed back toward Rampart. The second car continued on Dauphine. She wasn't being tailed after all.

The relief left her limp and exhausted and aware that her knee hurt. She touched it lightly and felt a tear in her slacks, probably done when she was floundering over that brick wall.

She made a left on Rampart and began to compare what she'd accomplished this night to what it had cost her. She'd learned that Woodley and the two Guillorys were indeed partners in some clandestine enterprise. If the house where they'd met didn't belong to any of them, the owner was probably the other guy, the one who'd had his back to her. In the latter case, his name could easily be determined. She had no idea how to get the identity of the remaining partner. But from the vote taken, he'd better watch his step. The thought of the vermin exterminating one another had a poetic ring to it.

That talk about a side effect meant there was a drug of some kind at the heart of all this.

Of course—*that's* why Woodley needed a tech who knew chromatography. He was planning to digest the original molecule—whatever that was—enzymatically and purify the resulting fragments for testing. Had she not screwed up so badly tapping his phone, she'd have probably been the one to do that work. And she could have made off with enough of the sample so Tabor could have it analyzed.

Could have—can't put "could have" in the bank.

Viewing it objectively, she hadn't learned a helluva lot and had almost lost her life—for the third time. Enough—she'd had more than enough of this. She'd tell Tabor what she'd heard and keep her nose out of any more of it.

She put her car away and walked home through streets choked with tourists clutching hurricane glasses from Pat O'Brien's and plastic bags from one of the T-shirt and souvenir shops that occupy every other storefront on Bourbon Street. Turning to watch a guy wearing a giant fabric crawfish on his head, she noticed for the first time a pain in the back of her neck, her body finally admitting the toll placed on it. And there would probably be more countries to be heard from. She stepped into the street to avoid a crowd around three little kids tap-dancing on the sidewalk. The asylum is always open.

As she returned to the sidewalk, a high-yellow black man with a face full of freckles and his hair in dreadlocks approached her with a tract in his hand. "Have you met Jesus, miss?"

She waved him off. "I'm not really dressed for it."

What she wanted now was to lie in bed wrapped in Teddy's arms and never get up. But he was far away. The next-best thing was hugging Lucky. She checked her watch: 9:20. He'd still be walking with Nolen and Mitzi. Nuts. A shower while she waited for him—that would be good.

She passed the photo gallery and unlocked the gate to the courtyard, already feeling the hot water of that shower running over her and hoping she wouldn't run into Eunice Dalehite. Her luck, which had waxed and waned all day, turned her way again, for Eunice's apartment was dark. She unlocked her own front door, went inside, and flicked the light switch.

No lights. Great. With this place, it was always something.

She shut the door and made her way to a nearby lamp. Eager to get out of her damp, filthy clothes, she was already unbuttoning her blouse at the same time she switched the lamp on.

"Now close the drapes," a voice said from behind her.

It couldn't be. It wasn't possible.

"I said, close the drapes."

She turned and saw Tom Ward sitting against the wall in a wooden chair he'd pulled over from the counter serving the kitchenette. In his hand was an automatic with an extension on the barrel that she assumed was a silencer.

"How did you find me?"

"I'm not gonna tell you again about those drapes."

Head spinning, she turned back to the window and drew the drapes.

"Now the other pair."

She did as he ordered, her thoughts now centering on the Ladysmith and how she might get at it.

"Now come back and sit there." With the gun, he motioned her to the armchair at his end of the room. "But straighten it up first."

She walked to the chair and turned it away from the TV. Ward got up and pulled his chair into the center of the room so they faced each other across eight feet of carpet.

"I'd have thought a woman with your looks could do better'n this," Ward said. "I particularly like that touch." He jerked his thumb over his shoulder at the brace behind him propped against the ceiling. "Real class. You could have parlayed that body of yours into practically anything you wanted. Instead, you had to go and get yourself killed."

Kit estimated it would take at least three seconds to get at the Ladysmith and fire off a round, which was about three seconds longer than it'd take Ward to fire. She told herself to stay calm, use her wits.

"How'd you escape the freezer?" Ward asked.

"So *you* did that."

"I never liked the idea from the start. But they wanted it to look like an accident. They're big on that. I should have argued harder, but I'm just the hired help."

"You saw me go into Woodley's office?"

"I was catching up on some sleep in one of the darkened rooms off the main lab when you came waltzing in. I'm surprised you didn't hear me leave."

"I did."

"Yet you stuck around. Bad decision."

"If I'd known you were in the building, I never would have gone in there. How come your car wasn't in the parking lot?"

"It was three blocks away, getting a tune-up."

"How'd you find me tonight?"

"You never answered my question about how you got out of the freezer."

"Professional secret."

"Oh, you won't answer my questions, but I'm supposed to answer yours?"

"I set off the temperature sensor by breathing on it. Somebody came to check on things."

"That's the way all IQ tests should be conducted. Then there wouldn't be so many morons throwing their chewed gum on the sidewalk and cutting you off in traffic. I'd like to kill 'em all."

"Now do I get an answer?"

"The Guillory sisters saw your reflection in a mirror when that screen fell over. We called the sheriff in Courville and he gave us your address."

"Why kill me? It's all over. The police know everything. Better for you to strike a deal with the DA before the others do."

Ward shook his head. "If the police knew, you wouldn't have come out tonight alone. Who sent you?"

"I told you that."

"Look, here's the deal. I can kill you fast or slow. Tell me what I want to know and it'll be fast. Otherwise, we can start with your knees and work up. I'd hate that. It'd be like that guy who took a knife to the Mona Lisa. You can't imagine the pain a gunshot causes, especially when it hits bone. The slug will shatter your knee and deflect, tunneling into your leg like a burning iron."

Three seconds with his guard down, that's all she needed. She unfastened another button on her blouse and folded it back so he could see the cleavage between her lush breasts. "Maybe we could arrange a trade. My life in return for . . ." She ran a finger down between her breasts.

Ward shook his head. "Only way a guy survives in this business is by remembering one rule: Follow your head first, your heart second, and don't listen to a thing your dick says. See, you just gotta accept the fact you're dead. And it really ain't that bad. Nobody knows when they're dead. Only pain matters."

Kit's outlook for getting out of this unhurt was so bleak, her thoughts shifted from escape to retribution and how she could take Ward with her. He'd said he was going to start with her knees. With the ensuing pain, it would be natural for her to bend over and cover them, gripping her ankles. With a little luck, she might be able to get off a shot before he caught on. She was glad now the dog had knocked the gun from her hand before she could use it. Otherwise, Ward would know she had it.

But she was frightened of the coming pain, afraid it would be so bad, she wouldn't be able to function.

No.

She *would* function. Even if he killed her, she'd simply refuse to die until she'd done the same to him.

"So what do you think?" Ward said. "Slow or—"

A floorboard creaked in the hallway leading to the back door. Ward rose out of his chair, turning fast in that direction. Before he got fully around, Brian Tabor stepped into view and fired three rounds from his own silenced automatic. The bullets slapped into Ward's chest and he dropped his gun. As he went down, his sideways momentum carried him into his chair, which fell backward, knocking the ceiling brace behind it loose, so it crashed into the TV set and clattered to the floor.

Glancing quickly at the loose plaster overhead, Tabor circled the spot and stood looking down at Ward's body.

Kit found this unbelievable. She wasn't going to die. She was going to live. She leapt from her chair and started toward Tabor, wanting desperately to hug him in gratitude. Before she reached him, he lifted his gun and fired two more rounds into Ward's head.

Perplexed at the need for this, she stopped a few feet away.

"Why did you do that? He was no longer a threat."

Tabor looked at her. "Maybe not to you."

Confused as to what he meant, Kit just stood there, working on it.

Then a pall washed over her. "The governor—*he* was the other partner."

Tabor raised his automatic and pointed it at her. "This is a poor way to show it, but he'll be grateful for your alerting us to that meeting tonight. We were concerned the others might overreact to his demands. But we had no idea they'd go as far as they did."

"You were there?"

"By the time you arrived, I'd already disabled their security system and slipped a couple of needle-nose bugs through the cracks in the French doors of the room they met in and the one next to it. I had to do both because I didn't know which one they'd use."

"How could you get there so fast from— Oh, you weren't *in* Baton Rouge."

"Right."

"Killing me won't help you. I called Andy Broussard in Memphis as soon as I got home and told him what I'd heard. He'll—" Realizing that rather than helping herself with this story, she could be hurting Broussard, she faltered.

"By now he's out of the picture, too."

"What do you mean?"

"Just what you're thinking."

The possibility that Broussard was dead was incomprehensible and horrible to contemplate, but facing the same fate herself, she couldn't dwell on it. All day long, she'd been yanked in and out of life and it was wearing on her. Where, she wondered, would salvation come from this time? Certainly not from the gun on her ankle. He'd never let her get to that.

Her whirling mind locked on an idea. Coming in, Tabor had glanced at the loose plaster. Maybe . . . She lifted her eyes to a spot over Tabor's head and cringed. Before he could catch himself, he, too, looked up.

Seizing the moment, Kit pushed his gun hand to the side and kicked him solidly in the groin, doubling him over. Afraid he'd recover before she could get her own gun out, she ran for the door and bolted onto the porch. There, she realized if she went down the steps to the courtyard, he'd have plenty of opportunity to pick her off before she got there. Impulsively, she went the other way and ducked around the corner into a dead-end alcove, hoping she'd have time to get her gun before he found her.

But she'd no sooner turned the corner than she heard him come onto the porch. It would take only a glance for him to see she hadn't gone down the steps, and then he'd figure out where she was. Needing more time, she started up the ladder to the roof. As she reached the top and threw herself onto the slate shingles, she heard the now-familiar *thwack* of Tabor's automatic firing from the bottom of the steps. At practically the same instant, a slug hissed past her ear.

Scrambling and slipping on the slate, she tried to put some distance between herself and the ladder, frantically looking for a hiding place. But on this part of the building, there were only a few small pipes coming through the roof, nothing large enough to shield her. On the older section, there were chimneys.

The pitch of the roof made for precarious footing and slowed her as she sprinted for the unrenovated wing. Tabor fired again from the ladder as soon as he could see her, once again narrowly missing the mark.

By the time he'd reached the roof himself, Kit had made it to the old wing. The first chimney was no more than ten feet away. As she ran, she planned what she'd do when she reached it. Take cover facing it, brace with her left leg. . . . Her thoughts raced, compressing time. If she used both hands to get the gun, she might slide off the roof. . . . Hold on to the chimney with her right hand and get the gun with her left. . . . No, she'd never hit him if she had to fire with her left hand.

Then there was a loud crack, followed by a cacophony of collapse as the roof gave way and she fell through. When the shock passed, she found herself suspended, slightly turned away from the chimney she'd been chasing, jagged roof slate surrounding her at chest level. Her left leg, hidden below, dangled in air; her right was bent at the knee by some kind of debris that had kept her from slamming into the floor of the room below. Her left arm rested on the roof; her right was in the hole.

She tried to leverage herself out of the hole with her supported leg, but the debris under it gave with the pressure.

"I can't stay up here long," Tabor said from behind her.

Tabor . . . Jesus . . . The gun on her ankle—her right hand was practically touching it. She inched her hand down and found the cuff of her slacks already lifted by a protruding splinter or nail. She unsnapped the Velcro strap, cringing at the sound, which, though muffled, seemed all too audible. Her fingers closed on the butt of the gun and she lifted it from the holster. Praying Tabor couldn't see it, she brought the gun up, sliding it against her chest.

"I want you to know there's nothing personal in this," Tabor said. "It's business, that's all. I actually—"

Kit twisted her head and torso in his direction. At the same instant she saw him, she fired—once, twi—

Her brain howled in shock.

Nothing.

Nothing was happening. The hammer was just clicking away like a kid's toy.

She fired again with the same result.

"Afraid I'm responsible for that," Tabor said. "After your shooting lesson at the range, I reloaded your gun with shells fitted with dummy primers. Now, I've got to go. Please don't look at me."

Left with no other way to resist, Kit stared into his face, determined he should know he'd killed a person, not merely conducted business. If giving him nightmares about this moment was all she could do, she'd take satisfaction in that.

"You, up there, drop the gun."

A voice from the courtyard . . . Kit couldn't turn enough in that direction to see who it was.

Suddenly, Tabor was running past her, headed for the end of the roof, where he was obviously planning to jump to the next building. The voice from below shouted again. "Stop or I'll fire."

Tabor kept running.

Before the owner of the voice could make good on his threat, the roof under Tabor gave way and he dropped from view. A second later, Kit heard him hit the floor of the room beneath. There was no further sound from that direction.

Very shortly, she was helped onto the roof by the smaller of the two cops who had saved her. Against the other's advice, he then edged his way to the hole where Tabor had fallen through, playing his flashlight into the room beneath. He studied the situation briefly, then looked at Kit and grinned. "I love it when that happens."

26

"Word is, if the governor doesn't resign, the legislature is gonna impeach him," Phil Gatlin said across Broussard's table at Grandma O's.

"That was quick," Kit replied. "He hasn't even been indicted yet."

"Sure he has," Gatlin said, "by every paper in the state."

Broussard took a sip of his iced tea through cracked lips and put the glass down. "Nothin' gets the legislature's hackles up like a crooked politician," He paused for effect, then added, "who's gettin' away with more than they are."

Gatlin feigned a shocked look. "I hope when the swelling goes down, you'll be the sweet old geezer we used to know. I'm sure you realize that by hitting this woman in the stomach, it makes you a danger to the entire fabric of society."

"I liked the world better the way it used to be—when at least a few issues were black and white. I hate gray."

"What'd she look like?"

"She was actually quite attractive."

Gatlin's eyebrows rose. "I was wondering how she got you to believe that goofy story about a cabin in the woods."

"It wasn't her appearance. I was just too slow mentally. I had everything I needed to link Tabor to the murder of Anthony Hunter when I came out of the reptile curator's office at the zoo. But I didn't realize it. If I'd made the connection right away and followed up, I'd have probably stopped everything at that point and"—he looked at Kit—"you could have been spared a lot of what you went through."

"The final result is all that matters," she said. "But those cops who saved me at the end really cut it close."

"I hate to think about that," Broussard said. "A half hour before I called Phillip and told him you could be in trouble, I was sittin' lost in the woods, my car hopelessly stuck in a mud hole, with no idea Tabor was involved. I'd decided to spend the night in the car and worry about gettin' out in the mornin', when I finally realized you were bein' set up, too. Then, I *had* to get to a phone. I guess it was desperation that showed me how to get the car movin'."

"How'd you do that?" Gatlin said.

"Jacked the rear wheels up and put the trunk liner under 'em. That gave me enough traction to get on solid ground."

"Should have thought of that a lot earlier," Gatlin said. "Or you could have gone back for the shovel and used it to throw some dry dirt under the wheels."

"Next time I'm in a jam, I'll be sure you're along."

Grandma O arrived and distributed the food they'd ordered.

"Anybody need anything else? No?" Her eyes stopped on Broussard. "Ah ain't got time now to hear how your face got like dat, but Ah'm nosy enough dat Ah *am* gonna know what happened. So keep it all fresh in your mind."

"It'll be awhile before it fades," Broussard said.

She went off to attend to her other customers.

"What was the connection you found between Tabor and Hunter?" Kit asked Broussard.

"When we first met Tabor in my office, he gave me a business card on the back of which he'd scribbled the phone number of someone named P. Bates. I've done the same thing myself—written a number on one of my cards, then mistakenly given it away. I figured it might be important to him, that he'd need the number. But by the time I'd noticed it, he was already gone. I gave the number back to him over the phone the night before I was taken out to the woods to be killed. That's what precipitated it. He was afraid I'd figure out who P. Bates was."

"Who was it?" Kit said.

"It wasn't a *who*. It was a *what*."

"Okay, *what* was it?"

"The toxicology lab in Memphis had determined that the poison used to kill Hunter was derived from a type of dart-poison frog, belonging to the genus *Phyllobates*."

"P. Bates," Kit exclaimed.

"Tabor apparently didn't know how to spell the genus, so he abbreviated it. The phone number was for an animal importer who could supply wild-caught *Phyllobates terribilis*, the most toxic frog known. Tabor wanted me killed before I figured that out. I actually became a target the day I called the prison board to start an investigation. I dragged you into it when I sent you up to Angola. I'm sure they intended to kill us both eventually."

"That's why Tabor gave me a gun loaded with dud cartridges. Insisting I take a weapon made it look like he was concerned for my safety. But he knew at some point, after I'd helped him keep tabs on his crooked friends and he was ready to get rid of me, I might try to use it on him. That day at the firing range, I wondered why, when he reloaded the last time, he used a different box from the one he'd been using, even though the first one was still half-full."

Gatlin swallowed a mouthful of turtle chili and waved his spoon at Kit and Broussard. "You both could have avoided all this trouble if you'd confided in me. You should have caught on when they requested you deal only with Tabor."

Broussard gave Gatlin a critical look. "I'll bet the Saints never lost a game you couldn't have won for 'em if only they'd asked for help."

"Well, there was maybe that one, when the whole starting backfield was out with the flu."

"How did Tabor recruit a Memphis homicide detective?" Kit asked.

"I wondered that myself," Gatlin replied. "I asked my friend in the department up there what they knew about it. She's not talking, but my friend said it probably goes back to when she and Tabor worked Vice together in Baton Rouge. Rumor is they were both dirty."

"And she was still able to get a job in Memphis?" Kit said.

"Nobody told Memphis. They were never charged with anything, so it was all speculation. You prevent somebody from getting work by passing along rumors, you open yourself up to a lawsuit."

"How dirty were they? She was prepared to commit murder."

"She apparently always had an eye for things she couldn't afford. And with the scheme the governor and his friends were working, Tabor could have offered her plenty."

Broussard put his oyster po' boy back in its lattice basket. "Sounds like you know exactly what they were up to."

"The only one stonewalling is the governor. The rest are singing like they're auditioning for the Met. The deal is, this guy Woodley discovered an ingredient in red wine that can reverse hardening of the arteries in mice. He figured out that the effective substance is made by yeast in the presence of alcohol and something I can't remember found in grape skins. Anyway, after learning how to make this stuff in large quantities, he arranged a tentative deal with a German pharmaceutical firm that agreed to pay him—get this—one billion dollars for the rights to all his notes and the knowledge of how to make it—*if* it proved to be effective and safe on humans. So where could they get some human subjects nobody would miss if things went wrong?"

"The prison," Kit said.

"They thought about just picking up street bums, but Woodley didn't want the deck stacked against success by starting with drug addicts and winos."

Remembering what she'd heard at the meeting, Kit said, "But in humans, it had a side effect."

"Brain damage," Broussard added.

Gatlin's eyebrows jigged together. "If you two already know all this, why am I talking so much?"

"I don't know all of it," Broussard said. "You're too edgy. I'm aware of the neural effects because I saw 'em in Ronald Cicero's brain when I did his autopsy. He was obviously one of their test subjects."

"Yeah, but he escaped before they could get rid of him and he somehow made his way to New Orleans, where he ran amok with that knife. If I'd known the governor was so dumb, I'd never have voted for him. To bring you two right into the heart of the conspiracy like that was nuts. Oh, sure, to hear Tabor tell it, they had it all thought out. They figured you were just gonna keep picking at the Cicero situation, so they thought by taking you into their confidence and getting you to report only to them, they could keep you corralled for a while, maybe long enough for their deal to work out. But sending Kit into Agrilabs as their agent was just asking for trouble, even if Bellair *was* afraid for his life and believed she was the ideal person to tap the director's phone. Lunacy . . ."

"Not that I'm interested in defending them," Kit said, "but I can sort of see it from their perspective. Most of the people at Agrilabs didn't know what was happening behind the scenes. And Woodley sure wasn't going to put *me* in a sensitive position. I suppose Tabor felt safe with me because even if I did manage to capture an incriminating conversation from Woodley's phone, I didn't have any way to play it back."

"Yeah, and look what happened," Gatlin said. "It was just greed. Instead of using their heads and closing down when all the signs pointed in that direction, they just couldn't do it."

"Did you know Tabor had a daughter?" Kit asked. "He showed me her picture at the firing range—a beautiful kid, deaf from birth. And now her father is going to prison, maybe worse. She didn't do anything wrong, but she has to pay, too."

"The ripples created by evil acts touch many shores," Broussard said.

Gatlin looked at Broussard and blinked. He pointed at him with his chili spoon. "That's just what I was gonna say."

"Anybody tell you how the governor got involved?" Broussard asked.

"He and Woodley used to be fraternity brothers in college. And remember, we're talking a billion dollars."

Broussard shook his head at what people will do for money. "You question them about Anthony Hunter? I'll bet he discovered the same substance."

"He did. So . . ." Gatlin drew his index finger across his neck. "That's the kind of thing that'd happen to me. If I discovered something that could make me rich, it'd be about two days before half the city stumbled onto the same idea."

"But that's the way science works," Broussard said. "When the database reaches a critical mass, the next step becomes almost inevitable, which means simultaneous discoveries are common."

"I guess that explains why Woodley recruited somebody at NIH to watch out for competition and alert them," Gatlin said.

"Who was that guy?" Broussard asked. "Another fraternity brother?"

"Just someone Woodley knew. The story they told him was that all he had to do was lose the grant application so Hunter would miss one grant cycle. They didn't tell him Hunter was to be killed. When they did it, they tried to make it look like a heart attack so there'd be no investigation of the death. In addition to all the other advantages of that, the guy at NIH wouldn't get nervous."

"Didn't he think Hunter's death was quite a coincidence?" Kit observed. "Dying like that right after being brought to the group's attention."

"He wanted to believe it was just that, a coincidence," Gatlin said. "And the way it was done made that possible. Then Andy proved it was murder."

"So everything began to unravel," Kit said.

Gatlin sucked his teeth. "That billion dollars made everyone want to hold it together."

"The whole enterprise was doomed from the start," Broussard said. "I'm surprised they couldn't see that."

"What do you mean?" Kit said.

"Too many people involved," Gatlin replied, enjoying the opportunity to supply Broussard's punch line. "Bags of crap that big always spring a leak."

"But I think we can be proud of ourselves for the role we played in bringing them down," Broussard said. "A real team effort." He looked at Kit. "And I wouldn't mind keepin' that team intact."

"I'm no good at this. I made so many mistakes. For days, I carried a useless gun around, thinking it could protect me. I—"

"I didn't say it was flawless performance. Look at me. Does this face look like I didn't make any mistakes? Life is imperfect. We all fall short of the ideal. But the best of us compensate, keep diggin', and finally find a way."

Kit could sense he was getting very close now to a direct compliment, was about to say she was one of those people. She waited eagerly for his next words.

"so if you wanted to, you know, come back to work, I wouldn't mind."

As usual, he couldn't give her what she needed. Almost choking with disappointment, she pushed back her chair and stood. "I have to go now. I'll talk to you both later."

"You haven't finished your lunch," Broussard said.

"I've had all I wanted."

"Well, it's my treat."

Longing for her old life and wishing she wasn't so damned incompetent, Kit went to her car, started it, and joined the traffic on Tulane Avenue.

At Broussard's table, Gatlin rubbed his big mitt over his face, fuzzing his eyebrows. "Don't you know *anything* about women?" He gestured to Broussard's visible injuries. "Look at you—of course you don't. Saying you wouldn't mind having her back—that was so lame. She was waiting for you to tell her how well she'd done. And you know, she really *was* a formidable adversary. You could have pointed out how she saved herself when her car went into the bayou, how she was alert enough to see the hearse that brought Cicero's body back to Courville, how she saved herself from that freezer by breathing on the heat sensor, how she dealt with that guard dog, how she—"

Broussard lifted a limp hand in surrender. "I get the picture."

"And you should have said you *wanted* her back."

"She knows that."

"Women need to *hear* that stuff."

"I meant to say it, but it just wouldn't come out."

"Broussard, you're a sorry case."

"I suppose *you* could have done better."

"Couldn't have done worse."

"Okay, you're such a paragon of sensitivity, say something nice to me."

"What do you mean?"

"We've been friends for thirty years and you've never said anything nice to me. So do it now."

Gatlin's face flushed. "Don't be crazy."

"See, you can't."

"I could . . . if I wanted. I just . . ."

"Then do it. What's so difficult?"

"It's a dumb—"

"Hey, anybody in here own an old Pontiac or a '57 T-Bird?" a guy yelled from the doorway. " 'Cause a kid just poured gasoline on 'em and set 'em on fire."

Gatlin jumped to his feet and started for the door, but Broussard grabbed his arm. "It's a trick, engineered by Grandma O to get even for our pelican prank."

Gatlin hesitated. "You sure?"

"Why else would it only be our cars on fire?"

"That's right." He went back to his chair.

The guy who'd brought the bad news left and ran back toward the parking lot, joined by a few curious customers. Knowing Broussard couldn't expect him to say something nice with his mouth full, Gatlin hurriedly picked up his sandwich and took a bite. Broussard also returned to his food.

A minute later, they heard the distant sound of a siren. Gatlin put his sandwich down and listened. "It's coming this way."

"Got nothin' to do with us," Broussard said.

The siren grew louder and Gatlin jumped up. "Look at that."

Broussard turned and saw billows of black smoke boiling past the front window, near the parking lot. He threw his chair back and bolted for the door, Gatlin close behind.

They piled out of the restaurant and ran for their beloved automobiles, charging through the black smoke with abandon. The sight greeting them when they emerged from the smoke brought them to a standstill, their jaws agape.

The billowing black cloud was coming from a smoke bomb on the sidewalk under the front window. In the parking lot, Bubba Oustellette was cranking a siren whose sound was muffled with a big towel. Seeing them, he stopped and sheepishly pointed behind him. "She made me do it."

Towering over Bubba like an unbottled genie, the sun glinting off the gold star inlay in her front tooth, was Grandma O, grinning hard.

While the police were saving Kit from Tabor, the loose section of ceiling in her apartment had finally fallen, covering everything in plaster dust and soot. The plasterer had put the finishing coat on the repair just before Kit had left to meet Broussard and Gatlin at the restaurant. After leaving them, she'd intended to go home and take another crack at cleaning the place. Instead, she found herself getting off the elevator on the floor of Charity Hospital housing the ME's offices.

In truth, this section of the building was a dreary place. Because of perpetual dampness, the wall across from the elevator would never hold paint for more than a couple of weeks, so it usually looked as if it had psoriasis. In summer, the monstrous air handler hanging from the ceiling clattered so loudly, you could barely talk in the hall. And the floor was a patchwork of unmatched tiles. Who would want to spend their time here?

She walked down to her office and unlocked the door. Opening it, she was met by the sweet smell of fresh paint. She flicked on the lights and saw that the drab off-white she had lived with for two years was gone, replaced by a bright parchment color.

Everything else was just as she'd left it. She went to her desk and sat behind it, remembering what life had been like before she'd had to leave. There had been moments she'd been frightened out of her mind, others when she'd been repulsed at something Broussard had shown her. Mostly, it had been a time of fulfillment, growing from the knowledge she was doing important work with people she respected and, in Broussard's case, even loved. She was as aware of the positives in her behavior over the past two weeks as Gatlin was. She just couldn't give them the same weight, which left the scales tilted to the negatives. If only she *could* come back.

She opened the drawer where she kept the copy of the book she'd been writing on suicide. It, too, was still there . . . still unfinished . . . a dream unrealized. She picked up the first page, intending to read it, but then, fearing she'd see only childish prose and poorly thought-out ideas, she leaned over and let it slip from her hand into the wastebasket. With the first page in there, it seemed like the rest should follow. She took the remaining manuscript out of the drawer and held it over the wastebasket.

But she couldn't let go. All the work she'd done on those pages and the minuscule possibility she was being overly critical of herself, that somebody, somewhere, might find the work good, kept them in her hand. She put the manuscript back on the desk and leaned over to retrieve the discarded page. In doing so, she saw something else in the bottom of the wastebasket—a card, with Broussard's handwriting on it.

She picked it up and read the message he'd left for her along with the flowers the day she wouldn't look at the new paint job.

"There's no one who can do your job better. Please come back. Andy."

Tears welling in her eyes, she slowly read those words

again. Twelve words, added to the scale measuring her worth. But how much do words weigh? she thought.

She propped the card against the phone and walked to the door. There, she turned and looked at the old venetian blinds over the windows, wondering if miniblinds came in parchment.

A MYSTERIOUS PLAGUE
AND A VICIOUS KILLER STALK NEW ORLEANS—
NOW THE CITY'S MOST BRILLIANT FORENSIC TEAM
MUST STOP THEM BOTH DEAD IN THEIR TRACKS.

LOUISIANA FEVER

An Andy Broussard/Kit Franklyn Mystery

D.J. DONALDSON

A lethal virus similar to the deadly Ebola is bringing body after body to the New Orleans morgue. As Broussard and Franklyn try to uncover the source of the virus, they come up against another killer—and this one is human. Now they must stop a modern-day plague and a malicious murderer before Kit and Andy become statistics themselves.

"His writing displays flashes of brilliance...Dr. Donaldson's talent and potential as a novelist are considerable."

—*The New York Times Book Review*

"A dazzling tour de force...sheer pulse-pounding reading excitement."

—*The Clarion Ledger*

LOUISIANA FEVER
D.J. Donaldson
0-312-96257-6___$5.99 U.S.___$7.99 Can.

ANOTHER DELICIOUS CULINARY MYSTERY FOR PETER KING FANS TO DEVOUR

The GOURMET DETECTIVE

PETER KING

In his first extraordinary outing, the Gourmet Detective must unravel the mouth-watering mystery of a TV journalist's sudden death at Circle of Careme, an exclusive London luncheon of foodie experts. Between dishy food-critics, rivalrous restaurateurs, and saucy chefs, Gourmet has to solve the crime—and make sure murder isn't on the menu once again.

A People magazine Beach Book of the Week

"This appealing detective serves up nuggets of culinary trivia and wry foodie humor."

—*People*

Be sure to read all the books by
Les Roberts
featuring Cleveland private eye
Milan Jacovich

THE CLEVELAND CONNECTION

Who hated an old man—a veteran of World War II—enough to kill him? When an old Serbian immigrant is murdered, Milan Jacovich must follow the old blood ties that lead to a world of hidden violence, family secrets—and old hatreds that die hard.

_____ 96218-5 $5.99 U.S./ $7.99 Can.

COLLISION BEND

When a television reporter is found strangled in her own home, Milan Jacovich's ex-girlfriend asks him to clear her current love as the chief murder suspect. But as Jacovich goes behind the scenes to uncover all the scandal and intrigue of big-city television, he comes closer to making the evening news—as a murder victim.

_____ 96399-8 $5.99 U.S./$7.99 Can.